NEW WORLD
ASHES

JENNIFER WILSON

OFTOMES PUBLISHING
UNITED KINGDOM

This edition published in 2016 by
OF TOMES PUBLISHING
UNITED KINGDOM

Wilson, Jennifer 1984-
New World: Ashes: a novel / by Jennifer Wilson.-2nd ed.

Cover design by KimG Design
Interior book design by Eight Little Pages

Summary: After seventeen-year-old orphan rogue Phoenix
sacrifices herself for her loved ones, her world takes an
unexpected turn. She may have forgotten her past, but it hasn't
forgotten her. A war is coming and her part in it is more pivotal
than anyone ever expected. That is, if she survives.

For Auston—
my best friend, the love of
my life, and my partner in crime.

1. SURVIVOR

FIRE. ASHES. REBIRTH.

Fire. Ashes. Rebirth.

This excruciating process happened over and over again until I pleaded for death to come. To make it stop. But it doesn't.

Fire. Ashes. Rebirth.

And each time... I'm a little less of the person I was before.

———

I NEVER SAW the faces of the men who took me.

Before being dragged to my feet, a black bag had been yanked down over my head, blinding me. The instant I attempted to retaliate against the restraining hands, my arms were pulled painfully behind my back, my wrists shackled by something metal. I remembered my injured arm screaming in agony as they forced me to my knees, but before I could cry out something hard was shoved into my side. Whatever it was shocked me with a voltage so high I was eventually rendered unconscious. Little did I know, that moment of comatose sleep was the only peace I would know for a long time.

When I awoke, I was here. Though I couldn't be sure exactly where *"here"* was. Undoubtedly, it was some kind of prisoner's holding chamber... but to me, it felt more like hell.

Everything but the ceiling was polished a perfectly glossy white. When I first roused, the smooth surface was soothing beneath my raw fingers, but I quickly realized the finish wasn't just for aesthetics. I sat up. Seconds after my head left the floor, hell opened its fiery gates. The entirety of the small room was devoured by a blinding white light emanating from exposed bulbs that lined the open ceiling. At first, I covered my eyes and recoiled, but no matter how I tried to block it out, the light still seeped in. Even behind my hands, my eyelids glowed a translucent red as I squeezed them shut. Purple veins shown through my thin skin. Sweat began to pour from my body at an alarming rate, my clothing becoming soaked almost immediately.

I buried my head in my arms.

If only it would stop.

As if the blazing light wasn't bad enough, the

music started. Not that the blaring noise could really be considered music. It was as if five songs were all being played at the same time, each one competing to be heard above the others. The sound was so loud it made my eardrums ache. Surely they would start bleeding if they weren't already. But if I moved to protect my ears, the light pierced though my closed lids again, making my head feel like it was on fire. Eventually, I compromised by huddling with my back against the wall while pressing my eyes into my knees and keeping my arms wrapped around my head.

In truth, it made little difference.

Through the constant onslaught, it was nearly impossible to think. Even my own name was becoming harder to remember. Only one thought kept rattling loose as the torture went on. They weren't going to ask me questions, to seek out my alliance like the Subversive once had. These people were going to break me and see what they could scrape off the floor.

I had to remind myself that *I* chose this.

That there was a *reason* I was here.

They were safe.

They were not being tortured like I was.

Sacrifice. What a heady notion. It had seemed like such a good idea at the time...

It still was. I reminded myself.

I tried to picture the faces I was fighting to see

3

again, the loved ones I had tried to save but it was so hard to focus.

I had a flash of memory, a glimpse of their terrified eyes pleading with me through that sewer grate. I know I had promised Triven I would stay alive, promised that I would survive this. But even now as I tried to think of him, his image began to slip away. Not even Mouse's round, sweet face could penetrate this unending mental and physical torture.

I was tough, always had been. My survival in Tartarus was proof of that. But this, this was killing me.

Less than a week ago, if someone had told me I would miss my time in the Subversive's underground bunker, I would have laughed. But today, *today* I did miss it. Soft beds, warm food, friends—well, not friends exactly, allies might have been a better word. Yes, there were enemies there too, but at least they had been civilized. More civilized than the Tribes.

More civilized than *this*.

The people of the Subversive didn't trust me, certainly not at first. (I still didn't trust half of them.) But over time, I had earned their respect and they eventually looked to me for counsel. They were why I was here in the first place—a botched recon mission.

They had sent us out to infiltrate The Wall and report back what we had found. No outsiders had seen The Sanctuary in six years and six years was a long time.

We had come in blind, not knowing what we would find here. Was it the city their leader, Arstid, remembered and had risked her life to escape? Or had it changed? Best-case scenario, we would find a city that had overthrown their tyrant. A place where everyday wasn't a battle to survive. A place where the refugees of Tartarus could live in freedom.

While I too desired freedom, answers were what I really sought. Answers about who I was and why my parents had given their lives to get me out. Either way, anything had to be better than Tartarus, better then hiding from the Tribes. Or so I thought.

Slowly, my body began to shut down. The steady ache in my lower back hinted my kidneys were most likely failing. The survival books I had once filched from Tartarus' library taught me what these symptoms might mean and none of it was good news for me. Every ounce of water had been drained from my body, pooling beneath me and clinging to my clothing. And no matter how badly I wanted it, no glass of water was going to magically appear to quench my parched body. At some point, I slumped to the floor. I couldn't remember doing it, and now that I was there, I couldn't find the energy to sit up again. My tongue scraped dryly across my cracked lips seeking relief. The only thing it found was the tang of blood. Even my eyelids found it hard to blink without sticking.

My body was dying.

I was dying.

I knew I had promised someone I would survive for them, but I couldn't hang on anymore. *They would understand… right?*

I had to let go…

My pulse was slowing, ready to give up.

Then just as suddenly as the onslaught had come, it stopped.

The world was plunged into utter blackness and the only sound I could hear was the painful ringing of my own ears.

At first, I loved the quiet. The dark felt cool on my parched blistered skin. The air no longer burned when I breathed. But that feeling of relief did not last. Soon the darkness became overwhelming. Its heaviness was crushing me, pressing in on my limbs, making it harder to breathe. In the light, at least I had a sense of being, but lying in the infinite blackness… it was as if I had just disappeared. As if a sea of nothingness had swallowed me whole. I wanted to curl myself into a ball, to wrap my arms around my knees, to hold myself together, but my body refused to move. Instead, I lay shivering in a pool of my own sweat. At one point, I vaguely remember my tongue desperately stabbing at the floor, seeking relief. The salty moisture did little to satiate my thirst. I wasn't sure if it was the lack of heat from the lights or if the temperature in the room was actually dropping, but it was getting colder. Then, as the ringing in my ears finally started to fade, the screaming began.

They were so loud.

I tried to pull my hands up to cover my ears but one arm was trapped beneath my fallen body while the other barely fluttered in response. I couldn't even lift my fingertips to scratch my nose much less cover my ears. Defeated, I did the only thing I could do and squeezed my eyes shut. As the screams echoed over and over, something familiar clawed at my mind. Slowly, I realized I knew these voices.

I struggled to understand. *Were they hurting people I loved?*

After what felt like an eternity, it clicked. The screams weren't another tactic derived to torture me. They were my own personal form of torment.

They were in my head.

As I made that jarring realization, I could now not only hear them but also see their matching faces flashing behind my closed eyelids. My mother's beautiful blood-spattered face was pale against her flowing blonde hair. Next was my father's, his face twisted in pain that distorted his usually handsome features.

I was sleeping. I had to be.

I *knew* these nightmares.

I had lived with them for over six years, awoke to

them every morning, relived them every night. But something was different now… They had changed.

There was another face, a *new* face. Black eyes stared back at me, overflowing with fear as the man died. A river of blood poured from his mouth, its crimson fingers creeping toward me. It felt like I was drowning in it. I choked, unable to scream. Maddox died to save me and now his death would haunt me just like my parents' did.

I tried to open my eyes, willing the ghastly apparitions to go away, but to my horror they were already open. In the darkness, there was no escaping the most tortured, inner workings of my mind. You can't hide from what's inside of you. The worst part about silence is that there's nothing to distract your mind. It didn't matter if my eyes were open or closed. I saw them. With great effort, I curled in further on myself, trying to disappear, to become nothing. And that's when the lights came back on, restarting the torturous cycle all over again. In the light I burned for my sins. In the dark they swallowed me whole.

Fire. Ashes. Rebirth.

IT FELT LIKE days, weeks, months had passed and still I was trapped in this hell. But by some cruel joke of fate, I didn't die. The fifteenth time (I was counting) the lights came on, something was different. The harsh lights were softer this time. It took me a minute to comprehend there wasn't the usual searing heat burning my skin, then another to realize I was no longer alone. Balancing on the thin edge of delirium, I could see the outline of a man standing before me, but it was hard to make out his face through the tangles of my hair and thickly crusted eyelashes. He was nothing more than a dark shadowy figure looming above me. I didn't bother lifting my head to get a better look. Instead, I just closed my eyes.

The toe of his shoe slid under my shoulder and then with a shove flipped me onto my back. As my stringy hair fell away from my face, he muttered something that sounded like a curse. My eyelids fluttered, but I couldn't focus. Stepping away from me he addressed someone else. His words sounded strange mixed with the residual sounds of the music still pulsating in my ears. They said something about taking me somewhere... to see someone. But before the words could register, my body shut down, casting me into a grateful unconsciousness.

SOMETHING COLD STRUCK me in the face. It rolled

over my skin, down my chest and into my lap. It should have been refreshing, but the chill of the water felt almost violent against my scorched skin, a million minuscule pins and needles stabbing my nerve endings. My head whipped back involuntarily before rolling forward again.

A groan slipped from my lips. My temples were throbbing.

I blinked a few times, trying to focus. Neither my body or mind felt under my control. *Keep your head.* I reminded myself. *My name was Phoenix. I had made a sacrifice. The Sanctuary had captured me. I didn't want to die.* As I stared at my soaked thighs, I tried to make an assessment of my fuzzy surroundings.

They had moved me.

The floor I could just see beyond my bare toes was grey now and I was sitting up—well, not so much "sitting up" as tied to a chair. While my instincts screamed at me to resist the restraints, I knew they were the only things holding me upright. As much as I wanted to be rid of them, I needed them for support. Without my bindings they would know how weak I was, but with them I stood a chance at feigning strength.

"Do it again." A snide male voice spoke to my right. I heard the movement of feet and the sloshing of another bucket.

"I would *highly* advise against that." I meant my

voice to be strong and confident, but what came out was cracked and raspy.

The sloshing noise stopped.

"So nice of you to join us, Prea." A different voice spoke this time. It was deeper, more refined than the first.

Using all of my strength, I pushed against the ropes on my chest and pulled my head up to face the man who said my name. It was like staring at him through a dark tunnel. I forced my eyes to focus.

He was old by Tartarus standards. His perfectly coiffed hair was streaked grey and white. The wrinkles embedded in his face had given way to gravity slightly, but there was something wrong about them. It was as if his face had been stretched back a little to keep the drooping lines tighter. There was something else in his features I couldn't quite place. Something… familiar. He had a sharp nose like a beak and the most piercing blue eyes. Even in my semi-delirious haze, their gaze sent a chill down my spine.

Focus, Phoenix…

His pressed suit was perfectly white, with a high blunt collar that stopped just below his angular jaw. Two silver bars were mounted on each shoulder. There was something round, shiny and silver over his left breast that I could not quite make out. The tailored uniform gave him an authoritative look, but it was not a soldier's uniform nor was it like the civilians' garb I had seen—that I had stolen—before being captured. The attire had been well calculated. He appeared to be a commander yet still a man of the people—white like a citizen's but cut like a soldier's. In his left hand he held a brass cane, but wasn't placing much weight on it. Possibly it was more for show than actual use. He may have looked older, but he carried himself with the authority and arrogance of a much younger man. Clearly, this was the man in charge. He was the one I had heard so much about and yet knew almost nothing.

This was The Minister of The Sanctuary.

This was Minister Fandrin.

As the tunnel of my vision widened, I took in more of my surroundings. We were not alone. Three other younger men stood in the room with us. While I was now aware of their presence, it was The Minister who still held my complete attention. He was the one who had spoken my name. My *real* name.

I narrowed my eyes at him.

"You must be confused old man. That's not my name," I lied.

His returning smile made my hollow stomach flip. "On the contrary my child, I am positive that your name *is* Prea. Prea Mason."

My throat clenched. No one knew my surname, not even Triven. That name had died with my parents. I concentrated on keeping my face calm. Emotionless.

"And what the *hell* makes you think you know anything about me?" I said through my teeth. My head was getting heavy again, but I forced myself to hold his cold gaze.

His smile shifted, looking more like a snarl.
"Even beneath all of that grime and filth…" There was loathing in the old man's eyes as they scoured over me. "Did you *really* think I wouldn't recognize my own granddaughter?"

2. EXCUSES

MY HEAD SUDDENLY felt lighter. Surely my mind was playing tricks on me again. I had heard him wrong. A sickness unlike anything I had ever felt clawed under my skin. It felt as if my soul had shivered. The smile that spread across his lips seemed to be an attempt at appearing paternal, but to me it was menacing.

"I think you must have me confused with someone else, old man." I lied again.

His smile faltered as he sighed. "It's truly disappointing how much you're like your mother."

He shook his head like the sight of me sitting before him tied to the chair was an embarrassment. Anger boiled in my veins. *How dare he insult my mother?* I wanted to scream at Fandrin that he was a liar. That there was no way in hell he and I shared any bloodlines. But the longer I stared at his smug face, the more I could see the resemblance. There was something in the shape of his jaw, in the hollow of his cheekbones, that looked so much like my mother…

So much like me.

But more than that—what really chilled me—were those eyes.

They weren't just bright and piercing… they were *my* eyes.

I tried to swallow. For the first time in my life, I had no quip to cut back. Instead I just stared blankly at the man claiming to be my grandfather. All I had ever wanted was my family back, but as I gazed at the man before me something within me churned. It was as if a tiny moth's wings fluttered against my spine, warning me something wasn't right. I tried to ferret out the source of those feelings but nothing came to my broken mind. My memories were too far gone. Whatever it was that my body seemed to remember, my mind could not.

However, one thing I had learned to trust over the years was my intuition. It was what so often kept me alive. While the man reminded me of my mother—of myself—I had no recollection of his face. He was nothing more than a familiar stranger, and a dangerous one at that.

Growing restless, The Minister paced the small space in front of me, his hand twisting over the top of his brass cane as he moved. His withered knuckles turned white as he gripped and re-gripped the handle repeatedly.

His voice was flawlessly controlled when he spoke again. Kind, gentle, just flirting with cold. "Imagine my surprise when I was informed that a band of the exiled had actually managed to penetrate The Wall. And not only had those parasites managed to infiltrate my city, but they had killed several of my troops *and* were being lead by none other than my supposedly dead granddaughter. Disappointing really."

I wasn't sure which he was more disappointed in—that I had acted against him or that I wasn't as dead as he thought I should be.

"You have come into *my* city, threatened *my* people and stolen from *me*. I have had people killed for much less, little girl." He turned to face me, but I stared determinedly at the barren grey floor. Pressing the tip of his cane to my throat, he jerked it upward forcing me to look at him.

"I have taken nothing from you—" I snarled, trying to disguise my rising panic. I knew almost nothing of this city. I had no bargaining chips here, nothing I could swap for my protection.

Then he gave it to me.

"Oh, but haven't you? That *child* is not yours." The tip of his cane pressed down harder, cutting off my airway as a dark shadow flashed across his features. Then he suddenly pulled back just a little, allowing me to suck in a desperate breath. "But unlike your mother, *I* can be forgiving. If you return what is mine, I will be lenient with you. After all, it would be nice to have my bloodline back at my side. We could be a family again." He eyed me possessively.

A young man in the corner shifted, drawing my attention. His eyes were filled with disdain as they focused on me. They were deep brown and despite their malice they reminded me of Mouse. She was the only one I had ever broken my rules for, the first person I had loved other than my parents. She was the sister I never had and the child I could never be. I sat in this very chair as my sacrifice to save her. *She* was what The Minister was asking for, what he claimed—like property—was stolen from him. *She* was my bargaining chip. My way out. At another time in my life, I might have taken that offer, but not anymore. He would never so much as lay eyes on her again.

As I stared at the older man before me I knew— deep down—that he wasn't lying. He *was* my grandfather. His blood ran in my veins. But regardless of blood, Mouse was more of a family to me than he could ever be. She and Triven were the only people in the world who mattered. And despite my selfish nature, I now would sacrifice everything to keep them alive—to keep them safe from the monster standing before me.

The longer I stayed quiet, the more impatient he

grew. The tip of his cane slowly pressed harder against my throat as he awaited my response. I could feel the bruise forming as my windpipe constricted further. I smiled warmly at him, batting my eyes before speaking.

"Go to hell."

I only caught a glimpse of rage as it flashed across his face before the brass cane smashed into the side of my head. But in that instant before I blacked out, I took pleasure in his frustration.

***

I DIDN'T KNOW how long I had been out, but regardless of the time, it was the pounding headache that woke me. It felt as if my head had been cleaved in two. A steady pulse beat in my skull. As I tried to roll onto my side, the pain flared, causing me to curl into myself in agony. I clutched my head trying to make it stop. There was a bandage just above my left temple. The flesh around it was raised and burning, the gauze sticky to the touch. I forced myself not to shake, scream, or vomit.

I lay still until the pain eased, counting the seconds as I focused on my labored breathing. Even without opening my eyes, it was easy to tell I had been moved to yet another room. Whatever I was lying on now, it wasn't the concrete floor of the room I had just been in, nor was it the high gloss surface of my personal hot box either. No, wherever I was, there was definitely some kind of mattress—if it could be called that—beneath me. Its scratchy material felt like sandpaper on my blistered skin. When the pain in my head finally subsided enough that I could open my eyes. I took in my new prison.

The floor was coated dark grey and the walls were thick cinderblocks that someone had painted white. In the corner of the tiny room was a silver toilet. At the other end of the room was a hingeless red metal door with a slot at the bottom about a hand's width high by two hands wide. I couldn't see the hall beyond it. And as the small gap had an opaque sheen to it, I would wager a guess it was an electrified force field similar to the door I had encountered at the Subversive. Stick your hand in it, and you would get zapped.

If I were to reach my arms out, my fingertips could just graze the wall opposite of me. The room itself was tiny. The whole thing was maybe half the size of my little closet in the old library. No windows. No vents. No electrified open passageways. They wanted to keep me isolated and blind. It felt like being buried in a cinderblock coffin.

Good thing I wasn't claustrophobic.

Other than my eyes, I hadn't moved an inch. But the tingling at the base of my skull alerted me to something. I knew that feeling. Six years of being alone, six years of constantly being on the run—on the defensive—had given me a sixth sense for these things.

I was being watched.

Feigning closing my eyes again, I looked up to the ceiling through my eyelashes.

I was right.

In the upper left corner of the room, just off the doorframe was a camera. I had seen many outside of The Wall in Tartarus. They were mounted in streets, falling off walls in decrepit buildings. There, they were old, fragmented and definitely not in use. But this one—while shaped a little differently from the ones I had seen and read about—was most certainly a camera and it was on. A tiny red light at the top warned me it was broadcasting right at this very moment.

I would bet my life there was one in my other torture chamber of a room too. I had just never been able to see it through the blinding lights.

They were watching me. They had *been* watching me.

I closed my eyes all the way, trying to forget that others were still watching, others who never closed *their* eyes. As I lay still, I took inventory of my body. Old wounds still hurt. The shoulder I was laying on was tender from the healing bullet wound. Aside from the splitting headache, raw skin, and injured shoulder, my body felt drained. Every muscle ached from dehydration.

My insides seemed to be withering into dust. Involuntarily, I licked my lips. They were still cracked and bleeding. If I was going to survive, I would need water. As if on cue, there was a grinding noise of something being slid across concrete.

I peeked at the door.

A glass of water had been pushed through the slot in the door. I felt a pang of relief, but didn't move for it. They knew I needed the water. They knew they had control over my life. We both knew it. But that didn't mean I couldn't control some things. I used the last bit of restraint I had and closed my eyes again. Eventually I would have to drink the water, but I wanted to do it on my terms, not theirs.

I lay still for a long time trying to think about anything except what I wanted to think about most—the ones I had sacrificed my life for. But the thoughts kept creeping relentlessly back into the forefront of my mind.

Were they still alive? Did they make it out? And the worst, and most wasteful thought—*were they coming back for me?* I had never wasted energy hoping someone would rescue me. And despite what Triven had promised, this was not the time to start.

Once again, I was on my own.

It was strange how time moved since my capture. A part of me felt like it had been just hours ago that I had watched Triven's face disappear into the shadows of that drain. But another part of my brain felt like it was a lifetime ago. Was it days? Weeks? Months? In truth, it was hard to tell.

What if Mouse and Triven didn't make it? What if I was holding out for nothing?

I shook those thoughts from my head. No. They *had* survived, they *had* gotten away. I had to believe that, if not for them, then for myself. Without them, my being here meant nothing. It meant I had sacrificed my life needlessly and I couldn't believe that. I surely would never have been careless enough to sacrifice myself if no good came of it. They were alive and I would survive this to get back to them. Mouse and Triven were my only excuse to live now, so they had to be okay.

A bright thought sparked in my slow mind.

They *were* alive...

The Minister's reaction had proven that. If he had them, then he wouldn't need me. But I was still here. *I* was still alive too. He was going to try and use me to get to them. So according to reason, if I'm alive then they are too. The more The Minister tortured me for information, the further Mouse and Triven were slipping from his grasp. A strange giddiness flared in my chest.

Grunting against the pain in my head, I leaned forward and took the glass of water. It shook slightly in my hand, the water sloshing in the clear cup. As much as I wanted to gulp it down, I hesitated. Normally, I would have sniffed it or just risked a fingertip taste, but they were watching me. This was a test, a challenge to look for weaknesses. For fear.

I firmly wrapped my fingers around the cup and raised it in a toast to the camera. My mouth spread into a dry and cracked smiled as I put the cup to my lips and drained it.

Challenge accepted. I'm not afraid of you old man.

Bring on the torture.

3. PAST LIVES

I STOPPED TRYING to calculate time, but since I had awakened in the tiny prison cell I had received four glasses of water and one sad example of a meal. It looked more like vomit than food. I didn't touch it. Instead, I spent the time reflecting on the man who called himself my grandfather.

My head was slowly starting to un-cloud, allowing me to think clearly again. At some point I realized Fandrin had never once asked about my mother's whereabouts. And the only reason he wouldn't need to ask, was because he already knew the answer. Why waste time asking about my mother or father when he knew they were dead? Heat burned in my cheeks, as another thought crossed my mind.

Did he have a hand in their deaths?

The man that I had just met claimed to be my grandfather and then nearly cracked my skull open with his cane. If he was capable of beating his self-proclaimed granddaughter into unconsciousness, then was he not equally capable of sending a Tribe that apparently worked with him to kill his own daughter? Obviously this man had no problem getting his hands dirty—or at least asking others to do it for him. Bile rose in my throat at the thought of his blood also flowing in my veins. I shied away from that thought.

Surely he was lying. It was just a coincidence we had similar features and he was using them to his advantage. Banking on the idea that if he told the poor orphaned teen that she still had family, she might cling to him and ultimately give him what he wanted. Too bad for Fandrin I didn't actually *need* anyone. What I needed was for the other people I loved to survive—but me personally, I had always been my best when I was alone. Against the odds. Bring on the solitary confinement, it felt like home.

I closed my eyes and took a deep breath. As much as I wanted to think about Triven and Mouse, it was a luxury I couldn't afford. They were my one weakness and if I was to survive this—if I was to return to them—I needed to shut them out for now. There could be no pining over my lost friends, or worrying about their safety. They were alive and if I wanted to see them again, I needed to leave my thoughts at that. Loving them had made me soft and now was not the time for weakness.

Just as I locked that allegorical door in my mind, the actual door to my cell opened. I didn't move, but stared expectantly at the opening as if bored. I was surprised that the boy who entered was not much older than myself. He was striking. The lines of his face were nearly perfect. He had a wide chin and prominent cheekbones that were accented by a long straight nose and high brow. The only imperfection on his otherwise flawless face was a small scar above his left eye. His uniform was similar to the one I had seen The Minister wearing. Slim fitted, tailored white pants and a sharply cut jacket enhanced his already broad physique. Only one silver bar adorned each of his shoulders but several metallic badges crossed the left breast pocket of his uniform, beneath the same round badge I had seen on The Minister. This was an officer. It became apparent officers wore white. Soldiers wore silver, like I had seen in the streets. He stood straight with his hands clasped behind his back as his bright blue eyes looked me over. His jet-black hair was as equally manicured as his suit. Short on the sides with a little more on the top. He was clearly a *high-ranking* officer in The Sanctuary's military.

I instantly recognized him from the room where I had been interrogated, but at the time he had seemed of little importance. Just another white suit in a room filled with uniforms. Now, however, I realized I should not have overlooked him so carelessly before.

"Get up." The soldier barked. The loathing in his eyes was nearly palpable.

I glared back at him unmoving. "What, the old man miss me already?"

His hand flashed out with impressive speed, the back striking my cheek so hard it felt as if my eye would explode from its socket. I fell face first into the mattress from the force of his blow and struggled to right myself. I wanted to laugh at him, to make him feel insecure about his strength, but my head was pounding again and my voice seemed to be stuck in my throat. His fingers coiled around the back of my neck as he pulled his lips to my ear.

"Say anything like that again and you will be dragged out of here in a body bag, *Princess*." His lips grazed my earlobes as he spoke.

Instinctively, I twitched away from him.

I am not sure what it was about the "princess" that bothered me so much, but whether it was the connotation the name carried or the way he said it, I instantly loathed that nickname.

"Got it?" His hissed giving my neck a sharp shake.

I glanced at one of the shining silver badges on his chest. The round emblem had two rigidly sculpted wings at the bottom. Three disjointed rings that arched over the top connected them. Tiny words were engraved on each of the rings. *Equality. Unity. Freedom.* In the middle, a strangely shaped spire jutted up cutting the pressed circle in half. Beneath that was a simple sliver nameplate. The inscribed letters read *R. James.*

"Yes *sir,* officer James." I put as much contempt in my voice as I could muster.

"It's *Major* James. And when a Major tells you to get up, you get up!"

Using my neck as a means of steering, he pulled me from the ground and marched me through the door. I only got a quick glance at the barren, all white hallway before a bag was once again pulled over my head. Simultaneously, shackles were clamped on my wrists. The black linen material was dense. I could just barely make out the heavy fabric as it flexed and restricted with each breath. There was no hope of seeing through the hood. I made a mental note to make better use of those few seconds of sight next time they pulled me from my cell.

Since I couldn't see, I counted. It was obvious from the sound of footsteps that there were five other guards walking with us. Apparently, they would not be underestimating me as I had hoped.

We took a right at sixty-five and then a left at one hundred and ninety-seven. At two hundred and thirty-nine steps I was jerked to a halt by the shackles on my wrists. The cool metal bit into my skin. As my stomach dropped I realized we were moving upward in some sort of lift. One hundred and forty-two seconds later the floor finally stopped moving. I heard the feet around me move again and was rewarded with a barrel of a gun jammed sharply into my spine when I didn't move forward fast enough.

The sound of our feet was different now, the echo magnified. After thirty more steps, my hands were freed from their restraints and I was shoved into a chair. As abruptly as it had been put on, the black bag was yanked from my head. I recoiled against the brightness, blinking rapidly.

The room was huge. Fifteen other soldiers lined the walls, including the boy that reminded me of Mouse. Three of the walls were solid white, covered with strange screens and monitors that didn't appear to have any depth to them. Moving images of The Sanctuary streets flashed intermittently across the screens. The wall directly in front of me, however, was made entirely of white beams and glass that bowed, curving sinuously into the ceiling. Beyond the glass I could see blue sky and a sea of beige and white buildings below.

There were large, white marble tiles covering the floor and the sparse furniture was made entirely of translucent materials, including the ornate chair I was currently seated in. While it was warm to the touch, it looked like glass, its rigid lines obviously not meant for comfort. Even the large desk in front of me was made of some kind of clear material, though not quite as see-through as my own seat. Sitting on the edge of the desk was a silver plate filled with small sandwiches. I looked away, suppressing my growling stomach.

It was easy to discern that all of this was a ruse meant to impress, to intimidate those brought before the great Minister of The Sanctuary. And while most would have ogled the room in awe, I appraised all of the surroundings in a matter of seconds while barely taking my eyes from the man sitting before me. His fingers were pressed to his lips as he studied me. I returned the stare, refusing to break the silence first. I searched his face, trying to find my features in his—or more accurately trying *not* to find them.

He finally settled his hands into his lap and broke the weighted silence. "Our first encounter did not go exactly as I had hoped."

"Really? And I thought we were doing *so* well." I slouched in my chair feigning an ease I did not actually feel.

The older man's face reddened but he held his composure. Sitting up a little straighter he spoke, "We are not barbarians here, but order must be kept."

Clearly this man believed his self-proclaimed aristocracy merited respect. I silently took an oath to show him anything but that.

"Right, because cracking your granddaughter across the face is an excellent way to prove you're not a barbarian. You're just freaking Grandfather of the Year aren't you?" I turned to the handsome stone-faced guard that had pulled me from my cell. "You should really get him a plaque or something. You know, so everyone knows how wonderful this man is. Hell, it might even make this place feel downright homey."

In a stoke of defiant genius, I leaned forward and snatched one of the small sandwiches from his desk and took a huge bite making sure to chew with my mouth open. If he was going to crack me in the head again, at least it wouldn't be on an empty stomach. I watched the young guard move to restrain me, but to my disappointment The Minister waved him off with a chuckle.

"I nearly missed your smart mouth." The Minister hesitated. "But I know the truth about that smart mouth of yours. That's just your way of hiding the rage burning inside of you. That hot temper I can see flaring in your eyes, you get that from me."

I nearly threw up my stolen sandwich. Swallowing it back down I said, "Lucky me."

"You and I are not so different you know." He spoke softer now, his blue eyes eerily penetrating.

"You don't know anything about me." I crossed

my arms in an attempt to shut him out.

"On the contrary my dear, I practically raised you. While you were more *refined* when under my watch, I guarantee that part of the girl I trained—that I nurtured—is in there somewhere. Despite your lack of memories, it's still there. Ingrained in you." He tapped the corner of his temple to emphasize his point.

I barked out a wry laugh, spraying some semi-chewed food, and seized another sandwich. I shoved it in my mouth but my throat was so dry I nearly choked on it. I had never questioned my natural abilities when it came to combat or to how I could analyze every situation in seconds. I just always assumed it was some kind of survival instinct. It never crossed my mind that I had been trained, *programmed* to think that way. My memories stopped before my eleventh birthday, before my parents' deaths. How many of those lost years had I spent being honed into a weapon? And what kind of parents would have let that happen?

I gagged down the last bit of sandwich before speaking. "You said it yourself, I seem to be lacking quite a few crucial memories. Like why the hell I should give a crap about anything you say. You're nothing to me. Not even a face I would notice in a crowd. How could you possibly delude yourself into thinking you have had *any* kind of influence over me."

The Minister laughed without humor. "Oh my

dear child. How could *you* possibly delude *yourself* into thinking that you could have survived one second outside of The Wall without my influence?" He folded his hands on the desk while leaning toward me. "You survived that city for one reason and one reason alone. You are what *I* made you."

My lip drew up in the corner with disgust. "Your lies only than flatter yourself."

Fandrin snapped his fingers at the blonde man standing near the illuminated screens. "Careful who you call a liar, child."

I opened my mouth to retort, but fell silent as the monitors all flickered to the same scene. There were two small children sparring in a ring while a younger Minister Fandrin watched over them. While the black-haired boy moved with animalistic ferocity, it was the blonde child that caught my attention. She was nearly half the size of the boy fighting with her, but it was clear she was the stronger fighter of the two. She was uncharacteristically graceful for a child. I felt my fingers go numb as I watched the scene before me. There was something familiar in the way she moved. I knew those moves. I knew that face, those eyes...

She was a younger version of...

She was me.

As the tingling spread up my arms, the scene changed and I watched in horror as the little girl sat at a table next to other children and reassembled a gun faster than her surrounding comrades. My throat tightened each time the scene changed—sparring, knife throwing, obstacle courses, shooting... It seemed to go on forever.

When The Minister finally spoke I couldn't tear my eyes from the screen.

"You were the best cadet at the Academy. Under my personal tutelage, you quickly rose to the top of your class. You were going to be the perfect soldier, a lethal weapon before you hit puberty." Pride dripped from his words.

I finally wrenched my eyes from the screen to glare at him. "I was just a child... You're a *monster*."

He shook his white head patiently. "I am not a monster, I am a *commander*. Before our rule, this city was no better than Tartarus. My fathers before me formed the army that now protects this city and it is I who holds it together today. An army is nothing without a great leader and I *am* great. I alone was bold enough to seek out children who showed potential and train them. And now our army is stronger than it has ever been. Children have proven to make loyal soldiers and loyal soldiers make for a great nation." He gestured to the uniformed privates standing in the room around us and to my horror they saluted with pride. "You were trained to rule by my side to be a stronger version of myself when the time came. There was once a time you believed me and I can see that passion, that power still burns in your eyes. Even now, you could join me again. Together, we can protect these people from the horrors outside of The Wall. We can keep the Tribes at bay. We can ensure that our peace here continues."

My eyes flickered back to the screens just as the younger version of myself broke her opponent's nose. Closing my eyes I spoke in a low, steady voice. "I would rather spend the rest of my days rotting in that box you call a cell than joining your ranks. How this city has not risen up to watch you burn for what you have done to their children perplexes me. You're not keeping the Tribes *at bay*. You're *working* with them. It's easy to appear the hero when the Ravagers are in your back pocket."

When I finally looked up, Minister Fandrin was no longer smiling.

His words were almost a snarl. "Sadly, my child, it appears your mind has been perverted by the world outside our wall more severely than I thought. I keep these people *safe*. This city is a working machine of cranks and gears. They turn and smash into one another in a whirl of organized chaos. And I—and I alone— stand in the center turning them as I see fit. Each person, powerful or pitiful, is under my control. Whether they realize it or not, they bend to *my* will. Because the truth is, I own this city and everyone in it. I am their governor, their minister, and their commander. Without me it would be chaos. People *need* to be ruled."

"You're not *ruling* them, you're *controlling* them. You are running these people's lives by keeping them in constant fear. You're not a leader, you're a tyrant." I spat the words at him, my answer rife with undisguised hate.

"Tomāto – tomäto. Those who seek power and safety will always support me. Like it or not child I *am* the ruler here, and if you won't adhere to my rules of your own accord then you will do so by force." His face cracked into a perfect smile that made my skin crawl. He casually leaned back into his self-proclaimed throne. "In my experience people always go one of two ways, they either bend or they break. Whatever the outcome, it's only a matter of time."

I leaned forward, closing the gap between us.

"Let me tell *you* something Gramps. I survived Tartarus *despite* you, old man. You may have succeeded in killing my parents, but you couldn't kill me then and you won't break me now. You can't break what's already broken. So bring on your worst. We will soon see who is stronger."

His eyes glittered. "Let's put that to the test, shall we? I think it's time for a little rehabilitation."

4. CONSEQUENCES

THOUGH I WOULD never admit it—not even to the internal voice nagging in the back of my mind—I regretted my arrogant words.

I worked my jaw, trying to loosen the clenched muscles. The barren room echoed with the sound of my labored breathing. Sweat clung to my clothing. It pooled on the black leather pad against my back and dripped from my temples. I shifted and the miniscule needles protruding from my skin vibrated painfully with the motion. Every muscle ached. Every nerve ending prickled with unseen fire, but still, these lingering flames were a reprieve compared to the agony that just stopped coursing through my body. This was the third electroshock "therapy" I had endured in barely two days.

Three soldiers stood alert in the room with me. A stern-faced woman stood in the corner, her gaze dutifully trained on the glowing screen before her. Her thin fingers hovered above the illuminated surface, ready to send the next wave of electricity through my body on her superior's command. A young man who guarded the door refused to meet my gaze, staring intently at his perfectly polished boots. I noted the minute twitch in his jaw every time the woman touched the screen. The last soldier stood behind me, just out of sight.

Minister Fandrin was nowhere to be seen, but only a fool would think he wasn't watching my torture, undoubtedly enjoying the pain he himself was too cowardly to inflict. I could see a glint off the monitor the woman was tapping on, a hint of a glass wall behind me. He was definitely watching.

"Come on *Princess,* just give up." Major R. James' smug voice spoke from somewhere behind me. "He *will* break you. You're weaker than him. We all know it."

The resounding laugh that burst from my lips sounded insane, even in my own ears. It was so nearly a scream that it was terrifying in the small room. The hairs on my neck rose as the sound echoed back to me. Instantly, I snapped my jaw shut to keep the building screams from completely breaking free. I had managed not to cry out in pain during their torture so far and the Major's taunting only intensified my resolve. His voice was like a dark beacon, reminding me of everything I stood against. Of everything I was fighting for. Of everything I hated. My determination burned, his words like fuel to the fire.

"*I'm* weak… Says the coward blindly serving a senile old cretin." I retorted.

"Again," the Major's cool voice instructed. The woman's fingers tapped the monitor.

My body arched against the straps restraining me, the nylon edges cutting into my skin. The electrical current surging through my body caused every muscle to seize, every joint to explode in agony, but still I remained silent. My teeth locked together so hard I was afraid they would break. Someone snapped their fingers and the current stopped just as suddenly as it had started. I collapsed back onto the strap-clad chair shaking with exhaustion. Spittle frothed in the corners of my mouth as the pain receded from my body again. A blotchy darkness crept into my vision. I closed my eyes in an attempt to stop it, willing myself to stay conscious. My chest ached. Even if I hadn't been able to hear my heart's irregular beat on the monitor behind me, I could feel it struggling to pump. A couple more shocks and it would undoubtedly stop beating. Someone moved behind me and I could feel hot breath on my face. Focusing my strength, I opened my eyes.

A face hovered inches above mine. Major R. James hid his emotions with the precision only a trained soldier could, but his eyes gave him away. An unbridled fury burned in those bright blue irises.

"You can make this end, Princess. All you have to do is pledge your allegiance to our Minister." He whispered. "Submit like the weak coward we all know you are. And just give him the girl and the traitor."

I snarled at him, bracing myself for the oncoming pain. My heartbeat stuttered on the monitor behind us. The Major's hand rose, his fingers poised to signal my torment, but just before dropping his fingertips he paused. Tilting his head he pressed his fingers to his right ear. I noticed the girl controlling the monitor do the same thing. Someone was talking to them. She moved before he did, her fingers flying over the screen as if she was twisting dials.

A deep frown set into Major James' features as he leaned further over me. "Apparently our dear Minister doesn't seem to think your heart can withstand any more high voltage shocks. So to accommodate your frail heart, Princess, we're going to turn down the voltage. But don't worry, this just means we get to play this game a little longer." He paused, leaning closer and dropping his voice so only I could hear him. "Minister Fandrin was right, you *are* weak just like your mother was."

I spat, smiling viciously as the spittle slid gratifyingly down his perfect face. He jerked upright, his movement staccatoed with anger. He unceremoniously shoved the female officer away from the monitor and twisted his fingers over the screen. The Major's blue eyes flashed for a second and then the most excruciating pain I had ever felt wracked my body. I couldn't even scream before the life was ripped from me.

I HEAVED FORWARD, sucking in a ragged gasp of breath, my eyes reflexively rolling back into my head. Voices were speaking near by. I wanted to open my eyes to seek out who was speaking but my body was unresponsive. My chest ached as if someone had dropped an anvil on it. Trying to quiet my breathing, to ignore the pain of every breath, I focused on the voices.

"See, she's back." It was the Major's voice. "Nothing lost."

"You're lucky, Ryker. You may be one of my best Major Generals, but you are not indispensable." My stomach rolled as Minister Fandrin's voice filled the room. "Due to your selfish insubordination, we can no longer continue her electrotherapy without risk of killing her today. I need my granddaughter broken, not dead. It would do you well to remember that. Keep your temper in check, or I will check it for you."

There was a tapping of receding shoes mixed with the offset rap of a cane, their sharp rhythms echoing as they faded down the hall. My eyelids fluttered open, but it took a moment to find focus. I stared at the Major, his bright blues eyes like flares in the dim room.

"Clean her up and take her back to her cell." He said coolly before turning to leave.

I passed out while they were moving me, but when I awoke in my cell someone had sponged the sweat from my body. My hair fell in wet but clean strands, clinging to my face and the back of my neck. My clothes were still dingy though. The stink clung in my nostrils, a foul acidic reminder of my torture. But there was another scent in the room, something sweet. Stacked just inside the door was a pile of dark linens. Without lifting my head I pulled the top most piece of fabric into the air. It was a shirt. Without having to unfold them too, I could see the other loose fabric was a pair of pants. My captors had given me the choice of changing myself. No one had forced me into a shower or stripped me of my clothing. It seemed strange that the same people who had just forcibly stopped my heart with an electrical current found morality when it came to undressing me. An unwanted memory pushed its way to the front of my thoughts.

Maddox's dark eyes flashed in my mind, the hungry lust burning in them as he had watched me shower. Then suddenly they transformed, the life draining from his black eyes as death crept over his face as he took his last labored breaths. I buried my face into the stiff mattress, pressing until white spots popped into my vision, trying to erase the tormenting images. They were getting worse.

Why did he push me out of the way? Why did he sacrifice his life for mine? I still felt a burning hate for Maddox. As the anger flared up, I couldn't be sure if it was only the hate I felt for Maddox or if it was simply all the anger I felt for everything in my life. The fury that consumed me came on suddenly like a flash of lightening. I was angry with my parents for dying, with Fandrin for being a monster, with myself for loving Triven and Mouse when I knew it would only lead to pain, with Maddox for his leering eyes and worse still for saving me, and with Triven for not having come for me already. I had tried not to think about him, but these past few days I was losing that battle. Triven promised he would come back for me, just as I had promised I would survive this place. But as my body ached with pain, I had the sinking feeling we had both made false promises. A Tribal death would have been kinder than this. Violent, but faster.

I wanted to fight for them, to see Mouse and Triven again, but I wasn't sure how much longer I could last here. Tears burned in my eyes. I squeezed them tighter refusing to let a single one escape. The Major's— Ryker I vaguely remember the Minister calling him— harsh words floated back to me. *"Minister Fandrin was right, you are weak just like your mother was."*

My mother was not weak. She had escaped this nightmare disguising itself as a utopia and she did it to save me. If my love for Triven wasn't enough to get me though this, then my love for my parents had to be. Tartarus might have killed my mother, but she had survived Fandrin and that meant I could too. Strange how kindred I felt to her now. For so many years my mother had been little more than a face in my dreams. And while I was aware of how much we looked alike, there was little other connection I had to the woman who haunted me. I had inherited her blue eyes, her blonde hair, her sharp cheekbones and her thin lips, but that was it. While still aggressively protective of her memory, I had always connected more with my father. He was the one whose words spoke to me everyday, whose knowledge had kept me alive.

I longed for my father's journal, hoping it was still safely in Triven's care. Had he found it yet, nestled in my abandoned backpack?

As much as I wanted my father's writings here to comfort me, I was glad they were far away from Fandrin's reach. Besides, there was little good they would do me here. My father had never written about The Sanctuary or how they had escaped. All of his words of survival were for the world outside, here they meant nothing.

Today had proven one thing, despite the

torture—despite the threats—Minister Fandrin wanted me alive. He restarted my heart, validating the fact that I was more valuable to him alive than dead. This meant that if I could hold out mentally, if I could stay true to who I was, I had a chance at surviving this.

I sat up and pulled the fresh clothing toward me. Turning my back to the ever-seeing camera, I stripped off my soiled garments and put on the fresh ones. The fabric felt rough against my still sensitive skin but at least they smelled fresh.

Shoving my old vile clothing away, I curled up on my cot. Crossing my legs beneath me, I leaned back against the cold cinderblock walls for support. The red light of the camera winked at me before I closed my eyes and let my head fall back.

I had been wrong before.

For so many years I had suppressed my emotions. Pushed away everything that could make me weak, make me human, but now I needed them. I needed those memories, those feelings to give me strength. Hate could give me drive, but I needed more than that. I needed the most dangerous feeling of all.

Hope. Hope gave you strength when all else was lost. Hope gave you a glimpse of a future even when there might not be one to be had. It was a reckless and dangerous emotion and for the first time in my life I let it into my heart.

Just because electroshock was off the docket for now, that didn't mean they wouldn't have a new torture worked out for me tomorrow. So, for the first time since I was captured, I let myself think about Triven and Mouse. Then I drew upon the few mental images I had of my parents. Keeping my eyes closed, I slowly drifted into a restless sleep.

Dreams quickly turned to nightmares. I was the child I had seen on the screens. I was sparing and I was winning. The faceless little girl before me took hit after hit until she couldn't get up again while Fandrin watched smugly from the sidelines. A strange pride washed over me. I stood triumphant over my opponent's fallen body, but something felt wrong. I looked down at the girl again. My smile wavered. Her brown hair fanned out around her unmoving head. Her thin neck was exposed. A scar. My hands shook as I turned her over. There was blood. On her face... On my hands... It trickled from her open mouth as her lifeless eyes stared up at me. I choked.

Mouse...

The screams from my nightmare erupted in my cell. They echoed, slapping me in the face, but the nightmares didn't stop. I could still see her. Still feel the blood on my hands. Screams turned to sobs and I began to claw at my own eyes to make the images go away.

5. CONTROL

I **STARTLED AWAKE**, causing the muscles in my neck to twinge. I had just barely dozed off.

It wasn't until the door swung inward that I realized that's what had awakened me.

Major Ryker James stepped into the cell sneering contemptuously down at me. His eyes traced over me with a look of disgust. Despite the washed hair and change of clothing, I was sure I looked anything but healthy. I stared blankly at him.

"What, no smart comment for me this morning, Princess? I'm disappointed." He said.

"I had a few quips in mind but dumbing them down for you takes too much energy." I smirked sardonically as I stretched lazily. "So what do we have planned for today Ryker, ripping off my fingernails, poison-tipped needles?"

He stooped, snatching my upper arm in a tight

grip and yanking me toward him. He towered over me. I stared down at his hand on my arm and was shocked to see that his fingers could close entirely around my bicep. I knew I had lost weight but I hadn't realized until that moment just how much. He yanked my arm again, forcing me to meet his eyes.

"That's Major James to you, Princess. You *will* respect me within these walls." Keeping a firm grip, he hauled me though the door. The familiar black bag was over my head before I could lift my gaze. The hands forcing my wrists into the shackles were far from gentle.

"While your ideas sound enticing, we had something else in mind." I could hear the malice in Ryker's tone. Taking a restricted breath, I began counting our steps.

My guard still consisted of at least five other soldiers at all times, but I could tell by the variance in footsteps that it was a rotating guard. Ryker seemed to be the only constant in the group. I wondered mildly if he was assigned to my demise in particular or if he had just taken a perverse liking to overseeing torture. I felt the familiar drop in my stomach as the elevator rose again, but unlike the time I visited The Minister's office, we stopped after only a few seconds. The gliding doors were nearly soundless as they opened, but the blast of noise from beyond caused me to start with surprise. The sounds of combat hammering my ears were all too familiar. Ryker forced me forward and the noise magnified.

A hand roughly yanked the bag away from my head. I was prepared for the change in lighting this time. My eyes adjusted. It looked like a warehouse. Everything was painted the same lackluster dark grey. There were clerestory windows surrounding the space, diffusing the room with muted sunlight. Aside from a few sparse bulbs and the dimmed sunlight, everything in the room was heavy and dark. It seemed the absolute inverse of The Minister's office. While I did not remember standing in the cavernous room myself, this was the same room I had seen my younger-self sparring in just days ago on the monitor screens. My eyes darted to the sparring rings scattered in the room and my heart sank. Older soldiers dressed in customary silver stood outside of the rings overseeing the matches. The fighters poised inside, however, were much younger.

They were children.

My eyes flitted from sparring match to sparring match. Most of them appeared to be under ten, dressed in matching drab grey uniforms. The dream from last night came racing back.

"Cadets!" Ryker's voice rang out, echoing back in the open space. All sparring teams froze in their matches. Their supervisors snapped to attention, saluting their superior.

"Line up!" The female solider on my left cried out. There was a scramble as the young cadets ran to assemble before us. I could not help but stare as their curious eyes flickered toward me. My throat swelled as I took each face in. Based on my short time spent around the Subversive's children, I roughly gauged their ages. The oldest child was maybe thirteen, the youngest bordering on seven. Each child bore the marks of fighting—bloody noses, blackened eyes and jaws, fat lips, bloody knuckles—every one marred by Fandrin's edicts.

"We have a special treat for you today." Ryker said. Several of the children's attention flickered to me once more. "Our honored guest here used to be the best in her class. The fastest rising cadet in our militia. She was our fiercest fighter, best weapons expert and our most lethal hope for maintaining our utopian society here in The Sanctuary."

All eyes broke rank this time. They gazed at me in appreciation, but just as that faint light of admiration sparked, Ryker snuffed it out with his next words.

"BUT… it seems that our prodigy here has forgotten her place." He prowled down the line of children as he spoke. "WHO are we here to serve?!"

"The Minister Sir!" The cadets shouted in unison, their curious eyes snapping back to attention.

"And who do we protect?!" Ryker bellowed.

"The Minister Sir!" Their volume rose with pride.

"And who would we *die* for?!" His icy stare shifted to me.

"The Minister Sir!"

I repressed a shiver, as my chest heaved with hate.

"And *why* do we live to protect our Minister?" He held my gaze. I wanted to slit his throat.

The echo of their perfectly synchronized response made the flesh on my arms prickle. "We live to serve and protect our Minister because he is the glue that holds our society together. He is our leader and our savior. Equality! Unity! Freedom! Semper fi!"

My heart stuttered as their last words rebounded back to me, the translation racing through my mind. *Always faithful.* I knew that phrase from the history books I had read in the library. It had been used in the Old World's military. It was a phrase of honor, of loyalty to country and state. But to hear it from the mouths of children... Staring at their blank, obedient faces... They didn't know what they were saying, *couldn't* know the monster they were committing their lives to.

Ryker turned to me, barely concealing a grin. When he spoke, his words were only for me. "The Minister owns them. Their every breath, their every thought. They have already been molded into his perfect little soldiers. He owns them, and soon he will own you too, Princess."

I lunged forward, feeling my wrists bruise as I pulled against my shackles. Just before I could reach Ryker's face—which I intended to smash with my skull—someone yanked me backward, forcing my arms excruciatingly upward. I doubled forward trying unsuccessfully to alleviate some of the pain blazing in my shoulders. A few more inches of pressure and both my arms would come out of their sockets.

Ryker leaned forward, so he could see my face. "Save it, Princess. You're going to need that energy."

"Cadet Norris, in the ring." He barked, still looking at me.

I watched through the tendrils of my hair as one of the older children, a boy about the age of thirteen, jumped forward. With a salute, he moved to the nearest sparring mat.

"Today we will be reminding our guest where she comes from. You cadets will be fighting for merit and honor. But today there will be no resignations. There will be no conceding defeat. You will fight until one of you no longer can." Ryker said.

The children's nervous looks were prominent on their paling faces. Still, they each shouted, "Sir, yes Sir!"

Swallowing back vomit, I stared at my shoes. They were going to make me watch as these children beat each other to a bloody pulp. Honestly, I would have preferred the electric shock. I had done this same thing as a child, but I could remember nothing of it. It made no mark on my memory, but my dream last night made me think of Mouse. She did remember her life here, and it haunted her. Every child's face I stared at, I saw hers.

"There will be one other change to our normal training." Ryker's deep voice rang out once more. In one swift movement, the manacles were released from my wrists and I was shoved forward into the ring. I staggered, nearly colliding with the equally surprised boy. "You will be fighting against a trained soldier who has survived with the savages outside of The Wall. She may look weak, but don't underestimate her. She is as lethal as any Tartarus Tribesman."

The children visibly stiffened, but to my astonishment their rigidity did not appear to be from fear but from determination. I was no longer the pride of their city. I was the enemy. I was everything they feared, everything they had been raised to hate. I was what they were training to keep out.

Rubbing my wrists, I drew myself up to full height and squared my shoulders against the Major. They couldn't make me do this. This was not a nightmare. I had a choice.

"I *refuse* to fight."

"You *will* fight, or they will suffer the consequences." To my surprise, it wasn't Ryker who responded but a soldier at the back of my guard. I had not noticed him before now, but as he moved forward through the pack of soldiers I recognized him. He was there the night I first met The Minister and again later in his office. It was the boy whose eyes reminded me of Mouse. Before, among the older soldiers, he had seemed so young. But now surrounded by children, I realized my first judgment had been false. He was young, yes, but no longer a child. Maybe fourteen or fifteen, but small for his age. Yet, he wore a white suit and his shoulders were adorned with silver epaulettes. He was not a mere soldier, but an officer—despite his young age. There was something in his tone that set my nerves on edge as he spoke again. "And I doubt your conscience can handle the repercussions of your actions."

I prickled as his large brown eyes glazed over like ice. My mind raced, searching for options. If I fought weakly, if I let the children get in a few good hits and ran out the fights until they were too exhausted to fight... Or if I could fake a knock out, maybe I could spare them. The soldiers seemed to think I was still a strong fighter but they had not seen me fight in years. Witnessed me fire a gun when we had tried avoiding capture—yes, but engage in hand-to-hand combat—no. Maybe I could fake loss of technique.

Six months ago, I would have fought these children. On the streets of Tartarus, the old Phoenix would have engaged anyone who came across her path and demolished them without a second thought. But I wasn't that girl anymore. Not after Mouse, after Triven. And especially not after meeting The Minister.

I met Ryker's sharp eyes and nodded once. As I turned to face the blonde-haired boy in the ring, a small fist thrust toward my face. Instinctively I dodged sideways, and popped my wrist out catching him in the side. An involuntary yelp escaped the boy and my heart plummeted. The many years of training and fighting to survive were hard to ignore. Synapses fired in my brain, my muscles twitching with the urge to fight, but I repressed them. The boy bobbed twice, swinging sloppily with his right hand. He threw too hard. His left hand dropped leaving his entire left side open, but I did nothing. Instead, I let his fist collide with my jaw. The sound was much more impressive than the actual punch, but I went with it, staggering a little, allowing the boy time to regain his own balance. The crowd of on-looking cadets cheered, but Ryker's and the threatening young soldier's eyes narrowed. They were not deceived.

I loosened my stance, tried to make my form look poor.

Think novice. I reminded myself.

I threw a punch, stepping forward to warn the boy of my intent. To my relief, he read my body language and stepped back letting the blow glance off his shoulder. I let my body fall forward with the force of my throw, leaving my head exposed. Careful not to let any anticipatory flinch cross my features, I prepared for his next assault. He took the opening and landed a clean blow to the back of my head with his elbow. Stars popped in my eyes, but his hit was not yet as strong as an adult's. Still, I dropped to my knees feigning a concussion. I let the boy punch me in the jaw and collapsed forward pulling my hands around my head like a novice fighter would. The boy went in for the kill and began assaulting my midriff with kicks. Despite his smaller size, I felt a rib crack. Even then, I stayed down and continued to take the beating.

I could hear his fellow cadets cheering him on, but a roar rose above theirs. "Enough!!!"

I rolled onto my back just in time to see the young, brown-haired officer rip the blonde boy away from me. The officer pointed a stubby finger at me. His eyes were ablaze with wild cruelty. "I warned you. You chose to fight like coward and now they will pay the price."

Horror sucked the air from my lungs when he punched the boy in the throat. As the child doubled over in pain, grasping at his neck—desperate for air—the officer began to pummel his face. I jumped to my feet just as the child's nose broke. I lunged forward but arms bound me like an iron cage.

He was going to kill the little boy.

6. FISSURES

I SCREAMED AT the young officer to stop, struggling against the arms holding me back. My legs flung out to kick the person restraining me, but he squeezed tighter. My broken rib blazed but I ignored it.

The young officer had snapped the boy's arm nearly in two. The child's screams were like razorblades against my eardrums. My attempts to free myself became erratic. I knew this wasn't how I would normally act, but I couldn't stop. One name kept thrumming in my head.

Mouse, Mouse, Mouse…

I yelled louder, so loud my throat felt like it would tear. With all the screaming and thrashing, it took a moment for me to hear the soft, sinister voice in my ear.

"Gage will kill that boy, Prea. He doesn't care if there is one less cadet in the ranks. He will sacrifice that boy or any other child to teach you a lesson." Ryker's voice made my blood run cold. "You can stop this. You may hurt one of them, but at least then you're in control. Unless you're too weak to handle it, *Princess*."

The Mouse-like young man—Gage, as Ryker called him—raised his fist to deliver the final blow to the limp boy dangling in his grasp.

"I'LL FIGHT!" I screamed. Gage paused to look at me. The pleasure in his eyes made my insides clench. I spoke softer now. "Okay… I will fight for real. No more feigning."

Gage dropped the boy with a triumphant smile. "Get this weak piece of trash out of my sight. He fights like a child. Who's next?"

"Good girl." Ryker crooned in my ear. I could hear him smiling as he said it.

Ryker released me, shoving me forward, as Gage stepped out of the ring and called the name of a new competitor. A girl no more then twelve stepped onto the mat. Gage pulled a gun from his side holster. Crossing his arms, he tapped the barrel against his arm with a pointed look. *You fight or I'll shoot her,* it said.

I readied my stance.

THE SCREAMS ECHOED off the walls of my cell, magnified in the tiny room. I knew the screams were mine, but still it took a while to quiet them. It had gotten worse over the last three days. The screams I could usually choke back or quiet once I awoke had taken on a life of their own. I would awake multiple times a night screaming so loud I could taste blood.

I never slept for more than half an hour. By the time I finally got my body to stop shaking and could doze off, it would start all over again. The nightmares that plagued me were of my parents, of Mouse and Triven and of Maddox's dead eyes. They were getting worse, more vivid and more violent with each passing day. Before when I awoke, I had always known it was just a dream, past memories that couldn't be changed, but now they seemed so real... so present...

Despite my resolve, they were breaking me.

My knuckles were swollen and bloody, my face blotched with purple and yellowing bruises and my fractured ribs ached every time I breathed. But this was not the worst of it. I could feel my mental stability crumbling. For the past five days I had been forced to fight child after child. I wanted to keep them safe, to keep them away from the boy who had once foolishly reminded me of my Mouse. I say *foolishly* reminded because he now resembled nothing of the child I had sacrificed my life for. Gage's brown eyes, which I had once found deep and pensive, were now hardened and cruel. He became the antithesis of everything I saw in

Mouse.

Each fight I told myself I was hurting that child to save them from a worse fate, but it was becoming harder and harder to believe that. At first I just knocked a few kids out cold, before they could even raise their fists to fight, but then I began to worry about the brain damage I might inflict doing that. So then, I changed my strategy to painful but reparable injuries, dislocated shoulders, sprained ankles, broken fingers and in one extreme case where the child was too stubborn to give up, a broken arm.

I hated myself for it.

For five days I had been hurting innocent children and even if it was to protect them, it made me sick. I couldn't remember the last time I had eaten, and my body was starting to show the signs of fatigue. During the last fight yesterday, I actually blacked out for a few seconds. Ryker's keen eyes watched me carefully, analyzing my every move. I was beginning to crack and he knew it. Gage stayed within sight of the ring at all times, his gun always ready, but he kept his distance as long as I continued to fight.

I pulled myself into a ball and stared at the red light on the camera above me. They would come for me soon and we would start this perverse torture all over again. I squeezed my eyes shut but not before a single tear escaped. Hope was nearly gone. It felt like my soul was dying. If I didn't escape soon, I would lose my mind. The dreams were also starting to happen when I wasn't asleep.

My mind was still churning when I heard the familiar sounds of footsteps outside the door. There was something different this time though. Unless my ears were deceiving me—which it was possible they were right now—there were fewer guards this time. Forcing myself into a seated position, I twisted toward the door, giving myself the best vantage point of the hallway when it opened. The seconds seemed to stretch as I stared at the steel door waiting for it to move. Eventually, I could hear the back of a hand brush the metal surface as it reached for the handle. I trained my eyes on the hallway behind the figure, my mind calculating as Major Ryker James walked into my cell.

"Having sweet dreams, Princess?" Ryker asked in a mocking tone.

I held my tongue. There were only two guards with him in the hall. It seems the arrogant prick was finally underestimating me.

Idiot.

"Oh, don't pout. We have another thrilling day planned for you, your highness. Besides it makes that pretty face of yours so unbecoming." He leaned over me smirking. I stared pointedly at his left ear, refusing to meet his eyes. My heart skipped a beat as something over his shoulder caught my eye. I smoothed my face to hide my excitement. "See, that wasn't so hard."

He thoughtlessly leaned closer as my heart rate began to spike. I hoped he couldn't hear it in the small room. I stared harder at his ear to mask what I was truly watching. The light on the camera just above his head had lost power twice now, the tiny red light flickering out and then back on. Whatever the cause of the power failure, it seemed the odds might be in my favor for the first time since I had set foot in this city. If the power to the cameras went off now, when there only happened to be two other guards watching me, I actually stood a chance of making an escape.

Ryker was speaking to me again, but I wasn't listening. I was recounting the steps to the elevator in my mind. Then I calculated the amount of time spent in the elevator to reach a floor above ground. Thirty seconds maybe, so at least three floors above where I was now. I could make up the rest as I went. Maybe even escape into the elevator shaft itself. I would be harder to track there. The light pulsed again, staying off for nearly five seconds this time.

This was it.

I turned my face to his, meeting his glassy stare with my own. A manic grin erupted on my lips and widened when he flinched in response. Sensing his blunder, he quickly leaned closer in an attempt to intimidate me and cover his own fear.

"Something funny, Princess?" His dark eyebrows furrowed as he studied my face.

Eight seconds this time. The power failures were increasing in duration, each time lengthened by three seconds. Next would be for eleven. That was all I needed.

He leaned in so close I could feel his hot breath on my cheeks. I held his gaze, but I was really watching the red light. His voice dropped so I could barely hear it. "Whatever you are thinking about, you had better wipe that smile off your face or Fandrin will do it for you. You are going to keep your mouth shut and do exactly as I say or else—"

I never got to hear the rest of his threat. The light flickered off as he spoke and I launched myself into action. I slammed my face forward, cracking the top of my skull into his perfect nose. There was a satisfying crunch as blood began to pour down Ryker's face, marring his perfectly white uniform. He staggered backward, arms flailing wildly for me, but I was ready for him. Kicking out, I caught him square in the chest sending him reeling backward into the silver toilet.

Eight seconds left.

Ignoring the pain in my ribs, I twisted to the door just as the first guard exploded through it, gun half raised and confusion on her face. Leaping into the air, I landed a foot on the doorknob while catching the baffled guard in the jaw with the other. Her eyes rolled back in her head as she slumped to the side clearing my path.

Four seconds.

After tipping forward to let my fingertips reach the doorframe, I then swung myself out into the hallway colliding with the second guard. We crashed to the ground with me astride his chest, the fingers of one of my hands already winding themselves in his hair as the other hand pulled back, poised to punch him in the face. Before I could strike, his gun went off and searing pain ripped across my left temple. Despite the warm blood I could feel dripping down my face, I knew it was merely superficial. I locked my jaw and punched him twice before his body went slack.

Time's up.

Precisely as the thought crossed my mind, a screaming alarm erupted through the barren halls. I reached for the guard's gun but snatched my hand back as the wall in front of me exploded into bits. Rolling sideways, I glanced back into my cell. Pulling himself up on the toilet with one arm, Ryker held his gun shakily in the other, his eyes crazed as they flickered to the camera in the corner of the cell and to me. I reached for the fallen guard's weapon again, but Ryker's hand twitched and the wall behind me exploded for a second time.

Cursing, I abandoned the gun and bolted down

the hall. My prisoner-provided linen shoes slid on the floor. I was losing precious seconds. My mind raced, retracing the steps I had walked so many times with the hood on. *Right at sixty-five. Left at one hundred and ninety-seven.* The steps were easy, more due to the fact that there were no other paths to take. The elevator came into view. Its doors were open. I pushed harder. The pain in my head was escalating, the alarms seeming to grow in intensity with the throbbing. I slid to a halt inside the elevator. My eyes instantly searched for the buttons, but the panels were all blank except for a scanner. I lunged for the opening, but the doors snapped closed with surprising speed, narrowly missing my hand as I leapt backward. My stomach dropped and I knew the elevator was moving upward.

"Damn it." I muttered.

I had just trapped myself in a metal gift-wrapped box for The Minister. Taking a deep breath, I searched the ceiling. It looked like a solid surface. There was no escaping. I raced through my options, the doors would open soon and I had to do something. Glancing around I kicked off my shoes and tossed them over the two small cameras in the corners. Now at least both of us were blind. The elevator was small enough if I stretched to my tiptoes I could just reach the opposite side with my fingertips. The progression was slow and painful, but I managed to walk myself up the walls in this strange, extended "x" position. Just as I reached the top, my back touching the ceiling, the momentum of the elevator began to slow. Had I not been suspended in the air, trying to hold myself up, I might not have felt the elevator stop. But as I was precariously perched on the walls of the moving box, I could feel my sweaty fingers slip just a little as the elevator halted. Blood dripped from the wound on my head. A small puddle had collected below me. I pressed my temple to my arm to staunch the bleeding. The doors opened slower than they had closed. I stopped breathing.

I waited. Sweat was beginning to pool on my face.

There were no words spoken, but I could hear the unmistakable sounds of fabric swishing together as someone gave rapid hand signals. Feet began moving against the hard floor outside. There must have been at least six guards by my count. Slowly, the muzzle of a gun protruded its way through the open door, followed by hands, then arms suited in silver. Just as her blonde head came into view, I retracted my arms and legs, launching myself onto the guard below. My hands wrapped around the barrel of her gun as my feet connected with her knees. The Master's training on how to successfully disarm someone flashed in my mind as my hands moved. Side-stepping the barrel in case she actually managed to get a round off, I pulled the gun toward me for just a moment dislodging it from her shoulder. As her muscles contracted instinctively to pull the gun back, I moved forward, using her own momentum against her. The butt of the gun popped her hard in the face. As her eyes swam, I twisted the gun up and over her head and spun her like a human top. I brought her to a stop, yanking her arm up behind her back until I could feel the tendons protest. She yelped, but otherwise did not fight me. The whole elaborate dance took barely five seconds and ended with my back to the elevator wall, the gun in my hand, and the unfortunate guard acting as my own personal human shield.

Five armed guards waited outside of the elevator, eyes and guns trained on what little of my face they could see behind their comrade. No one moved.

"Back off or I shoot her." I twitched the gun, regarding the woman I held before me. Her breathing had become more labored, making a strange gurgling noise. She sagged a little and I cursed for having hit her so hard. If I had to carry her weight as well as work the gun I would be in serious trouble. I pulled up higher on her arm forcing her to walk forward.

The guards moved with us. As I stepped to the edge of the elevator, I risked a quick glance of our surroundings. It was a small lobby of sorts, mostly painted grey and white with minimal furniture. It was empty but for the seven of us. Something moved to my left. A door off of the room opened and The Minister walked through. His face was smug, his white suit pristine as ever. The brass cane was tapping at his side. A pulse of hate rushed though me. Shoving my human shield to the floor, I took aim at Fandrin's chest and pulled the trigger.

7. FRACTURES

NOTHING HAPPENED.
My finger reflexively pulled the trigger again. Rapidly. Desperately.

Nothing.

I just caught a glimpse of Fandrin's superior expression as the butt of someone's gun smashed into my right temple.

I didn't remember falling, but I was suddenly on the floor with The Minister standing over me. He was twirling the gun I had stolen in his hand. I blinked back the blood flowing from my temple, trying to maintain eye contact with him.

"Great little toys these guns," he affectionately patted the firearm. "Your mother actually gave me the idea for them. Each gun is specifically formatted to work only with its rightful soldier. Every member of the guard has a unique microchip implanted in their wrist when they enlist. Each chip is then calibrated to its matching firearm. Ingenious really. No one other than a soldier can ever fire a weapon here."

He pressed the barrel of the gun to my head and pulled the trigger. Despite the knowledge that it wouldn't fire, I still flinched. Fandrin laughed while tossing the gun to the nearest soldier. As he began walking away he spoke over his shoulder. "Take her back down to the training room, I have a *specific* lesson in mind for my granddaughter."

I DIDN'T EXACTLY black out as the guards dragged me along the white halls. To my surprise they didn't bother putting a bag over my head this time, but the truth was it didn't really matter. With my vision going in and out, it was unlikely I would remember much anyway.

It startled me when my face hit the black sparring mat that smelled of blood, sweat and rubber. It took a moment for the familiar stink to completely infiltrate my hazy brain. It wasn't until I heard the whispers of moving feet around me that I realized we were already in the training room.

Had we really gotten here that quickly? How much time had passed?

Someone was talking but I couldn't quite make

out the words. I twisted my head to the side and pushed myself up onto my palms and knees. Big mistake. My eyes popped open, roving the black surface of the mat to find purchase, to find something to ground my spinning head. Blinking twice, my swimming vision finally fell on something small and white. I stared hard at the oddly shaped object until it stopped moving. The instant my vision focused I regretted my choice of anchor. It was a tooth... and based on the size, a child's. Red blood was still fresh on the porcelain surface. I breathed deeply through my mouth to quiet the roiling in my stomach.

Something in the room had changed. It was silent now. Staying on all fours, I tilted my head to see young Gage standing at the edge of the mat. A manic grin spread across his face as he gestured to me like a psychotic ringleader. I was to be his next performer, the main attraction of this freak show. Something white shifted next to him and my gaze slid to the man standing to his side. The Minister's hand was cupping Gage's bony shoulder like a proud father. Hatred welled within the pit of my stomach.

Pushing the nausea aside, I focused on that hate and pushed myself unsteadily to my feet. My temple pulsed where the blood continued to ooze, but I stood my ground. There was a bigger crowd than usual. There were many older soldiers now mixed with the young ones. This was not merely a sparring class. It seemed my punishment was to be a spectacle for the entire academy. Well, if they wanted a show, then I would give them a show.

Assuming my fighting stance I grinned at Gage, letting the blood trickling from my temple run over my lips and into my bared teeth. Surely I looked crazed. I stretched out my hand beckoning him to come fight me. The result was exactly what I had wanted. Several cadets took tentative steps back while Gage lunged hungrily forward, eager to contest me. All I needed was fifteen seconds in the ring with that psychopath. Fifteen seconds and I could snap the neck of the Minister's prize pet. An all-consuming rage surged within me, a fiery desire to put that rabid dog down.

To my utter disappointment, The Minister's hand clasped tighter, holding Gage back. Fandrin's white head tilted as he whispered something in his left ear. A glint sparked in Gage's eyes that made my scalp prickle.

"Private Riggs front and center." Gage bellowed, grinning at me.

My heart stopped.

Struggling to keep my stance firm, I felt the entirety of my body run hollow. A tiny child had stepped into the ring, her brown hair pulled into a low ponytail, her large brown eyes wide with fear. Her tiny frame shook slightly, but her mouth was set in a thin line of determination. She was so small, the youngest child yet, maybe seven at the most. I choked back the tears threatening their way to the surface... it was Mouse. My nightmares were becoming reality. They had captured her!

No... no that couldn't be right.

I stared harder at the little girl. Her eyes were too light, her mouth was too small. I knew all of this, but still, all my exhausted mind saw was Mouse. The girl's mismatched features blurred from existence and standing before me I saw only my friend.

A door banged open at the far end of the room and while every head turned toward the sound, I couldn't tear my eyes away from the child standing before me. I could hear the crowd parting, the steady march of heavy boots. It wasn't until I heard ragged breathing through his broken nose that I realized Major Ryker James had finally made it to the party. He stopped close, his body's heat radiating against my back. Ryker's labored breathing was the only sound in the room for a few seconds. Then there was a hiss of fabric and whoosh of moving air. I recognized the sounds of an arm raising to strike.

Please... yes, let him end this. I couldn't help the thought as I stared at the child in front of me. *Not her...*

"NO!" The Minister's voice rang out. My hair moved with the force of Ryker's swing as his fist came to an abrupt halt.

"*Please* sir," Ryker's voice was distorted by his

broken nose.

"Your carelessness, Major, is what started this little fiasco in the first place. Now stand down and let a true leader show you how to handle a hostile criminal." The Minister's words were simple, but I knew their true meaning. He was tired of playing with me, tired of being patient. He meant to break me, tonight. "Cadets pay close attention! This fight will show where true loyalties lies, that desire for self-preservation will always wither under The Sanctuary's power. We fight for the *many*, not the *few*."

Liar, I thought.

Ryker hesitated a moment longer before stepping away. While I could no longer feel his presence against my back, I knew he had not removed himself very far. The tension and anger emanating from his body was still hot against my skin.

I only vaguely heard Gage call out to the cadets around me. "Who do you fight for?"

"The Minister!" The resounding cry echoed off the ceilings. A clap of thunder made from hundreds of voices.

"And what do you trust in?

"The Sanctuary!"

"And how do you fight for it?"

My ears began to ring so loudly I didn't even hear the response, but I read it on the girl's lips.

TO THE DEATH!

My palms felt slick, while my throat went dry. I could feel the muscles in my neck spasming as I tried to swallow. *To the death...*

This wasn't just another fight in which I could break an arm or render someone unconscious. The Minister meant for me to kill the child or to succumb and let her kill me. Which we both knew would never happen, or at least it couldn't happen... could it?

Before my mind could fully process the lethality of the situation, the tiny girl was advancing. Her blows were calculated and surprisingly fast. The child fought better then most others twice her age. I backed away, losing my ground as I parried her advances. I was trying to think, to figure some way out of this, but I couldn't focus. If I let the child win I would lose everything. I would never see Triven or Mouse again and I would be turning this little girl into a murderer, for what? To appease my demented grandfather? To ease my own conscience?

I lashed out twice unconsciously. My survival instincts were clawing their way to the surface. The girl fell back cradling her head before resuming her stance. She spat out a mouthful of blood and began advancing again muttering, "For The Sanctuary."

I could hear Fandrin laugh from somewhere nearby and my vision went red. Someone had to make him pay for this. I *had* to live, if just to see that he died.

I remembered moving toward the girl, closing my eyes so I didn't have to look at her face—at Mouse's face—but I didn't remember any of my actions after that. It was as if someone else took over my body and I let it happen. It wasn't until I heard the clatter of the knife at my feet and the call to "Finish it," that I felt the blood on my hands. My eyes fell to the floor. A small body lay at my feet. It was like watching the world from the end of a long tunnel. My breathing was angry and ragged, while the girl's was shallow. I stared at the black handled knife that lay between my feet. My fingers slid together, her blood slick against my skin. This was the point where every other fight had stopped. The point when they carried away their comrade and placed another before me to break. But it was different this time. There would be no reset, no going back. The knife at my feet proved that.

I had promised Triven I would survive for him, promised that I wouldn't abandon him and Mouse, but at what cost? Could he forgive me for this? My whole life had been about nothing but survival. Seventeen years of doing anything it took to survive, but was *this* worth it? If I killed a child for my own selfish motives I would be no better than my grandfather... My head snapped up and I met the old man's eyes.

That was it.

That was what he wanted all along. To prove how much I was like him. To prove I would do whatever it took to survive. Just like he had taught me all those years ago. He wanted to prove to me that surviving for what I thought was right, was more important than the lives of others. He wanted me to see that I was the same as him, that I was still of his blood.

For one spectacular moment I fantasized about throwing the knife into his skull, but there were at least forty guns pointed at me and as my vision swam I could not guarantee actually hitting my target. I stared back down at the knife again and then at the child.

I smiled to myself. He was right about one thing. One life was not as important as the cause. *Please forgive me*. I silently pleaded to Triven and Mouse.

I stooped for the knife, swiftly snatching it up and with a mighty thrust aimed the blade directly at my own heart.

8. SHATTERED

"**N**O!" **THE MINISTER'S** cry could be heard above the ensuing chaos, but it barely reached my ears.

A large body collided with mine, grabbing for the knife in my hands. The blade nicked the top of my collarbone, scraping across the bone as it split the skin. Muscular arms wound around me in an attempt to crush me into submission. My body reacted to the assault with violence of its own. My hand flashed out, redirecting the blade toward my attacker. I caught a flash of jet-black hair as the knife found purchase, nipping Major Ryker James in the arm. Everything I had been holding back exploded to the surface. My fists moved with a speed and mercilessness even I had forgotten they were capable of. Ryker was equally skilled, our hands and limbs colliding violently, hard enough to break most people's bones. With the knife in my hand, I was gaining the advantage. He couldn't take my death from me and if he was a stubborn enough to try, then he could join me. I wouldn't kill a child, but I had no aversions to killing monsters.

Our entangled bodies crashed into the crowd of onlookers, sending them scattering in every direction. The running children were soon replaced with armed soldiers. Little red lights began flickering to life, dancing over our bodies as we fought.

A cry broke out over the din, "ARMS READY!"

My head turned in the direction of the cry and I caught Gage's eye for a brief second as his mouth twisted into a vicious sneer. Something moved behind Gage and I faltered. The Minister's arms were raised, in a silent attempt to halt the escalading disorder. There was something in his eyes I had not seen before, something he had kept hidden, but I saw it now.

I had lost focus. I had made dire a mistake.

In the seconds of my brief distraction, Ryker's hand grabbed my wrist holding the knife. The world flipped as I was lifted into the air and then slammed face down on the mat. The knife slipped from my hand as my arm twisted unbearably high behind my back, but that pain was nothing compared to Major Ryker James' knee colliding with my forearm and snapping the bones in two. I screamed in agony. In some kind of accidental, sick-minded mercy, Ryker granted me asylum by punching me in the head so hard the world and the pain slipped away with the darkness.

MY BODY JOLTED awake as the ice water burned against my skin. I gasped and sputtered, choking on the freezing water. My arms threw wide in self-defense, only to be pulled back instantly with a stifled scream. My arm felt like it was ripped in two. I shuffled backward until my back hit the wall, cradling my broken arm to my chest. It felt over-sized and heavy. I glanced down to see a clumsy black cast covering my right arm from elbow to knuckles.

"I figured the pain of slow healing might be a good reminder of who created you."

I turned my head toward the door of my cell. A dark figure stood blocking the doorway. Even though I couldn't see his face through my swollen eyes, I knew the voice.

I laughed through gnashed teeth. "I suppose a broken arm is a pretty accurate representation of a pitiful, *sick* old man."

The responding silence was heavy in the tiny cell. I looked down at the floor, smiling. "What's the matter Gramps? Not the response you had been hoping for?"

"You *will* respect me child." He snarled. "You wanted death today, but I *chose* to spare you. Without me you are *nothing*. I own everything your life is made of. I own *you*. Like it or not it is *my* blood in your veins, *my* voice that speaks in your mind and you *will* obey me. Or I will personally see that the end you so obviously desire comes as a long, drawn-out process that will make you wish your *mother* had never been born."

A laugh barked out of my chest sounding more like a cough. I could taste a coppery tang in the back of my throat. Closing my eyes, I let my head fall back against the wall. A weak smile crept to my lips and the words fell drunkenly from my mouth. "Seeing as how you can't even catch a librarian bookworm and an innocent little child, I'm sure you can understand why it's hard for me to take your threats seriously."

I was fishing and the rash old man took the bait. His polished shoes tapped across the cement floor stopping just as his hands clasped around my throat. I nearly blacked out as he yanked me to my feet, pulling me toward his face. "*No one* can evade me forever, child. Your mother is proof of that. I saw it in your eyes today, you're giving up. Little by little you are wasting away here and you have two choices. You can either remember where you came from and rule obediently by my side, *or* be disposed of like the disease-riddled vermin you have let yourself become. You *are* disposable, child."

My eyes flickered open, trying wildly to focus on his.

"You know *Grandfather*, I saw something in your eyes today too. *Fear.*" Grabbing the front of his shirt with my good hand, I pulled myself closer to him so my blood tainted breath washed his face. He began to recoil, but I held fast. "You can lie to yourself all you want, but I saw it. You *need* me. You are losing control of your city. Your people are turning against you, aren't they? The revolution my mother started didn't die with her."

My voice was rising both in pitch and volume as a manic high spread through me. Even as I spoke the crazed words, I knew they were true. Fandrin's hand began to shake with anger against my throat, trying to choke the words but I only yelled louder. "I can read it all over your face. You reek of fear and desperation. You need someone the people will love again. A long-lost prodigy bloodline that you rescued from the depths of hell itself, only to bring back to life and raise as your beloved successor. HA!" I cackled with sick delight. "You can't kill me, you *need* me."

"I DON'T NEED ANYONE!" The Minister screamed in my face, spit flying from his quivering lips.

My demented crowing echoed off the barren walls of my cell. "Yes, you do old man. But you know what? You will *never* have me. I have so many more reasons to live than to die for, and you can never take them away. There is nothing you can do to me now. I know your weakness. I own *you* old man and I will *never* be your lap dog. Trust me, the second you think you've got me trained, the instant you take my collar off I... will... rip ... out ... your... throat." I articulated each of the last words then lunged, snapping at him. My teeth just grazed his nose as he hastily shoved me back to arms length. True fear now burned in his eyes.

The crazed laughter filled the tiny room again. It vibrated the air and hurt my ears, but it didn't stop, not when he dropped me back onto the water-soaked mattress or even after the door closed. The hysterics lasted for what felt like hours and as sleep finally began to pull me away from my own deranged cackling, I realized this was what it must be like to lose your mind.

"PREA..."

I moaned, feeling the pain in my broken arm. I was shivering on the cold, still damp mattress. The room was finally quiet.

"Prea..."

My eyelids felt heavy with sleep. At first I could not tell if they were open or not. The cell was so dark it mirrored the backs of my eyelids perfectly. Surely they were still closed tight, but just as I thought that, a face came into focus. It was close to mine, laying on the pillow next to me, watching me with warmth in those hazel eyes. Tears welled in my swollen ones.

"Triven." I reached out to touch him but my hand fell on empty space. The tears began to fall in earnest now. I choked out a sob. "You're not real are you?"

He smiled softly, shaking his head. I closed my eyes, wanted to shut him out, but his face was still there. Swallowing, I opened them again.

"I'm losing my mind aren't I?" My voice broke and he nodded, frowning a little. I knew that lying here indulging in my mind's sick torments would only hurt me more, that I would awake in the morning still alone in this hellhole with no one to help me. I knew that keeping my sanity was the only way I might survive, but it didn't matter. I needed him anyway. Lifting my good hand, I laid it on the mattress next to his, not quite touching what I knew wasn't really there.

"You'll stay with me?" I asked the specter. He nodded, smiling sadly. Unconsciousness began to claim me again. "As long as you're here I will never give in to him... I'm trying to keep my promise..."

My sanity was slipping away and I was letting it. He and Mouse were my only reasons to survive, but I knew the truth. No matter how strong my will to survive, no matter how much I loved them, if help didn't come soon I was going to die in here.

9. ALONE

THERE WAS NO telling how much time had passed when I finally awoke, but based on the stench of my own body it had been at least a few days. My arm was throbbing and by reason, the heat radiating from my skin meant it was safe to guess I had contracted a fever. I buried my face in the mattress, breathing in the mildew stench. Tears were still clouding my vision. I pressed my eyes harder into the mattress, trying to staunch the unwanted waterworks.

I had been dreaming of Triven again. Every time I closed my eyes it was either his face or Mouse's that laid in the bed next to me, their patient eyes watching as I slowly slipped further and further away from reality. Every time I awoke it was torture knowing that none of it was real, that I was still here.

That they weren't coming for me.

No one had been in to see me. No torment had

been inflicted, but there had been no food either. My stomach had stopped growling, knowing its meager protests were futile. Every once in a while I would awake to find a small glass of water, but those moments were few and far between. It seemed I had finally pushed the old man too far, and now he was going to let me rot.

Maybe I had been wrong. Maybe he didn't need me after all. Maybe it was better this way.

Even with those thoughts rattling in my brain, something within me refused to give up. It was as if there was this minuscule flicker, this tiny, persistent ember that refused to be doused. And the only thing keeping that teeny spark still burning was the thought that despite what pain and torture The Minister could inflict on me, I was still defying him. Better than that thought, was the knowledge that the two people I loved were doing the same just outside of his reach. With Triven's and Mouse's triumphant evasion lingering in my mind, I managed to pull myself up a little straighter. If I died in here, at least I could die knowing my current life's mission was still being upheld. That somewhere out there people were fighting The Minister. People he could never touch.

The lights flickered to life, blinding me. I drew away, cradling my head against the assault. The light was painfully over stimulating after days in the dark, like tiny needles stabbing my eyes. Instantly, my head began to ache. The cell door opened, but I didn't move.

"Get her up." A cool voice barked from the doorway.

I lifted my head with curiosity. For the first time since my arrival, it wasn't Ryker who had come to retrieve me.

Gage stood in the doorway with a mingled look of pleasure and disgust. Two silver clad guards hurried past the young man and stooped to pull me to my feet. I hung limply in their arms at first, my feet barely working beneath me. It took what little strength I had left to stand, however shakily, in the soldiers' arms.

"What's today's torture? Babysitting you?" I muttered, my voice was like gravel.

Instead of the explosive reaction I had been hoping for, a wide smile spread across his pallid face. My skin prickled. The result was much more frightening than any threat he could have spouted.

"Let's get going. This is one appointment you don't want to miss." Gage turned, leading the way back down the hallway.

Someone shoved me face first against the wall. They fumbled for a minute with the handcuffs, my cast proving to be quite the hindrance. Eventually, they compromised by handcuffing my hands in front of me. One side was so tight it pinched and the other just barely encircled the cast. Before the bag was slipped over my head, I noticed that the size of my personal guard had grown. As I stepped through the door I had counted at least twenty soldiers before being plunged into blackness.

The boots seemed too loud as we moved down the hall, causing my head to pulse. I wanted to ask questions about this so-called appointment, to say something rude and demeaning, but it took all of my focus just to walk. In truth, I was leaning too much on the arms carrying me despite my best efforts to appear strong, the two soldiers half carrying me cursing whenever I fell into them. The elevator ride seemed excruciatingly long, my eyes staring unfocused at the black canvas breathing against my face. I was trying to count the seconds, but they seemed to be drifting in and out. When the door finally opened, it wasn't until we stepped outside that I realized we were in a place I had not yet been.

Internally cursing myself, I forced my slow eyes to blink a few times. *Pull it together!*

I closed my eyes, forcing my ears to listen.

The sounds echoed here, not like in the gym or like The Minister's refined office. It sounded hollow, with metal reverberations. The ground beneath my feet was coarse, gripping the bottoms of my slippers and grinding beneath the guards' shoes. I could smell something too, but could not place it... A metallic tang in the air maybe... or more chemical based? Then there was that whirring sound... I knew that sound. I had heard it before. My brain struggled to recall what seemed like a lifetime ago. It was that sound on the streets, the noise those strange vehicles had made.

I was jerked to a stop just as the bag was yanked from my head. I was staring at a pair of metal doors, their tops towering a good two feet above me. The two guards in the front pulled several levers and the doors swung open to reveal an encased, windowless room made of steel. There were two metal benches on opposite sides with fortified rings affixed strategically to the floor below them. I scanned the room. The step up was nearly a foot off the ground, but stranger yet there were wheels of some sort protruding out from underneath it. The whole thing seemed to be vibrating slightly. It clicked. The smell of chemicals, the humming noise and the vibrations—this *was* one of the vehicles I had seen that first day.

My jaw tightened.

They were moving me.

Not just from one holding cell to another, but outside of this monstrous building. My mind spun with the thought.

Outside...

"Step up," a soldier ordered in my ear. When I did not comply right away, the two men grasping my arms lifted and thrust me forward in the vehicle. The floor reverberated with a resounding thud as my feet connected with the metal surface. As the guards pushed me forward, the strange vehicle groaned and swayed under our weight. The men shoved me down onto the hard bench. They wasted no time securing me. As one guard alertly pointed his gun at my chest, the other took out an extension of silver chain and locked my handcuffs to one of the rings on the floor. He then attached the larger cuffs to my ankles. Once assured I could not escape, the guards hopped out of the container. It rocked again in their wake, making me feel a little seasick.

I could feel my heart rate begin to rise, pulsing rapidly in my temples. I was used to living in confined spaces, crawling through metal-encased air ducts, dwelling in windowless rooms, but this was something different. This was a metal box on wheels. A box I had no control over. I pulled at the chains restraining my hands. They barely rose to my bent knees. I pulled harder until my casted arm screamed in protest and the cool metal bit into the skin on my good wrist. As the pain escalated, my mind became clearer. Adrenaline was an amazing drug.

Think…

I kept the tension on my wrists taut. A slight boyish-frame jumped into the back with me. I glowered at Gage as he sat on the bench across from me. The doors slammed behind him, closing us in. For a brief moment, I could see nothing. Then as the vehicle lurched to life, a dome light illuminated the moving prison cell with an eerie blue hue.

Gage's face looked like that of a ghost's in the dim light. His porcelain skin was nearly opalescent. We stared at each other as the automobile trundled along, whirring in its oddly high-pitched tone. Neither of us spoke. Every few moments the corner of Gage's mouth would pull up in a sneer before returning to its usual smirk. He knew something and this silent treatment was his personal attempt at torture.

My silence, on the other hand, was due to the fact that every ounce of strength I had was focused on staying conscious. The past few days of dehydration and of sleepless hallucinations had drained me. Even the short, impromptu walk to the transport garage had left my knees shaking. Each time my eyelids blinked a little too slowly or I saw black rimming my vision, I pulled harder at the restraints. My feet were becoming slick as my blood trickled to the floor. But the harder the restraints cut, the more alert I became. I *had* to stay conscious. Thanks to the subdued lighting, Gage didn't notice.

Finally, he broke the silence. "Why a man who could have *anything* is so obsessed with *you*, I will never understand."

Gage's words hung in the air as we went back to

glaring at each other. This time, however, my mind was working. There was a truth to his words. The Minister was a man who got what he wanted—whatever he wanted. He never lost…

The vibrations in the floor began to slow. We were stopping. When the engine cut off, the light went out again. I took this brief opportunity to close my eyes, smothering the threatening tears of pain and exhaustion. I barely managed to open them again when the back doors sprung open. A blast of night air hit my face. I couldn't repress a tiny smile. It smelled like the night, like life, like… freedom. I stared out at the dark calling to me.

A cold finger caressed the side of my face. I yanked backward, but Gage's hand wrapped in my hair. With a thrust of his fist he jerked my head to the side, exposing my neck. A hungry look blossomed in his gaze as his free hand traced a line across my throat. I pulled violently at my manacles but they didn't yield. He pulled harder. I could feel the follicles separating from my skull. Every fiber of my being froze as Gage leaned down and trailed his nose along my exposed neck.

He sniffed me.

His thin lips traced behind his nose, catching on my skin. When his lips found my ear he laughed quietly before speaking. "Tonight—when you wish you were dead—come find me. I will be happy to oblige."

Giving my hair one last yank, he threw my head to the side and stepped back. I bared my teeth as I lunged for him like a wild animal. He merely laughed coolly as I struggled against my chains. With a skeletal smile, Gage turned and strode from the metal box.

I slumped back against the wall, letting my eyelids fall half closed. I could feel the heat boiling in my veins as the guards came to gather me. Gage thought I would want to die after tonight's new torture. If I *was* going to die tonight though, it would be on my terms. That little piece of crap would *never* feel the joy of being the one who finally beat me down. I didn't have a lot of choices here, but I could choose one thing. I could choose my own demise. It was better to die trying. I closed my eyes, took a deep breath, and let the untamed beast within me take control.

There was a heavy clanking on the floor. My feet were unbound. As the chain restraining my handcuffs clicked free, I sprang to life, surprising myself as well as the two guards. I dove forward, smashing the top of my head into the kneeling guard's face. There was a satisfying crunch before he slumped to the ground holding his nose. The metal box exploded with a deafening noise as the other guard's gun went off. I felt a lightening bolt of heat sear the tip of my right ear before the bullet ricocheted off the wall behind my head. In one clean move, I slammed my casted arm into his face.

There were two distinct crunches as I broke his cheekbone and my own newly set arm. We both bellowed in pain, but as he fell back, I leapt forward. The blackness was creeping in again; the pain in my arm was no longer keeping it at bay. My feet were moving, but I could barely sense what I was doing.

I flung myself from the back of the vehicle, tackling the nearest body. It wasn't until my fingers snagged a fistful of brown hair that I realized it was Gage. We tumbled into a tangled heap. The world seemed to spin as I lashed out, kicking, biting and punching whatever I could reach. With well-timed strikes, I slammed his head into the pavement as we rolled. Finally, we slid to a halt tumbling apart. Gage's body was sprawled on the ground face down, struggling to push itself upright. He was nearly unrecognizable. Blood stained his pale skin. A flap of flesh hung loose below his right eye. I somehow managed to come up in a crouch about five feet away. I was sure the injuries my body had sustained were substantial, but I felt nothing.

I chanced a glance upward. We were in an alleyway. Smooth walls blocked both sides in front and behind me. To my left, a foreboding bright light seeped into the mouth of the alley. The transport vehicle blocked my right, its oversized body nearly scraping the alley walls. In the little space, new guards were emerging from around the front of the truck in total disarray.

Everything had happened so fast they seemed at a loss, guns pointed in the truck, at Gage and at me.

Fire. I pleaded. *Just fire and get it over with…*

But they didn't. They had been instructed not to shoot. Gage was stirring, reaching for his own firearm. I knew he would not hesitate.

Not him, I reminded myself. My mind shut off and for the first time in my life, I chose flight over fight. Without a second glance I took off toward the pool of light.

It was a surreal feeling, like my body and mind were no longer one. I knew better than to panic. Panic gets you killed. But that was exactly what I was doing. My body scrambled down the alleyway, staggering drunkenly with exhaustion, while my mind screamed for it to stop. *NO!!! That's the wrong way! You're going the wrong way!*

My body recoiled as it burst into the brilliant lights, my retinas searing as they tried to adjust. I barely caught sight of the glinting silver uniforms patrolling the area before my feet collided with something heavy on the ground. There was an exhilarating moment of freedom as my body became airborne, but as quickly as the euphoric feeling began, it vanished. The concrete met my body with shattering force. I could feel each collision— each mind-jarring connection—as my individual body parts collided with the ground. When the shocks of pain finally stopped, I lay still unable to move. My fingertips were the first things to regain sensation. I scraped them over the rough surface. It felt oddly warm. I pulled my hand away from the concrete. It was slick. I blinked into the haze of white. Something was going in and out of focus, the oddly shaped blob blurring red and white. Slowly, my palm and fingers began to define themselves. My breath caught.

Blood.

Not only was my hand covered in the fresh vibrantly red blood, but it was all over my body, blotching my skin like a sick abstract painting. I gagged as the coppery tang suddenly overwhelmed me. I must have been shot. That was the only logical way to explain such an amount of blood. I pulled myself to my knees, waiting for the real pain to start.

My head swiveled idly toward whatever had tripped me and the world stopped.

It didn't just stop. The entire universe imploded.

No... no it was not *my* blood...

My soul—if I still even had one—was being sucked into oblivion. The pain was greater than anything I had ever felt in my sad existence of a life. The ground seemed to fall away and the only sound I could hear was a cry like that of a dying animal.

The blood looked like a river flooding the pristine street. It was everywhere, but all I could see were the bodies.

Two bodies...

Two disfigured and damaged bodies... but I knew those bodies.

I knew them...

There was a larger, obviously male body and a smaller one next to it I couldn't bear to look at. The larger body was turned, shielding the child next to him in their last moments. I could feel the last piece of me splinter into nothingness as I stared at the larger body with the perfectly sandy hair. There was blood staining the sun-kissed locks like a grotesque Tribe statement. I knew those broad shoulders, those oddly gentle calloused hands...

Those hazel eyes that I would never see open again.

The screaming got louder as I thought his name.

Triven...

My eyes traced his body to the small brown head cradled in his arms. I couldn't look any further—to see if her body too was riddled with bullets. I knew it would be. I couldn't even think her name. I couldn't handle any more.

The screams cut off as I retched. There was nothing in my stomach to throw up, but still my body convulsed and heaved as it tried to expel what it knew.

They were gone...

Just like my parents, they were gone. I could not survive this again, not this time. I felt it—my soul was dying. The vessel that was my body was just that—an empty container and nothing more. This is what it meant to be broken. This is what it meant to die inside.

I began to reach for the bodies, a perverse need somewhere deep within me that needed to know they were real. That had to touch them. My fingertips grazed the lifeless back of Triven's jacket.

It was solid.

It was still warm.

The screams morphed into sobs of hysteria, the sound echoing in the square. A part of me could sense the soldiers around me moving away in fear or in shame. It didn't matter. Nothing mattered. I began to crawl closer to the bodies. The only thing left in life I wanted was to lie down and die next to them, but someone stopped me.

Vise-like arms constricted around chest pinning my hands, dragging me to my feet. As he pulled me away from the bodies, I screamed and kicked and snapped at his arms, all coherent thought now gone. One large hand released me just long enough to slap my face so hard I saw an explosion of stars. My body went slack as my screams cut off. It was as if he had smacked the last bit of life out of me. Everything went numb. The man holding me grunted with the effort of holding my limp body upright.

Ryker's cool voice swam in my ear. "Damn it *Princess*, you had better stand up or you're going to regret it."

His words meant nothing to me. He was speaking to air—to a hollow shell. It wasn't until I heard the smooth, crooning voice that I found my feet again.

"You realize this is *your* fault, Prea." The Minister appeared before me, his spotless white suit making him look like an apparition under the bright lights. He leaned in to emphasize his words. "If you would have just done what I asked and given them to me, your little friends here wouldn't have had to die."

I lashed out, managing to free my unbroken arm. Ryker pulled me away just a fraction too slowly. Curving my hand like a claw, I slashed into Minister Fandrin's face, leaving behind five angry red streaks that were already beading with blood. The Minister howled in rage as I continued to writhe in the Major's arms.

Pressing his hand over his cheek The Minister glared at me. "Remember child, their blood is on *your* hands." He pointed at the bodies next to us.

"Now, get her out of my face before I kill her myself."

"Yes, sir." Ryker barked.

A soon as Fandrin was no longer in sight I went limp again. Ryker half-dragged, half-carried me back to the transport vehicle. I didn't notice if the other guards were still there. I didn't even care if Gage was there or not. I didn't care about anything. I didn't exist anymore.

I was only half conscious when Ryker threw me back into my mobile prison. My head made a loud banging sound as it struck the metal floor, but I didn't feel it.

I vaguely heard Ryker say, "Your chariot awaits," before he slammed the doors and cast me into the darkness.

The floor hummed and the light came on. I stared at my unshackled hands. The loose chains bounced on the floor next to my head. They hadn't even bothered to restrain me. I watched the shackles move, less out of interest and more out of the inability to look away. As my ear pressed deeper into the metal floor, an explosion painfully vibrated the surface beneath me. Then the chains and my arms were suddenly airborne. My entire body was floating through the open space of the empty container. Then it struck a surface. The world rolled, banged and exploded around me. I let gravity pull and push my body without opposition, barely acknowledging the cracking and splintering I felt as I collided with unending metal surface after unending metal surface. It was dark when it stopped.

I was no longer lying on the floor but on the ceiling of the truck, the barely flickering dome light pressing into my temple. I groaned, tilting my head in the direction of a sound coming from outside.

Without warning the doors sprang open. Two large shadows began to pull at me, dragging me away from the overturned transport vehicle.

There was fire engulfing the street and arms were lifting me. Someone was talking to me, but I didn't care. I didn't even fight or call out. Instead, I just closed my eyes and let the darkness take me.

Maybe it was Death's arms, finally come to take me away. I hoped it was. Sometimes, it was better to be the ones who died, than the one left to live...

10. ILLUSIONS

SOMETHING COOL TRICKLED down the side of my face. The droplet trailed over my jaw line and behind my neck before being absorbed into the cushioned surface beneath me. The cold trail left a tingling sensation in its wake. It should have felt refreshing, good against my hot skin, but it didn't... I felt nothing. I couldn't remember what had happened or where I was. There was something lingering at the edge of the hazy fog. Something I should remember... something I didn't want to. Tears were beginning to leak from under my closed eyelids.

There was something wrong... something had happened... *what was it?*

A cooled surface touched my forehead as something else large and warm grazed my cheek. The result was like an electric shock. My body surged back to life as my hands flew out, knocking away whatever had touched me. There was a clattering and the startled sound of shuffling feet. It was a reflex. I was abruptly on my feet staring wildly about a dimly lit room. My heart pounded so hard against my chest it hurt.

The surface beneath my feet was padded, the springs of the bed squeaking as I shifted my weight. My arm felt lighter. Twisting my wrist, I was vaguely aware that the cumbersome cast was gone, as well as the pain. In fact, all of the pain was gone. The room blurred in and out of focus. When it finally cleared, I fell back against the wall with a cry of despair. I realized what had touched me. Unbridled horror trapped the scream rising in my throat.

A sandy-haired figure stood in front of me, his eyes bright.

I was staring at the boy I loved. The boy I had gotten killed.

Triven stared back at me.

Everything came rushing back. Everything I had done, everything I had lost—*My fault, all my fault*—and now it would haunt me forever. It was my hallucinations all over again. He looked slimmer than I remembered, his usually handsome face tired and pale. But I knew it was an illusion. My mind was punishing me for what I had done. Tearing my eyes away, I cast them down at myself. I was still wearing my dark prisoner's uniform. Blood—his blood—stained the dark fabric.

I recoiled in defense as he took a step closer, halting him on the spot. I loved him, but I couldn't take this anymore. I couldn't stand to look at his face every day and know that I had caused his and Mouse's deaths. Anger overwhelmed me. Hoping to make the specter vanish, I struck out, intending to sweep away his illusion.

Instead, the room echoed with a sharp smack as my hand met not air—as I had expected—but solid, warm flesh. I yanked my hand away, clutching it protectively to my chest. The palm was stinging. Triven's face mirrored my own, shock and pain evident in his hazel eyes. There was a glowing patch of pink blossoming on his cheek.

"Prea?" His voice was honey, so much deeper and stronger than any of my hallucination's had been.

I flung myself from the bed, slamming into his body. Triven's arms wound around me, gathering me to his chest as his hands roamed over my body. They moved soothing my hair, tracing my face and holding me to him.

He was real. He was alive. Tears sprung to my eyes.

My fingers fumbled numbly around his waist, trying to pull him closer. They brushed against something hard and metal, the hilt of a gun. My hands jerked away from the weapon as the image of Triven's and Mouse's dead bodies flashed in my mind. I tangled my hands in his shirt, clinging to his chest, hardly able to stand on my own.

"You were… *dead*." My voice broke on the last word. My chest constricted painfully. "Mouse?"

"She's fine, perfectly safe. I sent her to get some rest. It wasn't us…We tried… We didn't know… I'm *so* sorry Prea." He took a steadying breath, but whatever he was going to say never made it past his lips. The moment Triven's mouth opened to continue, the door to our tiny room opened.

My heart stopped.

Standing in the doorway with blood running down the side of his face and a poorly applied bandage wrapping his head was Major Ryker James.

With no hesitation I shoved Triven. Spinning him out of the way, I unsheathed the gun from his belt and pointed it into the face of the Major. Unlike my aversion to touching the weapon earlier, my hands now curled eagerly around the gun like it was a long lost friend. I snarled and pulled the trigger just as something large knocked my arm sideways.

Ryker barely moved as the wall next to his head burst into tiny bits. The fragments scattering to the floor sounded like rain after the echoing thunder of the gunshot. I yanked my arm to fire again but something was holding my wrist, keeping the gun pointed safely at the floor. I stared incredulously at Triven's iron grip on my wrist.

I pulled again trying to free myself.

"Let *go* of me! Do you have any idea who this is? WHAT HE HAS DONE!" I shrieked. Practically growling, I turned my rage on Triven only to find his hazel eyes full of guilt and confession.

"I know who he is. His name is Ryker James." Triven's hand loosened slightly on my wrist. "Prea, he's the one who saved you."

"Saved me? *SAVED* ME?!" Triven flinched as I screamed at him. "If you call electrocuting me until my heart stopped, breaking my arm nearly in half, starving me for days on end, and then making me think you were dead, *saving* me. Then I guess this man is one *hell* of a savior! I *must* owe him my life!"

I dropped the gun, letting it clatter to the floor and yanked my arm away. This time, Triven let me go.

"You have *no idea* what hell I have been through! And *this* man..." I pointed a shaking finger at Ryker. "*This man* saw to every second of that torment!"

Despite myself, tears of anger and betrayal sprang to my eyes. I clenched my fists until the nails bit into my palms. I burned with desire to kill Ryker for what he had done to me. To hit Triven for letting it happen.

A multitude of emotions flashed across Triven's face. Finally, his eyes hardened turning on the Major. "You *tortured* her?"

Ryker, who had remained silent during the entire exchange, finally shifted his weight. His eyes traced the floor, not able to meet ours as he spoke. "Regretfully, I must admit that I had a part to play in order to keep my cover. I played it well. Yet, everything I did—no matter how seemingly cruel at the time—was done to save your life." Ryker now pulled himself up to full height, no longer looking apologetic. "You have every right to be angry with me for what I did to you Prea, but given the choice I would do it again. My calculated brutality kept you alive and without my protection, you would not have lived to see today. It was the same thing you did for those children."

Ryker's words hung in the air like a fine mist. I stared at the spot on the wall where the bullet had struck. I could feel both men's gazes on me, waiting for me to make the next move. He was right, I did do the same thing to try and protect those kids. But *I* hated myself for it.

Pointedly, I marched up to Ryker, jutting out my chin as I closed the gap between us. It pleased me to see him flinch at my approach. My whole body shook with anger and emotional fatigue as I spoke. "I owe you *nothing*. Consider us even. You *literally* took my life from me once, and now you have given it back. We're square."

I strode past Ryker without a second glance and into the hall. It wasn't until I was several steps down the dimly lit hall that I realized I had no idea where I was going. I paused. From behind me there was a gratifying thud of a fist meeting a face, followed by a muffled groan. I could just make out the low hiss of Triven's words.

"I am grateful you brought her back to Mouse and me, but that is the *last* time you lie to either of us."

Triven strode through the door rubbing his knuckles. He muttered something that sounded like, "Not even close to being square…"

Moving past me, he walked away down the empty hall expecting me to follow. I smiled faintly at the point between his shoulder blades. *Chivalry wasn't always that bad.* After only a few steps, I reached for Triven's arm, my gentle touch halting him in mid-stride.

"Triven… I have to see her. I have to know she's…" I swallowed, unable to say the word *alive* aloud. As always, he understood.

Triven's breathing was heavy as he glared over the top of my head down the hall. Ryker was undoubtedly standing there, watching us. Hesitating only briefly, Triven gestured to the hallway on his left, letting me walk ahead. His hand brushed against the lower part of my back as I stepped past him.

Once we were out of Ryker's sight, Triven took the lead again, taking me to a door much like the one we had just left. Pressing his finger to his lips to request my silence, he soundlessly turned the handle and pushed the door inward. The room was dark, but the shapes of two beds were visible. One bed was perfectly made. In the other was a small lump breathing steadily. I could see a crown of brown hair peeking out on the pillow. I took a strangled breath. Mouse's face was just as I remembered, perfect and unharmed. Peaceful even. A strange impulse overtook me. It was a nurturing desire to run to her, to touch her body, to hold her in my arms, and ensure that she was in fact safe and whole. I watched her deep breathing and pushed those feelings back down. My eyes lingered on Mouse for a moment longer, as if she would disappear when I blinked. Slowly, reluctantly, I stepped away. Nodding once, I pulled back from the dimly lit room and let Triven close the door again.

I looked gratefully at him. Triven touched my shoulder lightly in comfort and then began to walk back down the hallway again.

I followed, smiling sadly to myself. "When did she start sleeping *in* the beds?"

I remembered the little hands so often creeping around the edge of my cots as Mouse sought reassurance in the night from beneath me. It seemed a part of her had grown up in my absence. I had missed it. Triven's hand reached back, seeking to reassure. I took it.

"She started sleeping like that the day we made a plan to get you out."

"Thank you for protecting her." I said staring at my hand in his. His fingers squeezed mine and we both fell silent again.

They're alive…

Triven led me to another smaller room, not far down the narrow hallway. He pushed the door open for me and stepped back.

"I will wait *right* here." He promised.

When I stepped into the room he pulled the door closed behind me, sealing me in. I turned abruptly and stared at the door. The room felt oddly suffocating but I couldn't seem to make myself move. I knew I was in a bathroom. That Triven's intent was meant to give me privacy, but I could feel that irrational fear rising. I didn't want to be locked in. I didn't want to be alone. I must have stood there for some time, frozen in panic. When I finally managed to move, there was a soft knock and the doorknob began to turn of its own accord. Triven's voiced carried in before his face appeared in the crack.

"Prea, are you alright? I couldn't hear the water running and just wanted…" He trailed off when his modest eyes at last met mine. The anger that had burned in them from our encounter with Ryker was gone, now only understanding and shame shone through.

I stared blankly at him, still marveling at his gentle face and unharmed body. *He's safe. He's still alive.* I reminded myself again. Even after witnessing with my own eyes that he and Mouse were alive, I could still see their dead bodies in the street. I could still feel their blood against my skin. It felt like every time I lost sight of Triven—even just for a moment—that this was all fake, that I would wake up and find them dead again. I wondered if that feeling would ever go away.

"I can't..." There were no words to finish the sentence, or maybe it was that there were too many words to pick just one. Mercifully, he seemed to comprehend.

Moving swiftly, Triven slipped into the room and shut the door behind him. He locked the door before pulling me into his arms. I didn't resist. Normally, he was so careful about not touching me, but right now neither he nor I cared about politeness. We both needed the physical contact to remind us this was real. I rested my head against the hollow of his chest. Slowly, my body began to thaw, melting into Triven's as his steady heartbeat thudded solidly beneath my ear. He smelled good. He smelled real. Alive.

"You're really alive." I finally mumbled into his shirt, breaking the silence.

"*You're* really alive." He whispered into my hair, kissing the top of my head.

I clung to him as I stared blindly at the sink. "It was... The bodies were so..." I took a deep breath. "Who were they?"

Triven sighed sadly. "Two unfortunate citizens. Fandrin chose them because they looked like us. He murdered two innocent people because they fit a mold... *My* mold." His arms tensed around me, both protective and angry.

I blinked trying to purge the images from my mind. I had been too quick to believe. Not in my right mind, I had not questioned what I saw. The bodies were so like my friends, but now I realized that their faces had been so brutally damaged to hide any potential flaws. They weren't my loved ones, but they were *someone's* loved ones. That innocent man and child had been unjustly killed simply to teach me a lesson. They were used merely as fodder in The Minister's personal vendetta. Hate raged in my heart and my body shook with anger, but my heartbeat was steady. I meant my next words, committing to them wholly.

"I will kill Fandrin, if it's the last thing I ever do."

11. ANSWERS

MERCIFULLY, TRIVEN SEEMED to feel the same way I did about being separated from one another and agreed to stay with me. He slipped out of the room for only a moment, allowing me to disrobe and get behind the white shower curtain before coming back in. Part of me wanted him to join me in the shower. To hold me close, our skin touching as he helped me wash away the real life nightmares that ate at my brain. But I couldn't. As much as I needed him in the room with me now, I could not stand for him to be too close while I was in the shower. While I knew it was Triven standing on the other side of the white curtain, I was afraid if I peeked out it would not be his face I saw. Maddox was dead, but the dead have a funny way of haunting you. My skin rippled at the thought of those black eyes leering at me. I doubted I could ever stand being exposed in front of someone like that again.

So even though I felt horribly alone and exposed, I stayed hidden behind the curtain like a coward. Hiding from ghosts that weren't there. Focusing on my breathing, I let Triven's deeply velvet voice tether me to reality. *He was alive. I was free.* I reminded myself periodically as he spoke. His stories slowly distracted me from my own haunting memories. Soon, Maddox's face disappeared back into my subconscious, leaving us alone again. As I washed away the grime of imprisonment from my colorless skin, Triven spoke, answering my questions both asked and unasked.

"Mouse and I managed to survive on our own for nearly two weeks. She was so amazing, Prea. You would have been really proud of her. We kept mostly to power systems beneath the city, but had to come up for food and water." He paused, remembering his own imprisonment within The Wall. "There were a few close calls… but… well, we managed."

I made a mental note to ask more about those "close calls" as I rinsed the soap from my hair.

"Part of the problem was we were a little *too* good at hiding. Ryker and the other rebels were looking for us the moment we crossed through The Wall, but they had to shut down the security cameras in the tunnels to keep us safe. That's how we managed to get as far as we did, when we first came in. The rebels created rolling camera blackouts throughout the city. The Minister was blind, but unfortunately so were they. Mouse and I had no clue at the time. In our attempts to evade The Sanctuary guards we also successfully evaded the good guys."

Good guys? I froze mid-rinse, thinking of Ryker's face.

Triven must have sensed my tension because he added quietly, "The rebels *are* the good guys, Prea. I promise."

I stared at the grime built up beneath my jagged and broken nails. There was still blood caked underneath them. I dug my fingers into the soap bar. He sighed and I could hear his feet pacing the floor as he continued. "If I hadn't gotten shot, I'm not sure they would have ever found us."

I stuck my head out of curtain and stared at him. "You got shot?!"

Triven waved his hand, brushing the seriousness of it away. "It was nothing, I took a bullet to the leg trying to keep Mouse safe during a food run. It was stupid really, my fault. I let hunger cloud my judgment. We weren't being as cautious as we should have been. I'm not *you* when it comes to surviving… To be honest, I'm not sure anyone could match your skills."

He smiled lopsidedly at me and I pulled my head back inside the steam-filled shower, shaking my head in disagreement.

"I'm not as good as I used to be." I murmured.

Either he didn't hear me over the running water or he was choosing to ignore my last comment. "When I got shot, we had a hard time stopping the bleeding and couldn't move very far. We were trying to break into a medical facility when the rebels found us. At first, I thought we were dead, but when Ryker stepped forward... Mouse ran to his open arms. To be honest I wasn't sure if I should scream, shoot or give up. They all seemed like rational responses at the time."

I snapped off the water. A towel was promptly thrust into the gap behind the shower curtain and the tiled wall. My fingers grazed Triven's skin as I took the stiffly bleached towel. We both pulled our hands away as if an electrical current had passed between us. I quickly wrapped the towel around my body, suddenly feeling shy. Triven continued to talk as I dried myself.

"The rebels took us in, fed us, and healed me. It was strange. There were faces I knew—people I remembered from my childhood. They seemed like ghosts of my past. My mother thought all of the rebels died when we entered Tartarus, but some of them were still here, biding their time. There are so many more of them than I thought possible and yet so few when you think of the entirety of the population here."

I wrapped the towel tightly around myself and reached for the curtain. When I pulled it back Triven was still speaking, but he trailed off when he looked at me. I stepped out of the shower and his brow furrowed in pain as his warm eyes fell over my body. He moved forward, wrapping his hands around my upper arms. His fingers seemed longer than I remembered.

"I swear to you, I have been doing nothing but trying to get you back since that day. I'm so sorry, Prea... I failed you. So much has happened to you and I wasn't fast enough. It's my fault." His eyes dropped to the floor in shame, tears visible under his dark lashes. It was the first time I had seen him so vulnerable.

I turned my head to look in the small mirror and was horrified by the face that stared back. I hadn't looked at myself when I first came in and in fact, I couldn't remember the last time I *had* seen myself. The girl staring back at me was shocking.

My face had become too thin, the cheekbones protruding grotesquely through sallow skin. The eyes staring back looked hollow, sunken into dark rings surrounding them. My once slight frame now looked outright emaciated. I might as well have been a skeleton. Adorning my skin were a smattering of yellowing bruises and freshly healed pink scars. The healing-serum had not completely fixed everything.

"How long?" I said staring at the mirror. He needed no elaboration to understand what I meant.

"You were held captive for thirty-four days." His body shuddered with a silent sob.

Thirty-four days... It had been over a month.

Not wanting to look at the sickly girl anymore, I turned back to him and placed my hand under his chin. It took a moment for his eyes to meet mine again. My stomach sank when they did. Not only had The Minister managed to break me, but in doing so, he had also managed to hurt Triven.

"You and I have been through hell and back—probably twice—but despite it all, we are still standing here, together. And the truth is, I would go through it all again if it meant yours and Mouse's safety. I do not regret my decision to sacrifice myself for you both and I *forbid* you to take the weight of my choice onto yourself. It was your face that got me through many long nights and it was the knowledge that you were still out there that helped me survive. I am not the same person I was before I went in there—I know that—but I was also not the same person after I met you. You made me a better person, Triven."

He swept down with a practiced movement, his fingers winding in my hair as he pulled my body tightly against his. As it had so many times before, his mouth stopped just before it reached mine, waiting. I barely had to move forward and his lips claimed mine for the first time since our reunion. A part of my broken heart healed a little. For six years I hadn't needed anyone. I would never admit it out loud, but right now, I needed him.

And from the urgency in his lips, he needed me too.

THE WATER RUNNING in the shower behind me nearly drowned out our low voices. But that was the idea. Triven had pulled a grey silken robe from beneath the sink. I felt naked wearing it, its light fabric strange against my skin. Its sleeves were much too long. I was perched on the edge of the tub, shivering occasionally, but not cold. Triven sat stoically across from me on the floor, his knees bent in front of him as he watched me. He looked smaller somehow than I remembered.

We had been locked in the bathroom for nearly an hour. For the most part, I had retold what had happened to me. The torture I endured, what I was forced to do to those children. I had to stop several times to remind myself it was over—that I wasn't there any more. Still, if I closed my eyes I could see their faces, smell the salty blood on the mats, and hear their screams. There were always screams in my head now.

Out of a selfish need for preservation, I had toned down the parts when I feared I had become insane—mainly for two reasons. Irrationally, I thought Triven might not ever look at me the same if he knew. Being damaged was one thing, but being clinically insane... that would change things. And then there was the terrifyingly rational side—I had lost my mind in that cell. Even now as we spoke calmly, I would get residual flashes of rage and fear for no reason. They would come on like tidal waves enveloping my entire body, swallowing me whole until I couldn't breathe, until I couldn't feel anything else, all rational thought was gone. The girl I once was had become consumed, eradicated by the overpowering fear flooding my mind.

Then it was gone.

It was a struggle to keep my breathing regular.

After a particularly bad flashback, I had to drop my head between my knees, my long wet hair hung dripping on my toes as I tried to open my lungs. I clutched my head, pressing so hard it throbbed. Triven sat helplessly against the door, his fists curled. I asked him not to touch me, unsure if I might accidentally lash out.

"I hurt those kids… I told myself everyday that I was trying to save them from a worse fate, but I still hurt them. I can't even remember all of their faces or names. After a while I tried to forget, to block it out. Remembering only made it worse. It didn't really matter who they were, because to me every one of them was Mouse." I gagged.

"I can't even begin to imagine." Triven's voice ached with sympathy.

Something prickled at the back of my mind.

"You're a good fighter?" I looked up to find him staring at me. His forehead was pinched with stress.

"I suppose so…"

"But you were never recruited." It was a statement not a question. He had gone to school, he had told me about being in classes with other students. There had never been any stories about children soldiers. Unless he had lied to me by omission.

Triven looked uncharacteristically ashamed.

"I went to school here to become an electronics communications engineer, like my father." He bit his lip. "I was supposed to be a soldier. I should have been fighting in the same sparring matches you did as a child. I passed the assessment test to be a soldier with flying colors. Placing fifth behind you."

Words failed to form in my mind. Kind, intellectual, compassionate Triven a mindless soldier? It was hard to imagine. It was strange to think how close our lives had come to colliding years ago. I stared at Triven wondering how diffcrent it would have been. Would I have loved him at all? Would he have loved me? It seemed both of our pasts held secrets.

"I didn't know." He chewed on his thumb staring at the floor. "I don't think Arstid even knew about it. My father had altered my scores once the results were in. He didn't want me to be a soldier. He hacked the system and gave me a whole new life. But even the best hackers leave a trace. The rebels found out about it. Ryker showed me the test scores."

"What did your mother do when she was here?" It was a question I had never asked. Arstid was such a pillar in the structure of the Subversive it was hard to envision her as anything else.

Triven laughed dryly. "She was a school teacher. Hard to imagine, isn't it?"

We stared at each other. I could see Triven questioning himself the same way I had these past few weeks. All of our lives could have been so different. His father had given him a new life, just as my damaged memories had done for me. But who would we have been without those life-altering moments?

We came here seeking answers, but finding them was starting to feel like a curse. Like I was tainted now. I thought of Arstid—leader, bitter shrew, teacher and Triven's mother all rolled up in one. I had once considered her vile, revolted by her domineering nature. But now that I knew where *I* came from… she seemed like a saint.

"Fandrin… I'm his…" I couldn't say the word. My tongue stuck to the roof of my mouth. When I snuck a glace at Triven, he didn't look surprised. "Did you—"

"No," he cut me off. His eyes were round with innocence, pleading for me to believe him.

I did.

"Maddox is dead." I blurted out. I'm not sure why I said it.

"I know."

"I *hated* him, Triven. Hate isn't even a strong enough word. I wanted to kill him! Then he… He… He sacrificed himself for me. Why?!" I turned to Triven, begging him for an answer. "He saved my life and now his face haunts me every night. Every time I close my eyes. I *still* hate him!"

"No one would blame you," his voice was soft. "One act of kindness—no matter how sacrificial— doesn't erase all of the bad things a person has done. He was far from perfect."

"I see him all of the time," I admitted. My toes were going in and out of focus. "I see all of them… all the time. Do the ghosts of our past ever stop haunting us?"

I was staring at the floor again, trying to make it stop tilting.

His voiced carried to me from a far-away tunnel. It took great effort to focus on his words.

"You're not losing your mind…" I could hear him swallowing. He sounded guilty. "They drugged you, Prea. *We* drugged you. To get The Minister to lessen security on you, it had to seem like you were slipping. Like he was winning. The rebels on the inside used mild hallucinogens to help you… regress faster."

They had given me drugs to make me appear insane. I wondered if the poison still coursed in my veins. The room was spinning. Maybe their drugs had worked *too* well.

When I was finally able to sit up again, Triven's face was chalky. The lack of color deepened the sleep-deprived bruises above his hollowed cheekbones. Pain surged from his warm eyes. They quickly fell to the floor. There was more that he wasn't telling me. I could feel it. I was pretty sure I knew the missing words.

The drugs actually did make you lose your mind. You are permanently damaged.

The tempest of my emotions was rising again.

I pushed down the anger. It was not with him. My emotions were on an unbalanceable scale, tipping rapidly back and forth.

Anger.

Fear.

Anger.

Fear.

It was either that or an empty ache. Even when I was in Triven's arms I could still feel the hollowness eating at me from somewhere deep inside. I desperately wished those feelings had stayed locked in my prison cell, but like all undesired feelings, they had cruelly followed me. My fingers ran up my arms trying to suppress another oncoming chill. The tips of my fingers grazed something hard and rectangular in my left wrist. Hastily pushing back the sleeves of the robe I stared at my arm. It was nearly imperceptible to the eye, but if I twisted my wrist I could just make out a small section of raised skin. It was maybe the size of my thumbnail. I pushed back my sleeve, checking my other wrist.

There was one there too.

"They're microchips." Triven said. He held up his right wrist showing me his.

I stared at him in horror. *"They're tracking us?"*

"No," he immediately consoled me. "They are for weapons. Guns here—"

"Don't work if you're not chipped to match them." I finished his sentence staring at the miniscule bump under my skin. I had learned that lesson the hard way. "That's why I was able to fire at Ryker earlier."

"Yes, these are modified though. Any gun will fire for you here, not just the one calibrated to you."

"Why do I have two?" I stared at my arms in turn.

He smiled. It was so nice to see that smile again. "Because I am one of the few people who noticed you're ambidextrous."

"Oh…" I knew the chips would be a necessity, but I felt like it was just another way for The Sanctuary to put its mark on me. These marks were just more visible.

"I wouldn't tell anyone for a little while. I inserted them myself when you were healing. People here were worried you might... well they weren't ready to give you access to firearms just yet." He shifted his gaze to my newly scarred wrists. We were thinking the same thing. They weren't wrong, Ryker could attest to that. "But I knew you would feel better if you had the means to defend yourself."

He was right. I did feel a *little* better.

I sighed. There were still so many questions to ask, but I was struggling to find the energy. I should have wanted to know more, but for the first time since I could remember, I didn't want any more answers. Still, I pushed myself to ask at least the important ones.

I stared up at the concrete walls and squared ceiling. A dreamy déjà vu settled in my mind. "Where the hell are we? It feels like we're back in the Subversive—"

"But with intentional flaws?" Triven finished the thought for me staring at the squared ceiling too.

"We're in a rebel blockhouse. We're safe here." He paused before adding, "For now."

"Triven, what do these people want from us?" The scales were tipping to panic again. "Can we even trust them?"

For the first time since we were reunited, his eyes didn't quite meet mine. "I'm still trying to figure that out."

12. ECHOES

THE WHITE SHIRT and matching linen pants felt overly abrasive. Everything fit too loosely, making me feel like a child. I pulled nervously at my sleeve as I paced the tiny room. I was back in the cement-lined room I had awoken in. My father's returned tattered journal was clutched to my chest like a talisman to ward off fear. It wasn't working. Triven had left me to get dressed and went to wake Mouse. Despite myself, I was anxious about seeing her.

I wanted to know for certain that Mouse was safe, that she was the same perfect child—well, as perfect as any of us could be—I had risked my life to save. Seeing her sleeping had temporarily satiated me, but now I wanted to hold her in my arms, smooth her hair and know for sure that she was safe. Yet, after seeing the way Triven looked at me—and now knowing what I looked like—an underlying fear began to grip my heart, that seeing me might scare her. Mouse had somehow always been able *see* me—to look into my eyes and witness the person inside. There were times her brown eyes seemed to know more about myself than even I did. This time, however, I was scared of what she might find. If I had merely been damaged before, what did that make me now? Irreparable? Broken? Dead inside?

I chewed on what was left of my thumbnail, until I began to taste the salty tang of blood. Cursing under my breath, I spat and tucked my thumb into the hem of my sleeve. There was a light knock on the door. I froze, dropping my once cherished journal to the floor.

"Prea?" Triven asked, cracking the door slightly before entering.

My throat constricted, causing my words to sound strained. "I'm decent."

The door flew open and a tiny blur of white and brown exploded into the room. Mouse froze for half a second before launching herself at me. My knees gave out and I fell to her height just as her body collided with mine. She was still so small. I had forgotten how small she was. But somehow she seemed bigger now. As if she had grown stronger in our month apart. I ran my hands over her body, feeling her lean arms, checking to make sure she was truly whole and unharmed. When I was content with my assessment I pulled her away to get a better look at her face. Her face had thinned a little, some of the childhood roundness giving way to the young woman she would one day be. Her hair was longer, falling below her angular shoulders. But her eyes... those alone had gone unchanged. A single gold chain hung around her neck, at the end of it dangled my father's pocket watch. My heart warmed at the sight of it. Noticing my stare Mouse tried to pull it off and give it back, but I stopped her hands. Resettling the chain back in place, I shook my head sincerely. I liked that she had it.

A single tear slid down her cheek as she stared at me. Her frail hands cupped my face for a moment, then she began to sign.

Triven translated without hesitation. "You saved me."

I wiped her tear away with my thumb, "And *you* saved me."

We smiled weakly at one another. She signed again.

"We saved each other." Triven's voice caught a little.

I hugged her close and stared at Triven when I spoke again. "In so *many* ways."

WE SPENT THE next hour just the three of us. The

only outsiders now trapped within The Wall. It felt almost like being back at the Subversive bunker, except that we all looked different now. Stronger. Weaker. Older. Younger. Somehow all of these things at the same time.

Mouse recounted the stories Triven had already told me, her hands flying with such speed even Triven had a hard time keeping up. She was so animated, I found myself trying not to smile. I had missed her. Once she finished signing madly, her round eyes became fearful as she pointed inquisitively at me.

I raised my eyebrows. "You want to know what happened to me?"

My eyes flickered to Triven before returning to hers. She signed again.

"I'm not a child. I can handle it." Triven's voice was flat, obviously he didn't agree.

My mouth was suddenly full of cotton, my throat spasming as it tried to swallow. I looked down at my scarred hands, unable to find the words. Triven had gotten only a glimpse of what had happened to me in captivity and even then I had barely explained it. How do you describe living through your own personal hell? Hatred and fear writhed inside of me. I closed my eyes trying to shut out the vibrant memories of pain, of torture, and of hurting innocent children. My lips quivered.

When Mouse's little hands touched mine, I actually recoiled, jumping away and startling us both. She was motionless for a moment, then slowly moved forward again placing her hands over mine. I let her.

She signed again and this time I understood even without Triven's translation.

It's okay, I understand.

Her fingers released mine and traced the scar marring her throat. We squeezed each other's hands as Triven placed a comforting hand on her shoulder.

We started as a gentle knock sounded on the door. A woman's hand slid around the opening doorframe, followed by an unfamiliar long face surrounded by a curtain of silvery, golden hair. The woman's eyes were kind as they swept over the three of us, a warm smile rising on her thin lips. When she spoke her voice was soft, like what I would have imagined a librarian's to be. "I am so sorry to interrupt. We are all glad that you are finally awake, Prea. Dinner is ready. If you're hungry."

Triven's hand slid over my back in comfort as he felt me cringe at the use of my given name. He was the only one I could tolerate speaking it. "*Phoenix* has had a long day," he gently corrected her. "Maybe it might be better if we ate in our room tonight."

Her face fell a little, but the lingering smile remained gentle. "Oh... yes of course. How silly of me… Sorry, *Phoenix.*"

My stomach rumbled at the thought of food. As I glanced around at the solid cement walls I felt the sudden need for more space.

"It's okay," I said a little too quickly. I took a deep breath before nodding confidently at the woman. "It might be nice to get out of this room for a little while."

I regretted my words almost immediately. We had followed the silver-haired woman down the narrow hallway and up a set of tightly wound stairs. When she opened the door at the top, it was like stepping into another universe. The heavy door slid sideways and my steps slowed as we entered the new space.

I then watched in fascination as Triven pressed his hand to a faintly glowing rectangular spot on the wall next to the opening we just came through. The door slid shut again and once it touched the frame, it all but disappeared into the wall.

I stared at the seamless wall for a moment before glancing around the rest of the room.

We were no longer in a bunker but a house. It was a plain home, but a home nonetheless. The walls were all painted the same shade of white and all the floors were a consistent grey tile. Nothing hung on the walls except a plain white clock and one photo. It was the photo that made me halt mid-stride. Minister Fandrin was seated proudly in his glass throne of a chair staring down on us. I glared at the picture, with the growing urge to rip it off the wall and put my foot through it.

"Every house is required to hang his picture. *We* keep it there as a reminder of everything we are fighting against."

I knew the voice even before I turned toward its owner.

Ryker was standing in a doorway watching the four of us as we emerged from the stairwell. My body went rigid at the sight of him, my back teeth grinding together. His face still looked battered. I was pleased to see his left eye was nearly swollen shut and now a violent shade of purple. He must have seen the glint of pleasure in my eyes because one of his eyebrows rose accusingly.

In a shocking display of affection, Mouse let go of my hand and ran to Ryker. Her arms wrapped around his waist hugging him tightly. He returned the squeeze gazing affectionately at the little girl. Every one of my muscles tensed for attack. How dare he touch her? I flinched forward, but the fair-haired woman gently touched my arm, drawing my attention just long enough to distract me.

"Um... dinner is ready, Ryker." She chirped, obviously sensing my unease. "We should eat. You know how Mae doesn't like to be kept waiting."

Mouse hugged Ryker once more and signed

"*thank you*," before running back and taking my hand again. She beamed between the two of us and signed another word I knew.

Friends.

I smiled weakly at her, but when she turned away my cold glare returned. Triven, who had not said a word, gestured for me to follow while carefully inserting himself between Ryker and the rest of us. They were obviously not going to be friends anytime soon either.

The house was so much a home it was startling. There was simple furniture adorning each room, sparse but enough to seat a small family comfortably. There was very little that made the home feel lived in or personalized, however. In the living room there was a grey sofa, two undersized matching armchairs, a see-through monitor—like the one I had seen projecting images in The Minister's office—and a small coffee table. Everything was immaculate, looking untouched.

"Our house looked just like this," Triven said. "I remember sitting on a sofa just like that reading with my mother."

Suddenly the monitor glowed to life, causing me to start. An attractive woman in white was speaking, but I couldn't hear her words.

"The evening announcements," Ryker muttered as he passed us. "They broadcast every night—mostly just propaganda drivel. We keep the sound off."

Looking away from the woman on the screen, I stared a moment longer at the living room before moving on. I nudged my mind, trying to remember something.

Had I sat on a sofa like that with my family?

Nothing came to my memory though. The house felt strangely comfortable in its sterility, but I had no memory of ever seeing a house like this before. Voices could be heard coming from another room, accompanied by the warm smell of food. It didn't smell quite as good as Cook's had back in the Subversive but still it smelled pretty wonderful. I followed the voices and stopped in the doorway. A table had been set for ten and people were bustling about claiming chairs and passing dishes. The excited hum slowly subsided as all eyes fell on me. I backed up two steps until I bumped into Triven's chest.

"Well, now that everyone's here it's time to start eating. I will not have my food getting cold." A dark-haired woman with a round face pointed at us. There was a streak of silver running through her long unruly hair. It framed the left side of her face. "You four sit down now and make yourselves comfortable. I will not have my dinner held up any longer."

"Yes, Mae." Triven muttered leading me toward the crowded table.

"Sorry, Aunt Mae." Ryker apologized and moved to the other end of the table, pausing to kiss the woman on the cheek before taking his seat. My ears perked up at the word aunt. I stared harsher than necessary at the woman who shared blood with Ryker.

I was no sooner seated between Mouse and Triven, than a plate piled with food appeared before me. When I looked up, the gentle grey-blue eyes of the silvery-haired woman met mine.

"Um… thank you…?" I halted, not knowing her name. Politeness still wasn't something I was comfortable with. Neither was being forced to sit down with a bunch of happy strangers.

"It's Inessa, dear. You're welcome." She smiled sweetly, patting my shoulder. I tried not to flinch away.

I stared at the plate, not entirely sure what I was looking at. When we walked into the room I could smell food, but this didn't look entirely edible. There were spoonfuls of brown, grey and green looking mush plopped into little sections of the plate. It looked better than what I had been served in my captivity, but not by much. I poked at the mushy green lump with my fork.

"It tastes better than it looks, I promise." Triven muttered. I watched in awe as he placed a fork-full into his mouth and dutifully chewed.

"Well of course it tastes better than it looks!" The dark-haired woman named Mae barked down the table. "We may only get protein-based sludge to work with here, but I'll be damned if this old gal doesn't know how to make it taste halfway decent!" She tapped herself in the chest with her thick thumb. "And you, my girl, could use a little more protein in your life right now. I want to see that plate clean when you're done here."

I stared wide-eyed at the bossy woman who had just told me off like only a mother usually could. Normally, I would have picked up the plate and thrown it in her direction, but there was something so final about her speech that I actually scooped some of the mush into my mouth. Ryker snorted into his plate, earning him a light slap on the arm from Inessa, who smiled warmly at me in turn.

As my tongue pushed around the squashy substance in my mouth, I was shocked to taste earthy vegetables like the ones grown and harvested back in the Subversive. The sense was peculiar. The taste was right but the texture was all-wrong. The grey mush was something akin to a salty meat and the brown was close to a sweetened potato-like flavor.

"We still produce some foods here. Genetically modified fruit mostly." Inessa said. "But in the long run, raising and maintaining food sources proved costly and inefficient."

"According to our dear Minister," muttered Mae.

"But I ate a sandwich in Fandrin's office." I interjected. "A *real* sandwich."

"*Real* food is available to the privileged." Mae

snarled. "The Minister and his highest ranking officials don't actually eat what the rest of us do. Ryker is the only reason we occasionally see real food at this table."

I could feel Ryker's eyes on me. I refused to look at him.

Inessa filled the awkward quiet. "A few years ago, the general public's meals were altered to these. MNS's— Manufactured Nutritional Subsidiaries. They were less expensive to make, easier to produce and—"

"AND were meant to control the masses. MNS's may be stock full of nutrients, but they are also laced with mild tranquilizers." Mae interrupted.

I froze mid-chew. The entire table went silent.

"Not our food, dear." Inessa added quickly. "Mae oversees food processing. Only three-quarters of the food being processed is actually laced with tranquilizers. And the doses are mild. Most people simply feel content and happy. The rebels have been very selective as to who receives the treated meals."

Triven set down his fork. "So who *is* receiving the dosed food?"

"The schools." Ryker didn't look up from his plate. Triven let out a low hiss, but I thought I understood. "When dosed with small amounts of sedatives, the children tend to become lethargic. For the most part, their lethargy is then mistaken for ineptitude and the military deems them unfit as potential soldiers.

And Fandrin has no idea we're controlling the outcome of his little recruitment tests."

"And the rest of it?" Triven pushed.

Mae answered him, "The rest of it is being distributed to the public. Suspicions would be raised if there weren't signs of the drugs being effective. However, every rebel household is now eating clean meals. We are slowly dialing back the drugs to the general public. But it takes time to do so unnoticed."

The conversation shifted and I stopped listening. As I slowly worked on clearing my plate, I observed those surrounding me at the table. There were ten of us seated in total, five men, four women—including myself— and Mouse. Everyone was in civilian clothing, wearing various shades of white and grey. Aside from Ryker's battered face, they all looked similar. The men wore plain clean lined haircuts, while the women's hair was worn long, either slackly cascading down their backs or held back with simple plaits.

It struck me how different this was from not only Tartarus, but from the Subversive. Aside from the obvious physical differences, the behavior was also different. The first time I sat with the members of the Subversive to eat, every eye watched me with a wary glare. Here however, the eyes occasionally flickering my way were filled with reverence, recognition and curiosity. I was not used to being looked at that way. It made me squirm between bites. The conversation was mild, speaking mostly about each person's day at work or whether someone had seen the latest governmental propaganda. While I could constantly sense gazes shifting in my direction, for the most part everyone acted as if I wasn't there. Only Ryker's and Triven's eyes shifted to me apprehensively. Both men knew what I was capable of, and they were waiting for the ticking time bomb to explode. I knew they were both right. This quiet reserve I had fallen into would only last so long and sooner or later the fiery girl trapped beneath the surface would claw her way out again, demanding answers. I could already feel her anger stirring in my chest.

This felt wrong.

All of it.

These people were gathered around a table talking as if I wasn't even here. As if I hadn't just spent the last month being tortured by the man just a few seats down from me. My heart began to race. I closed my eyes trying to calm myself, but images of dead bodies and battered children flashed across my lids.

I pushed up from the table abruptly, making everyone jump. The conversation had stopped. Slowly, Ryker rose from his chair eyeing me, hands raised in front of him. It was only then I realized I was clutching my fork like a weapon. Mouse's eyes were round as the tip of my fork hovered close to her left cheek. Triven held out his hand next to mine. I dropped the utensil into his palm with a spastic reflex.

"I think I need some fresh air." I said to no one in particular. Mouse set down her fork and began to push away from the table. I opened my mouth to tell her to stay away from me but Triven spoke first.

"I'll take her up to the roof. You stay here and finish your dinner." He pushed her chair back in and kissed the top of her head. She watched us warily as we left but stayed put.

I followed Triven blindly until we reached a set of steps with a hatch at the top. When he pushed open the hatch I nearly knocked him over in my desperation to get into the fresh air. I burst onto the rooftop gasping for air. My heart was racing, its pulse thumping painfully in my temples. My body began to shake and my vision was blurring. Fear blossomed in my chest.

What was happening to me? Did they lie to me? Did they drug my food?

I began to stagger, looking for something to sit on. Triven's hands wrapped around my waist. I struggled to push them off. There was a strange wind gathering in my ears. I balled my fists in preparation to strike, but his hands closed tightly over my wrists, holding me like a vise. Pulling me into him, Triven curled his body protectively over my back and held me to his chest. After a moment I realized it wasn't the wind I was hearing but

Triven's shushes. Slowly, he pushed me forward until my head dropped between my knees.

"It's okay, Prea. It's just a panic attack. Breathe. You have to breathe."

I tried to focus on his words and attempted to match my breathing to his steady chest behind me. My heart rate finally started to slow and my vision began to clear.

"What's wrong with me?" I croaked. "I have survived *everything*. I was stronger than anyone else. I survived all of the nightmares, the torture, the deaths— but the echoes of it all... I can't seem to stop those. I can't stop seeing you dead, her dead, my parents, Maddox... Fandrin broke something in me, Triven. He broke me. I was weak... I was..."

Triven held me tighter, as if to keep me from falling apart. "You're not weak, Prea. You're one of the strongest people I have ever met. You're one of the bravest, most intelligent and frightening people I know. But you are *not* weak. I know you are hurting right now, but I also know eventually you will use that pain to become stronger."

I nodded mindlessly against my knees.

"What if I hurt one of you before I get to that point?" I thought of the fork tines too close to Mouse's cheek.

"I won't let that happen." His voice was so self-assured I almost believed him.

Almost. The truth—I *was* a ticking time bomb and we both knew it.

Tick... Tick... Tick...

BOOM.

When I awoke that night, it was to a room filled with silent screaming and blood.

13. REGRETS

THERE WAS BLOOD on my hands. Even in the dark I could see it. Glistening, vibrant and still warm.

So much blood.

My hands were still shaking, the fingertips quivering with anxiety and disgust.

It wasn't my blood. It was his.

Triven's.

The shame was so powerful my body didn't have room for any other emotion. It consumed and ravaged my soul. I stared at my shaking hands and a new emotion made its way into my mind. Repulsion.

I balled my hands into tight fists and cracked them, once… twice against my temples.

I had lost control. I knew this was going to happen. The poison in my mind had finally seeped out. It had been when I was sleeping, but I couldn't stop. Not even as I woke up. I couldn't even remember what had triggered it. What I had been dreaming about. But when I woke, Triven's blood was on my hands and I had him latched in a choke-hold strong enough to make his face turn purple. He wasn't even fighting me. Just tapping at my arms in a vain attempt to wake me as blood poured from his nose. When I finally came to my senses, I had leapt away, letting myself smash onto the floor. I could hear Triven gasping for air as I skittered away from him. My temple collided with the ground as I crashed down, making my ears ring.

That's when I saw her.

Mouse was cowering beneath her cot. Tears streaming down her face as her mouth twisted in a silent scream. I wanted to reach for her. To say I was sorry, but I couldn't. Instead, I whispered for them not to follow me and took off like a coward.

Somehow I had made it here, though I didn't remember exactly *how* I had gotten here. The living room was nearly pitch black. Only a faint glow was seeping in through the covered windows. I was curled into a tiny ball on the stiff pristine couch. I knew I hadn't hurt him that badly. Broken his nose, maybe. There was always a lot of blood when you broke someone's nose. It was Mouse's face that horrified me most.

I had put that look on her face.

I slammed my fists to my temples again. What was wrong with me! I had always been in complete control of my body, of my mind. But it was as if The Minister had strategically removed that control. Like his fingers were still wiggling in my brain. He had taken away everything that made me Phoenix and left this quivering mess in his wake. I knew now he had won. He had broken me. The question was—could I survive to rise again? Triven thought so, but look at where that got him.

Soft steps stirred me from my personal hell. I kept my head bowed but spoke a warning. "I want to be alone."

"I fear you have been alone for far too long." Her voice was gentle as her steps continued. "The mind is a dangerous place. When left alone too long with our own inner demons, we can easily fall prey to their deception."

She stopped before me and waited until I looked up. Inessa's eyes were bright in the darkness. In her left hand was an offering. A steaming cup of something that smelled like citrus. When I did not take it, she simply placed the cup on the table before me and moved to an open chair.

I stared at the rising steam. "And what would you know of inner demons?"

"More than I would care to admit." A sad smile pulled at her thin lips. She stared at me, her bright eyes burning. She glanced down at my hands. "He's okay you know? Triven's nose has already been mended. And Mae has helped calm down our dearest Mouse. There wasn't anything that happened tonight that can't be forgiven."

I stared at the blood drying on my skin. "I do *not* deserve kindness. Not after what I just did. Triven may be reckless enough to forgive me, but you didn't see *her* face…"

I buried my head in my hands again. Hate was easy. Love was hard.

"Oh child… That little girl has seen nearly as much as you have. Yet, she still has one of the purest hearts I have ever seen. Don't underestimate her."

Shame still plagued my thoughts. Inessa's keen eyes did not miss a thing. "Don't underestimate yourself either."

"It's not that simple. What if this is something I can't fix? What if I hurt one of them again or worse? What if I don't come to my senses next time?" My voice rose, vibrating with inner turmoil. "Ryker managed to break something out of that prison, but *what*? Triven sees the girl he fell in love with in a broken-down library, but I'm not that girl! I am a bomb!"

"Triven is not reckless. He cares for you, and that is the greatest gift he can give you right now. And the *only* mistake you can make, is to push him away. And no, it's not simple. Nothing is ever simple, Pre— Phoenix. Not even within The Sanctuary. In fact, despite our outward appearances, none of us are as simple as the clothing we wear. Life is *always* complicated. It doesn't matter which side of The Wall you're standing on."

I made a grunting sound in reply. She continued unperturbed. "The Minister has shackled us all in one way or another. Your mother was raised to believe she was a disappointment for not being the heir he desired. You were then raised as the child and successor he knew your mother would never be. Those outside have been bound by The Wall's isolation with nothing but their instinctual desire to survive. And those of us inside have been chained by the ideal we are all the same, but equality is not always equal."

She continued to speak in the absence of my response.

"Everyone here is meant to serve a purpose—to contribute to our *fair* society. Children with certain aptitudes become soldiers. Those with a knack for educating become teachers. Those who are technologically inclined work on keeping our systems secure. No one has a choice and everyone has a place. Males provide genetics and women provide new life. We are married under state-approved matches and those of us who choose not to procreate are deemed unmatchable. Love is a privilege, only acknowledged when it can produce the strongest offspring. Your mother and father were of the lucky few. They loved one another *and* were genetically a match. I on the other hand have been deemed unworthy of such an honor as love."

I finally looked up after her lengthy silence filled the room. She was staring at a simple silver ring on her left hand. I watched her caress it lovingly with her thumb. Inessa's eyes shone with tears when she finally looked up. "Mae and I have been in love since we were about your age. No matter how my mother pushed me to court boys, I knew it never felt right. You know, the government can mandate many things... but matters of the heart—they are ruled by a power all their own."

I looked back on every touch I had seen pass between the two at dinner. Every lingering gaze. How had I missed that before? Maybe because love wasn't an emotion I had seen very often.

Inessa looked back down at her mug. "Inside The Wall our love is considered a violation. But here— inside *these* walls, of *this* house—our love isn't judged. It is beautiful and celebrated."

I thought of Triven and Mouse. Of everything I was willing to sacrifice for them, despite my desire for self-preservation. Above all other emotions—above hate and vengeance, above fear and desire—love was the most formidable. It was the most honorable and always worth fighting for. I understood that now.

"My life has been filled with little else other than hate and violence." I steadily met her gaze for the first time that night. "But one thing I do know about love—

no one, *no one* has the right to tell you what your heart knows."

A sincere twinkle lit in her already brilliant eyes. "You know that is almost exactly what your mother said to me when I told her about Mae."

My eyes fell away when her stare lingered too long. She realized her intrusion with flushed cheeks. "Forgive me. You look so much like her now that you have grown. It's almost like talking to a ghost."

I grabbed the cup so I didn't have to look at her. "I am *not* my mother."

"It is hard for me to believe that considering how little you know about her." Inessa's eyes fell to my hands. Looking at the blood. My defenses rose automatically, as they did whenever anyone spoke of my family.

"What could you possibly know about my mother?" I snapped. "Or about me for that matter."

"About you? Unfortunately not as much as I would like, my dear." She paused to sip her drink. "About your mother? Aside from maybe your father, no one knew her better than I did."

My eyes narrowed, but Inessa's warmed.

"Jutta was my *best* friend." Her face fell when she said my mother's name.

I flinched.

Hearing my mother's name was always like a slap in the face. Worse still, the last person who spouted it at me in an attempt to find comradery was Arstid. And Triven's mother was the last person I wanted to be thinking about right now. She had been right about me—I was a loose cannon, a temporarily leashed wild dog waiting to lash out. I pulled my legs further into myself trying to contain the rage percolating beneath my calm façade. I had had some control before, but tonight… tonight I was anything but in control. I shouldn't be allowed near them—near anyone again. My stomach ached with sickness as their shocked faces flashed behind my lids.

"Don't do that." Inessa's voice was a whisper.

"Do *what*?" I bit back misplacing my anger.

"Blame yourself." She was staring at me.

I glared back at her. "How about you let me handle my own issues and just continue on with your little stories!"

She actually cringed, her aged eyes looking hurt. I suppressed the urge to roll my eyes. Everyone here was so sensitive.

"I'm sorry." I muttered into my drink and took a sip in a gesture to prove my sincerity.

"I sometimes forget you're no longer the little girl whose hair I used to braid." She said.

"Sometimes I wonder if that child *ever* existed." I stared at the swirling liquid, mesmerized by its languid movement. "All I have seen is the soldier child prodigy.

A weapon."

"Oh she did exist, and she was so much more than a weapon." Inessa smiled with memories. "And as much as I miss that little girl, I admire the woman she became. Your mother would have too."

Again, with my mother... I did roll my eyes this time. "You do realize the woman you speak of is little more than a fairytale to me? I have seen her face a thousand times and still I know almost nothing about her. Her face has haunted my dreams for over *six years*. Her words are the only reason I continued to fight for my survival." A tiny bubble of rage rose in my chest. "I am not sure if I should thank her or curse her for imploring me to survive this hell."

"You mother and father gave their lives so that you could live—"

I cut her off, "My mother and father abandoned me in a shit city with practically *nothing*! I had no memories. No allies. I had been *alone* for six years! I might have survived but to what point?! They left me with nothing but hate and fear all because they were, what... some kind of martyrs?! Arrogant militants who made a rash decision that got dozens of people killed along with themselves!"

I was practically screaming when I finally managed to staunch the pent-up words of resentment pouring from my mouth. In all my years alone, I never realized how truly angry I was at them for leaving me.

Inessa's words were barely a whisper. "You don't really believe that do you?"

I stared hard at a fabric pill on the sofa's seat by my little toe. The anger was subsiding, but my chest still ached with pain. I closed my eyes. "I'm not sure what I believe anymore."

"Can I tell you about them?" Inessa asked hesitantly.

I wanted to tell her to screw off and leave me alone. I also desperately wanted to know about the people who had raised me. I compromised by saying nothing. After a few minutes, Inessa took my silence as consent.

14. KINDRED

"**JUTTA WAS MY** oldest and truest friend. Until she died, my life had never existed without her in it. We were born three days apart, your mother first of course. She always had to do everything first." Inessa smiled, her eyes glistening in the dark. "Leyla—your grandmother—died during childbirth. It was a rare thing for that to happen in those days—what with our technologies—but sometimes the body just stops. It gives up without warning or reason and the truth is no amount of science can save a body that doesn't want to live anymore. I wonder sometimes if it's because she knew too late what a monster she had married. Either way, The Minister blamed your mother for Leyla's death.

"Unlike you, your mother was not born out of a love-bound marriage, but one of genetic opportunity. The Minister searched every citizen for a woman who could produce the most superlative genetic offspring.

Leyla proved to be his best potential match. But when she died, all of his hopes of producing a male heir died with her. You see, as by law, not even The Minister can remarry in the circumstance of spousal death. One mate. One chance. That is all we are given."

Population control, I thought. With no room to expand the population it had to be controlled. Out in Tartarus children rarely lived to see adulthood, so reproduction was never an issue. But here with modern medicines and limited resources it had to be regulated.

Inessa's long fingers toyed around the rim of her mug. "Jutta may have been the Minister's daughter, but he never saw her as his progeny. She was smart and resourceful, but never showed any interest in combat. Your mother was never taken into her father's inner circles. She was never trained to be a soldier. He ignored her and she resented him. Jutta knew little of how far his control extended both inside and outside of this city, but she knew of his corruption. Despite his glowing demeanor with the public, she saw what he was behind closed doors. One of the benefits of being invisible to her father was that he never noticed just how much she overheard."

Inessa shook her head. Her eyes glazed with memories from the past. "He treated Jutta like a plague for many years. Naturally she became rebellious. Eventually, that rebelliousness lead to mutiny. Many people blindly loved The Minister for upholding this false utopia. So many more hated him for it. Your mother was at the top of the second list. She even took your father's surname to further distance herself from Fandrin. It's rare for spouses to do that anymore and considered disrespectful of one's lineage. We are only allowed two children; the first bears the father's name, the second bears the mother's. Your mother chose neither. It did, however, prove beneficial when the rebels began to form. They might not have followed Jutta had they known her birthright."

"Why couldn't my mother have been an heir? It seems archaic that only a man could rule. Especially for a society that claims to be utopian." I bristled at the idea of being found inferior because I was born with different reproductive organs. I knew Inessa was only trying to distract me from my inner demons. Despite myself it was working.

Her eyebrows stitched together as she met my gaze. "I forget how little you know about our ways. Women are seen as equals in all ventures. We work alongside men—fight with them, clean with them, cook with them, program with them, rear children with them. The Ministry's council used to be comprised of an equal number of males and females. Six in total. They were a system of supports, meant to help guide and challenge the hand of the reigning Minister. Each of these members was selected at random on a rotating timeline to serve two years, before returning to their normal lives.

"The position of The Minister was the only constant in the group, that way with the rotations of the council at least one person was always unvarying. That role was meant to serve as the control—it created the tipping vote. *And* it was the only position passed on by blood. The original idea was that the bloodline represented resilience and unity. That together our lineage could survive. For many years it worked, because despite being the face of The Sanctuary, The Ministers could always be outvoted by their council if he or she was found incompetent."

I nodded at her that I followed.

"Over the last century, however, Ministers began to find proof that council members were 'corrupt'. Your great-grandfather began inquisitions into council members who did not agree with him. They were accused of wanting to overthrow the system—to rule the city and destroy the utopia we had created. There always seemed to be a damning amount of evidence compiled against them. Those that were found guilty were thrown out of The Sanctuary.

"The Minister was portrayed as a hero for outing the supposedly corrupt council members. Grateful for his righteousness, civilians began to call for new edicts. The Minister's face was the one they had grown up seeing, trusting—so for the first time in our history the people gave him total power over the selecting the council. Now, The Minister can hand pick his council members and the positions are for *life*."

"That doesn't explain why my grand—" My throat tightened stopping me from finishing the word. I forced a cough to loosen the restricting muscles. "*He* refused to recognize my mother."

Inessa held up a hand signifying she was getting there. "Sometimes you need to understand the past to prepare for the future. In the past we have had female Ministers, but the last three were all male. By sheer happenstance. Your grandfather wanted nothing more than to uphold this family legacy. He wanted a male heir to live in *his* image. He saw women as weaker, inferior creatures that could never live up to the standards he thought a ruler should uphold. It wasn't until he began to train *you* that he saw potential in a female heir."

My heartbeat was pounding in my throat. Too well, I remembered the way he had stared at me as if I were a prize. A thousand bugs crawled beneath my skin. The idea of having *any* potential to be like that man repulsed me.

"If The Minister basically abandoned her, who raised my mother?" For the first time I felt a small pang of kindred spirit with the woman whose face I saw every night. She too had been alone—parentless just like me.

"*My* mother," Inessa answered with an air of pride in her voice. "My mother was a caregiver. It was her job to help raise and educate the youngest children if their parents could no longer provide such supervision. Most children stayed with us only part time while their parents were working, leaving when they were old enough to be placed into society schools. Jutta however, lived with us nearly full time. She wasn't just raised as my playmate, but as my sister."

My heartbeat was escalating as my head blurred with information. I pulled at the strings connected to my lost memories, but they still provided nothing. I stared hard at Inessa's face trying to force some thought, some recollection, but as always, there was nothing. Everything this woman was telling me could be a lie and I had no way to disprove her. My defensive, untrusting mind screamed at my heart to shut her up, to make her stop talking. But my heart ached to hear more.

Inessa continued, unaware of my turbulence.

"My mother knew what Jutta might be some day—that she could be the next ruling Minister—despite Fandrin's oppositions. So everyday, after the other children left, my mother educated both of us with banned teachings. We read books that were supposed to have been burned. We talked about countries and wars that happened centuries ago. We even talked about governments and liberties. Back then I thought it was an exciting game we had to keep quiet about. In truth, what my mother did was considered treason. She would have been exiled for it. We all could have been." She shuddered. "Exiles were cruel and obscenely public then. Now we watch videos of the accused being dragged away by soldiers, never to be seen again. Ryker told me the exiled are sent to the Ravagers as part of the payment for their services. Innocent people are sold as prey to entertain those monsters."

I felt sick. How many of those screams from the hunted had I ignored over the years? How many of those people had been citizens from The Sanctuary? I dropped my head onto my knees. Why not pile that on too? Just one more horrific thing added to an already guilty conscience.

"Those public exiles were actually what brought your parents together." Inessa said thoughtfully, continuing as if she had not just proclaimed that my grandfather was selling off human victims to a gang of leather-clad, pierced savages.

"That doesn't seem to say much about my parents, does it?" I muttered, revulsion rising in the back of my throat. "I would think exiling a person to Tartarus doesn't exactly exude romance for most people."

"It wasn't romance that brought Jutta and Coen together, sweetheart." Inessa pinned me with a fierce stare. I winced at hearing my parents' names together like that. I barely thought them, much less said them aloud. "We were twenty when it happened. A supposed group of traitors had been found and the entire city was gathered to witness their banishment. There were seven people that had been found guilty that day. Never before had so many been banished together." She paused here, hand fluttering to her mouth as she gathered herself. Her voice was a little thicker when she continued.

"One was your mother's good friend from our childcare days. Another was your father's brother. It was all very ceremonial. The guilty are supposed to accept their fate and stand at the mouth to the city as the gates close, locking them out. But there were so many of them and tensions were too high. Three of the exiled panicked and tried to run back before the doors closed. They were shot on the spot. The automated doors pushed their dead bodies back. The bodies tumbled and rolled onto the others still stuck on the other side. Limbs were caught in the doors. The survivors screamed and clawed at the opening to get back in. There was so much screaming." She stroked her ear as if trying to quiet the screams from her past. "The intent of the mass exile had been to scare us into submission, but when the soldiers opened fire, outrage erupted in the crowd. Some citizens rushed the soldiers. Others ran fearing for their lives. Seventeen people were killed that day. Some were shot by soldiers. Some were trampled in the chaos. Any of those who remained combative afterward were put in solitary until deemed rehabilitated."

I flashed back to my personal experiences of The Minister's ideas of rehabilitation. My lungs struggled to work.

"It was the first outbreak of violence The Sanctuary had ever seen within its walls. The Ministry blamed the deaths on insubordination and fear. *'Chaos is what happens when citizens don't trust in their leaders…'*" Inessa mocked The Minister's deep voice as she rolled her eyes. "The old tyrant meant to quell ideas of rebellion, but really all he did was spark a fire. Your mother and father met through their shared hatred for her father…"

I had stopped listening. There was something nagging at my mind. Something she said that didn't add up. "If there was a location where they exiled people… why have I never seen this passageway?"

Inessa opened her mouth, but it was a deep voice behind me that answered. "Because it was *that* tunnel the rebels tried to escape through. The tunnel The Minister caved in on top of their heads to condemn those who rose against him. It was the tunnel that brought you and me into Tartarus." Triven sat down next to me.

Mae had healed his nose. Aside from a few bruises on his neck he looked unscathed. The mug began to shake precariously in my hands. I searched his eyes wanting to say something, but no words came.

Inessa cleared her throat and spoke softly to break the heavy silence. "I think maybe that's enough family history for tonight."

She rose from her chair and stretched. Walking toward us, she lifted a hand as if to place it on my shoulder but then thought better. Instead, she gently touched Triven's cheek before she took my still half-full mug. "Goodnight you two. Try and get some rest."

We watched as she descended down the passageway.

"Mouse is going to stay with Mae and Inessa tonight." I nodded staring at Triven's chest. "She wanted to stay with us—"

"No!" I jumped backward putting up my hands in defense before calming my tone. "No. I think it's better if she stays with them for a little while… Triven, you should—"

"I am *not* leaving you."

There was a finality to his words that even I couldn't challenge. Triven stood up and walked to the passageway before pausing. The message was clear. He wasn't leaving without me. Slowly, I rose and followed suit. We walked in our customary silence to the room. Someone had replaced our sheets, any trace of Triven's spilled blood now vanished. Almost as if it never happened. Almost. The room seemed much bigger without Mouse's bed in it. I stared at the space where her bed had sat. Her frightened face pierced my thoughts.

Brushing past Triven as he pulled off his long-sleeved shirt, I climbed into our bed, pressing myself as tightly against the wall as possible. Triven switched off the lights, casting the room into darkness. As he moved in the blackness, I pressed my forehead to the cool stone wall. I bit my lip when the bed shifted beneath me. At first, he was careful not to touch me, but as I pulled farther away his arm wrapped around me, pulling me closer. I twisted, grabbing the metal frame of the cot. My body jolted as a metal spur bit into the flesh of my palm. I didn't let go. Instead, I gripped it tighter.

Pain was real.

Pain could keep me awake.

Better my blood than his.

"Prea, I *know* that you could get through this on your own. That you could push everything that has caused you pain away and become the girl who needs no one again. I know that you don't need me." He swallowed. "But *I* need *you*. And despite how strong you are, we are better together."

"If I hurt you again—"

He cut me off. "I'd deserve it."

I let go of my hold on the frame and twisted in his arms. His breath was hot on my face. Our noses were almost touching. Even in the dim light, I could see his bright eyes.

"How could you say that?" I searched his face for an answer.

"I left you." His turned his eyes down in shame. "I should have made you jump first. I should have climbed back out and pulled you in with us... but I didn't. I *left* you."

There were so many things I was angry about. So many things that were eating away at me, but this was not one of them. Hesitantly, I touched his face. His skin was warm beneath my fingertips as I trailed them over his temple. "You did what I asked you to do. What I *needed* you to do. You saved Mouse. You saved yourself... Triven, the only thing that got me through that hell was knowing somewhere out there you and Mouse were alive. Free."

He clasped his hand over mine, pressing it to his face. Then his eyes shut, blocking me out. "It's more than that..."

I had never seen so much pain on Triven's face. An icy fear trickled over my heart.

My voice came out pinched. "What are you saying?"

Triven's throat spasmed as he swallowed. "It was my idea to give you the hallucinogenic drugs."

I recoiled from his touch.

"What?" I shook my head in disbelief.

He didn't try to reach for me.

"Ryker wanted The Minister to think you were slipping. He thought that if you showed signs of cracking they would pull back on your guard. And then we would have a better chance at getting you out. We had no way of telling you without giving away Ryker's position. Hiding your emotions is not your forte. We agreed it had to look authentic." Apologies hung on his every syllable. "I know you. I know that you're strong and would never crack on your own. So... I suggested we help your mind *slip* a little."

I could hear him swallow.

"I didn't know about the torture or the kids. Ryker only said they were holding you in solitary." Anger shook Triven's voice. "If I knew... I would have never—"

"But you did." I whispered. My eyes stung. The face that had given me hope was the same one that had caused me to lose my last shred of sanity.

"It should have been me. I would have gladly given myself up to save you from the torture they inflicted. What *I* did to you. It took us too long... sometimes I can see it in your eyes. We didn't get you out fast enough."

It was my turn to look away. I had tried to hide my pain. I had tried to hide the fact that while my body was free, a part of me was still trapped inside The Sanctuary's prison cell. But he knew. I hadn't deceived anyone. I wasn't okay. And he had a hand in it. Triven's betrayal hurt, but I couldn't take this pain too. Not right now. I shut my eyes and said the hardest thing I had ever admitted.

"I need you."

Triven's hands wrapped around my wrists like tender shackles. "I am *so* sorry, Prea. I will never do anything to hurt you, not ever again. I promise. I won't leave you like I did that night. I won't ever make that mistake again. I will die before that happens."

He pressed his lips to mine. I could taste the regret and sorrow behind his kiss and wondered if he could taste the fear in mine.

A foreboding sensation settled itself in my bones. Too many had already died to keep me safe. How many more would fall victim to the same fate?

Triven stayed in the bed with me for the rest of the night. And while I kept my palm pressed against the metal spur to keep myself awake—to keep him safe—I could feel a rift opening between us. Triven might have revealed a guilty truth to me, but he was still hiding something.

I could feel it.

15. TRAITOR

THE AIR FELT sharp in my lungs. It even burned a little as I inhaled. It was a welcoming feeling. After nearly a month of being trapped in a cell, the air—even man-made air—felt like freedom.

I had snuck onto the rooftop seeking peace. It had become a kind of refuge in the last few days. Once I had overcome the panic attack that first night, the wall-less rooftop space began to feel like a reprieve.

I stared at the city's skyline from my safe little crow's nest. Triven had informed me that the roof was protected, that we couldn't be seen, but I still shied away from the edge if there were people on the street below. The city was nothing like Tartarus. The buildings were all pristine. The genetically enhanced trees that released twenty times the regular amount of oxygen cropped out occasionally above the beige rooftops. Just as the day we first arrived, the sky was a perfect crystal blue, with a gleaming sun that actually heated my skin. Only the unavoidable horizon broke the illusion of it being real. Meeting the sky in every direction was The Wall. It towered above the homes with an austere authority. Even surrounding their beautiful homes and manicured trees, it still looked foreboding.

The city was bigger than I had anticipated. Nearly every building looked the same. Every building, but one. A solitary goliath stood in the center of the metropolis. The Tower, Triven had called it. The silver building loomed over its brothers. The windowless sides stretched straight up toward the false sky, while the front of the building was divided into three glass-covered fingers. The monstrosity curved at the top, peaking to its back. The center finger rose above the other two, giving the building the appearance of a wing.

I knew this building.

Not only had I been held captive beneath it, but I had also seen it on every Sanctuary crest. *He* was in there.

I turned away, glowering at the street.

I was avoiding people. I knew that. But how do you face a room full of people when you don't even know who *you* are anymore?

Triven and Mouse still looked at me with love and admiration, even after they saw how little of me was actually left. But there was something new in Triven's eyes now too. Regret. I hated seeing it there. It hurt. I had forgiven him. Or at least I wanted to. Deep down. But emotional pain doesn't always listen to what you want. It's irrational that way.

All the rebels, on the other hand, treated me with respectful reverence. But every time my eyes met theirs, they looked as though they expected me to remember something, or to know some past connection I had with them. Even Inessa's kind eyes had begun to bother me.

I hated it.

I hated seeing the love in their eyes, when inside I loathed myself.

I shouldn't be allowed around other people. The other night was the perfect example. My self-restraint was still spiraling out of control and I was just barely clinging to the edge. I knew somewhere inside the girl I had fought so hard to become was still there, but the layers of anger, drug-induced hysteria, and torment were burying her alive. In Tartarus I knew who I was. No matter how lonely or angry or spiteful I was—I was still always me. Phoenix. The girl who needed no one. The girl who could always survive.

Here, however…

In The Sanctuary I wasn't just a renegade trying to survive. I was someone they were looking up to, someone they had lost. I had a family and friends that I couldn't remember. Everyone here knew more about myself than I did. Inessa's stories proved it. Not even the girl in the mirror looked like the one I remembered. Her eyes were dead, her face sunken in. It was as if I had begun to wither away.

It was as if my reality was slipping away and I didn't know how to hold on. Less than two months before—what seemed like a lifetime ago now—I had desired above all else to come here and find answers. But I had never prepared myself for the consequences of those answers. I had wanted to know what life was like here. Who my parents were. Who I was. But every time I found more answers, the less I wanted to know. And the more I lost myself.

I pressed my fists to my temples, wrapping them with my knuckles. Trying to call on the warrior inside me. Trying to make the voices of uncertainty shut up. Everyone here wanted to talk war, to debate strategy. But as soon as the topic came up I couldn't get away fast enough. The old Phoenix would have never run away from a fight. She would have pushed her useless feelings aside and soldiered on. So why did that seem so hard now?

Triven had managed to keep going. Despite the fear over losing me—despite being forced into hiding— he had managed to keep moving. He went to meetings, was involved in plans about the uprising, but whenever the offer was extended to me I had feigned tiredness and disappeared into our room. Then as soon as I was alone,

I would wish I wasn't.

Part of me wanted to know the truth of the city. Like who were these people who had rescued me, but the other part of me was furious for how long it took them to break me out. Inessa had given me a taste of my past, but there were still so many unanswered questions and I had not seen her in two days. Mercifully, I had not seen Ryker since dinner that first night either, but his absence also made me apprehensive.

While my days were spent avoiding people, my nights were filled with sleepless hours. In those rare moments I actually managed to doze off, the night terrors were horrific enough to keep me from wanting to sleep. Mouse had not slept with us since the first night. I had tried repeatedly to send Triven away as well, but he refused to leave me alone to suffer. So instead we suffered together. Me with imaginary ghosts. Him with feelings of guilt. We were quite the morose pair.

Secretly, I was thankful and angry with him at the same time. We both looked worse for the wear, what with scratch marks and bruises from my nightly outbursts when sleep snuck up on me and then there were the growing circles under both our eyes. We had been in our room just a moment ago. Triven was trying to talk about the rebel's last meeting I had avoided when his words slowly began to slur. He was asleep within seconds. I felt excruciatingly guilty as I watched his eyes flutter beneath their lids. He was so exhausted. It was my fault. Dinner would be ready soon, but knowing that tonight would be hell again, I had pulled the blankets over him and snuck out to let him sleep for a while. Plus, I needed the space.

Still too ashamed to see Mouse alone again, I had let my feet carry me somewhere for a moment of peace. Which is how I had ended up standing on the flattop roof staring down at the streets below. Darkness was beginning to fall. A falsified twilight was blooming on the horizon, casting everything in an auburn hue.

I breathed again deeply.

The stark sweetness of the fresh air still felt strange in my lungs compared to Tartarus's polluted smog.

While I heard nothing, my senses began to itch. Only one person in this house could make my stomach burn white hot with such underlying rage. I felt a small pang of pride that not all of my senses had been damaged. I spoke without turning, "It's not smart to sneak up on people."

"Good to see your awareness of your surroundings is still intact." Ryker walked to the railing where I was standing, but kept a careful distance between us. I stared at him. This was the first time I had seen him out of uniform. He now donned simple white linen garb much like the one I had been provided. While his stance was still severe, he seemed more at ease than I had ever seen him. More human. He was also holding two cups of steaming liquid and offered one to me.

I was careful not to touch his hand when I took it.

I also had no intention of drinking it.

We stood in silence for a while watching the street below. Every nerve in my body was on edge. I had to remind myself that while the man standing next to me was certainly not a friend, he was no longer the enemy either. Mouse obviously put her trust in him and despite my own foibles she had trusted me as well. Out of respect for my small friend, I would have to try my best not to kill him.

A passerby on the street glanced up for a moment and without thinking I shrank away from the edge. Ryker glanced down at the civilian unfazed.

"He can't see you." He waved his hand idly at the passerby. The man gazed right through us and then continued on his way. I leaned closer to the edge to inspect the rooftop. I couldn't see anything but as I reached my hand out, Ryker shifted to stop me. I snatched my hand back automatically balling it into a fist and taking a fighting stance. He rolled his eyes and held up his hand in surrender. "Easy Princess, I was just going to tell you not to reach over the roof's edge. The holographic field only projects to a certain point. If you reach out too far, passersby are likely to see a disembodied hand floating above my roof."

"*Your* roof?" I raised an eyebrow at him. I had assumed this was Inessa's home. "And *don't* call me Princess."

He actually chuckled. "Yes, *my* roof. Did you really think I would entrust yours and Mouse's safety with anyone else? You know, you hated that nickname even when we were kids."

I twisted in his direction. Sarcasm soiled my tone. "You knew me when I lived here?"

For the first time since I met him, there was a sadness in Ryker's eyes. Ignoring my question, he turned away from me and moved to a beige chair someone had placed on the rooftop. I followed cautiously as he gestured to another one a few feet away. I positioned my seat in order to keep a better eye on him before sitting down. Once seated, I calculated my positioning between him and the edge of the roof. One wrong move and those passersby would not only be seeing my hand but a male body flying over the side of the building.

Ryker stared out at the street. "The rooftops are supposed to be for repair access only, but when the second rebellion began we installed this holographic force field as a sort of baby-step toward fighting back. Our people aren't allowed privacies here. Everything we do is monitored. Watched. This was the first place we could escape. This was the first place we could be unseen."

"What about *inside* your house?" I turned back toward the hatch imagining Fandrin's frosty eyes watching my friends.

Ryker waved his still bruised hand. "The cameras in the house are on a three month perfectly calculated loop. As far as Fandrin's concerned I'm living a stable boring life alone. To him I am nothing but a loyal and committed solider."

"Funny, I would have said the same thing about you. By the way, too manly to take a healing serum like the rest of us?" I asked glancing at his damaged face and hand. While he looked at his hand, I suspiciously sniffed the tea he had given me. Ryker watched with an amused smile. I narrowed my eyes and took a sip out of spite. It was a while before I could actually muster the nerve to swallow.

"The Minister thought it a fit punishment for letting you escape. All of the soldiers injured during your escape are healing in pain." He rolled his eyes and took a sip of his own drink. "It's not drugged."

"Do you say that to all the ladies?" I sneered, unable to help myself.

Ryker scoffed. He didn't miss my undertone.

"I figured your Boy Scout would tell you about that sooner or later. It wasn't in the food or water, just so you know. Anyone can refuse to eat, but everyone has to breathe." Ryker took a deep swig of his own mug.

I ground my teeth. *Of course it was in the air.*

Despite his stern face, the corners of his mouth pulled up. "It's nice to see that your charming wit hasn't changed though."

I scoffed and sat back in my chair. "You say that like you know me."

Ryker fixed me with a penetrating stare. He chose his words carefully. "I *do* know you, Prea. You and I were… *friends* before you… *left.*"

When I flinched at the use of my given name, he noticed. I snapped back to compensate for my reflexive reaction. "Friends? *Really?* How convenient. I can't seem to remember anything *and* you have no proof. You know I'm getting a little sick of everyone *thinking* they know me."

Ryker leaned forward and pulled something flat and shiny from his pocket. I stiffened. Sighing, he tapped the screen a few time before tossing it to me. I automatically caught the device. The screen was playing images like I had seen in The Minister's office, but these were not of children fighting. These were of a raven-haired boy and blonde girl laughing together. The scenes changed but the children's fondness for each other was clear. They were play fighting, the girl always coming out on top. Then they were swinging on swings in a backyard, laughing as they got higher and higher. They were sitting at a table, the boy looking at the girl with adoration as she blew out a candle on a small yellow cake. A woman appeared behind the smaller version of myself and kissed the top of my head before sweeping the dessert away. My heart yearned. My mother.

The screen began to shake as my hands trembled. These were moments of my past, of my life. Not someone else's memories recited to me, but actual moments I had lived. And yet, I looked on as if they were a stranger's.

I tore my eyes away from the lost memories to stare incredulously at Ryker. "When you said we were friends…" I trailed off unable to form a further thought.

"I meant we were inseparable." Ryker's eyes pierced mine, beseeching me to remember. When I continued to stare blankly at him, he broke the connection running his fingers through his hair with frustration. The stark difference between his jet-black hair and his pale fingers was mesmerizing. "Those are a few of the rare moments we were allowed to be children—they were almost always under your parents' watchful eyes. You really don't remember anything do you?"

"In my mind, you *never* existed until the day you showed up in my prison cell." There was an icy venom in my words. Ryker's well-trained emotions gave almost nothing away, but the slight tick of his right eye told me I had hit a nerve.

He stared at me with the intensity of a soldier. "When we first started training at the academy, I was the worst in our class. Just a small, scrawny boy who had only been admitted because his father was one of The Minister's highest ranking and most trusted officers. I was a failure and my father never missed an opportunity to remind me of how ashamed he was of his only son. Of the dishonor my weakness brought to his name." Ryker's jaw locked as he swallowed, his Adam's apple bobbing.

"One day, after a particularly bad performance in a match, a few of the older cadets thought that maybe they could *beat* some training into me since nothing else seemed to take. One of them damn near broke my leg when this tiny blonde spitfire came flying out of nowhere. She single-handedly managed to take down the three older boys like they were nothing more than rag dolls. Afterward, when I tried to thank her, she shoved a bony little finger in my bruised chest and proclaimed, 'That's the first and last time I save you. Either you learn to fight for yourself and keep up, or we're through here.' After that night, I spent every waking hour trying my damnedest to keep up with you. We trained together every day and hung out every other moment we were not in the gym. Eventually, I became second-ranked in our class. The only person I could never beat was you and it wasn't ever for lack of trying."

I frowned at his story. There were still too many holes. The mental image in my past was still broken. It was like staring at a constellation of dots that didn't connect. There were too many stories from too many people. Still I sought answers. "If my parents were so against Fandrin's rule, why did they let their only daughter enlist in his child army just to flee with me later on?"

Ryker paused in thought, staring out at the darkening sky.

"Honestly, I don't know the entire story. If you want answers about your parents, you should speak to Inessa. But if I had to wager a guess, they used you as a distraction. Fandrin was so focused on you—his star pupil, his bloodline—that your mother was able to start a rebellion right under his nose. You were supposed to buy her time, but things backfired." Ryker paused touching the scar above his left eyebrow, remembering something. His eyes met mine again. "You still bear your own scar from that day."

Reaching up, I touched the thin line running along the base of my skull. I narrowed my eyes. "How did you know about that?"

"I felt it one day in the cell, when I grabbed you

by the hair…" He looked down, unable to meet my gaze. "And I'm the reason you got it."

I held my breath as he abruptly leaned closer. His long fingers reached to the forgotten screen sitting in my lap. He tapped the surface again and a different video started playing.

It was another video of us, but we were sparring this time in the same room I had recently been forced to fight in. Other soldiers stood by watching us. Fandrin and his brass cane were in the forefront. My stomach cringed as the little girl took out the taller boy with one final hard blow. Blood pooled on the mat beneath his unconscious body, seeping from a deep wound above his left eye. With respect she bowed to her fallen partner then to The Minister seeking his blessing, but he did not return the favor. Instead, he threw a knife at her feet. It was nearly identical to the way he had presented the knife to me the other night. I couldn't hear his words in the video, but I knew what they were. *Finish it.* The little girl refused to pick up the knife, backing away to protect her friend. Fandrin advanced on her with the speed of a then younger man. His cane rose in the air threatening her as he pointed back to the knife. As his lips turned white with anger I could see the words "loyalty" and "for The Sanctuary" form on them. In a brazen gesture, the girl turned away from the older man and began to leave the ring. I wanted to cry out and warn her as his cane came crashing down into the back of her head. Her tiny body crumbled to the ground as blood poured down her skull, staining her flaxen hair crimson.

When the video stopped, I continued to stare at the blank screen. My brain was turning, clicking the gears back into place.

Click. Click. Click…

I understood. For the first time since my imprisonment began I started to understand Ryker's actions. Not justify them, but *understand* them. "That's why you stepped in the other night. That's why you broke my arm. You thought he might kill me this time."

Ryker's voice was soft, bordering on apologetic. "Or worse, that you might kill yourself."

My head swirled as every one of his actions took on another meaning. His goading me to fight harder, his stopping my heart temporarily to make the torture cease, all of the threats I now understood were actually warnings. My ears began to buzz with the flood of knowledge. I barely heard Ryker when he began to speak again.

"Even before all the tests confirmed it, it was easy to ascertain his blow had caused you severe brain damage. When you finally awoke, you could barely speak, your motor skills were impaired and you didn't remember anything. Not your name or your parents… or me. Not even your training. Our healing serums were not as effective then. They could repair damage, but not regenerate memories. The doctor said there was still swelling in your brain. That you might get better with time. I remember sitting in the ward with you, watching over you while you slept when Fandrin came in. He was still using that same brass cane. He had just wiped off the blood like it never happened. Fandrin made me salute him, and then he pressed a sergeant's pin into my hand and said 'For The Sanctuary.' It was supposed to be your pin, *your* promotion. I knew even then it was a payoff. A bribe to keep my mouth shut but for what, at the time, I wasn't sure." Ryker squeezed his palm as if still holding the pin. "I had been unconscious when he struck you. They told me it was an unfortunate accident but I knew something was wrong. Fandrin hid that video well, deleted all the copies from the archives and ensured no one in that room would ever speak of what happened. Those who might have let their tongues slip conveniently disappeared like your parents.

"If it hadn't been for your father's computer skills that video might have been lost forever. I received it in a coded message the day your parents removed you from the hospital. That night you and your family disappeared along with the rest of the rebels. It was your mother who sent the video to me… that and a copy of the letter from my own father offering me as a sacrifice to ensure your loyalty to The Minister. I was supposed to be the sacrificial lamb in the ring with you. A final trial to test your devotion to The Minister. Apparently, we both failed the test. After I watched that video, I vowed to see Fandrin and everything he had created burn."

His fists were clenched so tightly they were shaking. The white tint of his bones shone through the skin on his knuckles. I stared hard at his fists.

"At least we both have *that* in common." I felt the blaze of hate swell in my chest for The Minister. The dullness I had been shrouded in ebbed. Something sparked inside me. Something alive with anger and betrayal.

Ryker continued—it was as if now that he had begun to speak, he couldn't stop. Our shared past was pouring from his lips like an open tap. I repressed the urge to cover my ears.

"There were so many things Fandrin did, my father did... *we* did as soldiers in training that I never agreed with. But so many others followed suit I thought that *I* must have been wrong. Even you were a loyal soldier until that night. But when I got that message... when I saw *that* video... You were only a child and you stood up to him... It changed everything in my mind."

Neither of us spoke for a while, Ryker still worrying in the past while I tried to understand it. I could still see the desire in Fandrin's eyes when he discovered his bloodline wasn't in fact dead. He knew that he could win over his people again if I was at his side. Which meant only one thing—the people never knew that it was his own blood that started the rebellion against him. "Inessa, told me what they used to do with traitors. How did Fandrin cover the betrayal of his only heirs?"

"We were told that a band of rebels about to be exiled for treason had escaped the city and kidnapped your family in revenge. The rebels were accused of wanting to open the gates, to let in the Tribes as an attempt to overthrow our Utopia. The monitors buzzed with the falsified story for days. 'The rebels had overtaken the gates and Tribes were entering the tunnel. As the hellions bore down to destroy all we held precious, The Sanctuary's guard was able to blow up the tunnel, saving us all. But sadly The Minister's family had to be sacrificed to save the city. His only daughter and grandchild were buried alive with the rebels. A heroic misfortune to save their people.' The Minister managed to hide his daughter's treason, glorify his bloodline, quell an uprising, and silence all those who thought to move against him in one fell swoop. He falsely mourned his family's death and the city worshiped him again." Ryker shook his head, equally amazed and appalled.

"There were a few of us who knew the truth, but for a long time we were too scared to act. Eventually— when we realized the dust would never truly settle—we banded together again. The few original rebels left, joined forces with younger blood and we formed new plans. It has taken years to get to where we are. Personally, I have spent the better part of my life living in Fandrin's shadow, becoming his right hand man, and waiting for the right moment to strike. And for the first time in years, we're ready." Ryker's eyes were bright with hunger and rage.

"And you're confident of your rebels' loyalty?" I thought of how convincing his loyal soldier routine was. Loyalties can be easily feigned.

"Eventually you have to trust someone." Ryker's eyes glinted. "We have been exceedingly careful in choosing our numbers. And while there are those who will undoubtedly fight with us when the war begins, it was not wise to entrust them with our secrets. Not yet. Many of our supporters may not even emerge until after the first blood is shed."

"And what keeps those you have chosen so carefully from turning on you?"

He shrugged as if the answer were simple.

"Hatred. We have all lost someone unjustly due to The Minister." Ryker looked pointedly at me. "We all would rather die a gruesome death than live a prolonged life under his rule. Loyalty has secured Fandrin an army, but what he fails to see is that hatred can fuel a rebellion."

I thought about watching The Minister burn for his actions, about how good it would feel to strike that match myself. "How long?"

"We strike in three weeks' time." Ryker's voice was steady. His vibrantly blue eyes focused.

I nodded, realizing how short my time frame had just become. Three weeks. Apparently healing—both mentally and physically—would have to wait. I needed to be the fearless soldier I once was, now. If there was still a ticking time bomb inside of me, better I point myself in the right direction before it went off.

Ryker looked at his watch and rose from his chair. I threw my hand up to stop him.

"There are still a lot of things you haven't told me." I accused.

He pressed a hand to his flat stomach. "And there will be more time for that, but right now I am starving and if we're late for Mae's dinner she will skin us both."

He fished something else from his pocket and tossed it to me. My hand flashed out catching the small silver capsule with a clear lid. I shook the container watching six white pills rattle inside.

"What the hell is this?" I asked shaking the container at him.

"To help with the nightmares." Ryker said nonchalantly.

"I don't need—"

"*Please*," His voice dripped with disdain. "You both have bags under your eyes and based on your lack of physicality that's certainly not what's been keeping you up at night."

I muttered a curse at him and he smiled knowing he had hit a nerve. I chewed on the inside of my cheek but said nothing, not wanting to give him the satisfaction. Ryker moved toward the roof hatch. As he drew level with me I grabbed his arm forcing him to face me. He stared at my touch in surprise. Instead of letting go—like I wanted to—I tightened my grip until I saw him flinch.

"You *will* answer *all* of my questions about my past and the present alike. You *will* give me answers. You owe me that." I held him in a steady glare. My jaw set, shoulders squared. "*And* you will fix whatever it is that you and your cronies broke in my head."

His eyes shifted between mine, searching for something. "I promise, to tell you what I know. And I will do whatever it takes to get that fiery girl back that I first met in that cell. Because right now, this wisp of a girl standing before me is useless."

He was telling the truth, somehow I could sense it, but it was the flicker of a pleased smile that made something in my body tingle with apprehension. I let go of his arm.

Mouse trusts him. I reminded myself.

I followed Ryker to the hatch, pocketing the little white pills. My once dormant mind had started to work again. It felt rusty. "That night the cameras in my cell went out and I broke your nose—"

Ryker cut me off, pausing as he held back the hatch door. "That was first time I tried to help you escape. *Someone* screwed that up a bit."

His eyes glittered with mingled anger and irony. I cringed at the thought of how much sooner I could have been set free, of the two people who wouldn't have had to die if I had just trusted him. I turned my back on him and lead the way down the stairs, trying not to think of dead bodies.

"I still don't trust you." I said over my shoulder.

Ryker chuckled, his smile now evident in his tone when he replied. "I wouldn't expect anything less, *Princess.*"

"Call me that again and I will do more than break your nose." I growled.

"Just remember, Prea—Keep up or we're done here."

"Duly noted." I shot back.

16. AWAKENINGS

TRIVEN STEPPED THROUGH the panel in the wall just as we reached the landing. He eyed us with curiosity, but said nothing as we approached. His eyes narrowed slightly as he studied me before focusing on Ryker. He was calculating something. What, I couldn't be sure. Triven's face softened as his eyes met mine again. I stopped in front of him, standing too close for politeness but still not quite touching. He knew better than to reach for me, instead he waited for me to speak. Ryker left us and headed for the table. I did my best to again ignore him, but Triven's eyes followed his recession before returning to mine.

"I should have come to get you sooner, but you needed the sleep," I said. Even now after a few hours of rest there were still dark rings under his eyes.

"I'm not the only one." Triven observed my own weary face.

I shook my head, doubting that sleep would ever be an easy part of my life again. There were too many memories, too much time for my subconscious to chatter without distractions. No, sleep was never going to be easy.

I changed the subject before he could further object to my lack of sleep. "When is the next rebels' meeting?"

Triven's eyebrows rose, but he didn't look too surprised by my sudden change of interest. "Tonight, actually. After dinner."

"I want to go." I said firmly.

"I figured it was only a matter of time." Triven smiled his annoyingly all-knowing smile, but the warmth didn't quite meet his eyes.

Dinner was an agonizingly slow event, everyone chewing his or her mush with sluggish concentration. I finished in about five minutes and stared at the others, wondering what exactly it was they were still masticating since the food was primarily pulp. I tried once to bring up the rebels' plans, but was promptly silenced by the formidable Mae.

"No business at my dinner table." She glared hard over her plate of grey slop. Her dark eyes flitted to Mouse as if to say '*Not in front of the child.*'

I rolled my eyes.

"Technically it's *his* table." I jerked my chin in

Ryker's direction. He choked on his food, sputtering and prompting Inessa to smack his back in a motherly fashion. Next to me Triven stifled a smile. It seemed at least he still found my boldness amusing.

"*My* cooking, *my* table." Mae puffed out her substantial bosom. "You want to make the rules at dinner, next time *you* cook."

Triven did laugh this time, but at least had the good judgment not to meet my glare when I turned toward him. Even Mouse was grinning, her head bent over her plate.

"Fine. *Your* table, *your* rules." I nodded curtly at the dark-haired woman. My energy would be better served focusing on taking out The Minister rather than learning to cook. Mae could have her little dinner table talk. After all, was it not I who would be driving the next conversation? The *important* conversation?

Let her cook. I could prepare to serve up a war.

My table, my rules. I smirked to myself. We would talk war, she could do the dishes.

TO MY DISAPPOINTMENT, there was actually very little for me to plan in the way of assassinations. It seemed most strategies had already been set in motion. I sat in the back of the tiny room. A bead of sweat trickled down my temple. The room was crowded, crammed with fifteen bodies shifting and restless. I had chosen the seat in the corner, farthest from the main table and hidden from the pendant's rim of light. Mouse perched alert at my side, her skinny legs folding over themselves. Triven sat in front of me, not obscuring my vision but allowing me a reprieve from curious eyes. I never knew how he always seemed to understand what I wanted, but he did. He also seemed to be trying extra hard after his confession of drugging me.

Sitting on the outskirts of the dim light, hidden behind Triven's broad shoulders, I could easily see every face in the room. I could watch every movement, evaluate each person as they spoke. It reminded me of all the times I had watched the Tribes from above in Tartarus. Nearly invisible, but wholly present—I was a ghost in both worlds.

I had listened to them talk. Listened and watched. It felt normal.

We had been confined in the room for nearly half an hour now, and I was yet to speak. Triven had subtly steered the discussion, asking the questions he knew I would want to hear. He was buying me time. Giving me answers and letting me process things. In Tartarus I knew my place. I dominated the city with knowledge that was far superior to others, but here... I was in the dark when it came to The Sanctuary and

Triven was handing me a narrow-beamed flashlight. I clung to it.

Their plans were far more advanced than the Subversive's had been. Technologies here changed everything. Tartarus barely had enough power to light a few buildings, but here electricity ran their entire world. Even my mind had a hard time grasping the depth of it all. Cameras were in every home, on every street, watching every move these people made. Every second of their lives was accounted for. Every breath, every meal recorded. All of the rebels' homes had been overridden, of course. Loops played at random, cutting in and out as people left or returned from their homes. Homes were connected through facility tunnels like the one we had hidden in so long ago. Their precautions were well planned and meticulous. Their meetings were never held in the same blockhouse and the group never met in its entirety. They never risked losing the entire rebellion if exposed. Tonight's was being held in Mae's blockhouse—which was almost identical to the one in Ryker's home.

Their plans had been years in the making. Plans that had already been set in motion. Plans that could no longer be stopped. The rebels had grown in numbers over the last few years. Their infiltration of the city had been slow and well thought out. Like a cancer, slowly spreading its way through the lymphatic system until it was too late to take action against it.

In three weeks' time, The Wall was going to lose power. The grid was going to come down for the first time in nearly a century. The Sanctuary would be exposed to the city it once ostracized—and all of its inhabitants. It was then that the rebels were going to launch an attack, with the Ministries' forces divided and weakened.

My selfish anger had only allowed me to set my sights on The Minister, but the rebels weren't just looking for an assassination. They wanted a complete culling of the government. They were taking down the beast, not just cutting off its head, as I had once preached. Still, I wasn't sure they understood what their freedom might cost them.

I studied each person in turn. Some of the faces I had seen on other nights at the dinner table but tonight there were several I had not seen before. Among the familiar were Mae, Inessa, Ryker, and a man who reminded me very much of Doc Porters.

One light-haired male was tall and lean, with thick hands and a slow steady manner about him. His fingers were calloused, knuckles raw. My mind automatically ran through the labor-intensive jobs required by The Sanctuary. He was certainly manual labor.

A dark-haired female about my age sat next to

Ryker, her head bent, her shoulders curved in slightly. Her fingers were thin and nimble, but her hands steady. She caught me staring and surprisingly held my gaze before returning to the conversation at hand. Not a soldier, but not a manual worker either.

An older man with peppered hair and dirt under his nails—groundskeeper. A man with flaming red hair and matching raw skin up to his elbows—chemical laundry services. A flighty woman with tapping fingers—computer systems engineer. A middle-aged woman with severe posture and a stern face—soldier.

My brain mechanically clicked over each person. *Click, click, click, click*… A sensation of dread washed over me. It seemed my mind had finally begun to turn back on. A part of me was awake again. And it didn't like the math.

Four soldiers. Eleven civilians.

Eleven *liabilities*.

Rebels surrounded us, but there were only four trained soldiers among them. A shocking reality hit me. This wasn't Tartarus. These people hadn't had to fight for their lives. To kill or be killed. They were repressed, scared… and if they started a war, they might just die that way. I wanted The Minister dead. That was my end game. I didn't care about politics or running a city. After his death I could walk away. I could protect Mouse. Maybe even learn to live with Triven by my side. But what of these people? Killing The Minister meant nothing to them. They wanted to overthrow the entire system. But opening The Wall would be like unleashing hell into Eden. These people were innocent and naked with their naivety. If the Ministry fell they would be nothing more than lambs for slaughter. The Tribes were not a weapon that could be easily controlled. Once their part in the plan was complete, there would be no forcing them back into Tartarus. You can't just release the Titans from their cage and then expect them to go quietly back in.

My mind roared with thoughts, Ryker's voice barely carrying over my internal din.

"The Minister knows the rebellion is growing in strength, but thanks to Zeek and Fiona his mark is way off target. Currently soldiers are rounding up civilians at random, people of suspicion, relatives of those previously involved." His bright eyes fell on Triven pointedly, and then shifted to Inessa. "I fear some of us are at higher risk than others."

Inessa held her head high. "We knew the risk when we joined the rebellion."

"Do you? Do you *really* know what you're risking?" My voice was barely above a whisper, but the subsequent silence confirmed it was heard. Every head but Triven's turned to stare at me.

"Of course we know—" Mae began, but I cut

her off.

"*I'm* not sure you do." I shifted behind Triven, glaring at each person in the room as I spoke. "To ensure the death of your government, you are willing to unleash hell and all its demons upon your city. You may be able to overthrow the Ministry, but how many innocent lives are you willing to sacrifice to make that happen? How many of your women will be defiled? How many of your children will be slain before you achieve your victory? Tens? Hundreds? Because in the end their blood will be on *your* hands, not the Ministry's."

Several rebels looked away in shame, only Ryker and the other soldiers held my gaze.

The austere-faced female soldier spoke in a terse tone. "We are aware of what the Tribes—"

"*Really?* You are *aware* of the Tribes? Are you *aware* of how they hunt? That they play by no rules but their own? That their only desire is to survive and they will do anything to see that happen? How many of you have set foot outside of your precious Wall? How many loved ones have you witnessed raped and maimed? How many allies have you seen bleed out before you?" My voice pitched with a bit of hysteria. Triven's shoulders tensed, but he remained still, keeping his face forward. I forced myself to calm down and closed my eyes to fight back the onslaught of memories. I took a deep breath. *Steady...*

"I want nothing more than to see The Minister and everything he stands for fall—preferably at my own hands—but to involve the Tribes? The Ravagers are in the Minister's pocket for now. But regardless of their current alliance, once you open The Wall there will be nothing stopping them from turning on the entire Sanctuary—Ministry and rebels alike. This Tribe—these savages—will stop at nothing. And the other Tribes are equally unpredictable. It won't just be The Minister fighting a battle from all sides. You will be in the center ring beside him, a gun pointed at you from every direction."

Mouse's tiny hands took hold of mine, steadying them. I hadn't even been aware they were shaking.

Ryker spoke with the cool air of a military official. "Pre—Phoenix speaks the truth, as did Triven before her. The Tribes are not a weapon that can be honed for use. They are deadly and unpredictable, but still, enemy of thy enemy is thy friend."

I didn't like where this was heading.

Ryker continued. "The rebels have come to an agreement. While we know little of your world outside our walls, you know less of ours within. We will take care of *our* end, if you take care of *yours*."

I narrowed my eyes. "What exactly are you getting at, Ryker?"

Triven shifted in his seat his muscles flexing with

tension. This was what he had really been holding back from me. His words were like a weight crashing down on my chest.

"He wants *us* to unite the Tribes."

17. DOUBT

I SLAMMED THE door to our room with such force the metal frame was still reverberating. I wanted to punch something. To scream. To take off and let all of these morons die in their own self-righteous stupidity.

"What the *hell* are these people thinking?!" I was practically screaming. "Unite the Tribes? *Unite* the Tribes?! Does he have any idea how insane that is? Or that we spent the last two months pitting them against each other in an all-out Tribal war?"

I paced the room, prowling the small space and finding nowhere to escape. Both Triven and Mouse were watching me carefully. Mouse was perched on our cot, her skinny legs just barely reaching the floor.

The meeting hadn't ended well.

One thing that hadn't changed inside of me was my temper. Triven's words had hung in the air like tiny daggers waiting to drop. I had felt the blood rushing to my cheeks, the rage searing its way to the surface. When Ryker had confirmed Triven's proclamation, I exploded. I didn't really remember much after that. Several threats had been made on both sides and at some point my chair managed to get thrown across the room. Inessa said something motherly about giving me time and the word hero was vaguely pitched around a few times.

Evidently, my face had become the rallying point for the rebels, even before they knew I was still alive. The video of my insolence and then Fandrin's abuse had become a beacon for the resistance. They had all watched it upon recruitment with the same shock and horror that I had just felt on the roof. It was all part of their plan. The video would go live to the entire city just minutes before The Wall goes down. They were going to use me to show citizens exactly who their Minister *really* was. Since the rebels now discovered I was alive, they had wanted me to be the face of their rebellion. A living accolade to everything the rebels stood for. The hawk-nosed female solider even had the gall to promote our *mission* as if being given this death sentence was a blessing. "You would be considered our liberator, our hero."

I understood what they wanted. If I died trying to unite the Tribes, then I would be a *memorialized* hero and if I miraculously managed to succeed, then I would be the *warrior* hero for their people to follow. Dead or alive, I was of value to them. Whether I wanted to be or not.

That's when I had left. I vaguely remember flashing a few rude hand gestures before exploding from the room shouting, "Go find someone else who has a death wish to be your damn hero!"

Now, in hindsight, my reaction had been a little over-the-top. But honestly, what the hell were they thinking. That Triven and I would just skip off merrily to do their bidding because they had saved our lives? They weren't just asking us for support. They were sending us on a death mission while using us as martyrs to start a war. They wanted us to do the impossible—to unite the Tribes and worse, they wanted me to be some kind of hero to their people. It was better when the Subversive thought I was the enemy.

I stopped pacing and clutched my head in frustration. I stared at the barren concrete wall looking for answers. "I'm *not* a hero!"

I could hear the bedsprings creak, but didn't turn to see who had moved. Mouse's fingers pulled gently at my arms, forcing me down to her level. Her hands were steady as she signed.

"You're *my* hero." Triven's voice caught a little while reciting the translation.

She looked at me with warmth and pride. Signing again. This time I understood her.

They need us.

I couldn't meet her eyes anymore. "I know, Mouse. I know we should help them, but what they are asking is too much. I can't risk your lives. I can't risk you and Triven. I thought I lost you once already and it nearly killed me. You can't ask me to go through that torment again."

Mouse and Triven spoke over each other.

"And would you ask the same of us? We can't let you sacrifice yourself again."

Together.

We both looked at Mouse. Triven let out a heavy sigh. I knew he was thinking the same thing I was. She was too young. It was not her choice. Not yet. But he was right about his say in the matter. I couldn't make him stay if I chose to leave on this suicide mission. I couldn't ask him to suffer my loss anymore than I could endure his.

I fell back into a seated position on the floor and rubbed my head. Mouse settled herself in front of me. She was sitting ramrod straight, with her hands folded delicately in her lap. Her large brown eyes were intent as she stared at me. She touched the scar on her throat, then leaned in and grazed the one on the back of my head. She nodded once before signing again, her hands moving slowly so I could understand.

He can't win.

My heart twisted. I leaned forward and gathered Mouse to my chest, kissing the top of her head. I could feel my father's watch still hanging from her neck. "You know, for someone who doesn't speak, your words are very loud."

She pulled away grinning at me, but faltered when she saw my face. Mouse was my lifeline, my compass. She was right we should help the rebels. But it wasn't just help they were asking for, they were asking the impossible. Impossible was usually my forte but now... I was unsure of my capabilities.

I shook my head staring at the floor in shame. "I'm scared and for the first time in my life I don't know how to overcome it. I feel paralyzed. I have always been in control—of my body, my mind, my future. Even when the Subversive took me, I still had the upper hand. I knew more about the city, more about the Ravagers. But here... I feel like I'm in the dark. I have no jurisdiction—I can barely control *myself* anymore. We came here to start a war on our terms, only to find it has already begun and we are just along for the ride."

Triven crossed the room and folded himself down beside us. "*Everything* has changed. To be honest, as well planned as we were, we weren't prepared for any of this. None of us were equipped for it—not you or I, nor the rebels. I don't think they ever expected you to come stumbling back into their world. Or for any of us to survive out there for that matter."

Mouse put her hand on his arm shaking her head. She tapped her chest and nodded her head. We both stared at her. They had expected her to survive.

My temper rose again as I thought about how they had sent her out into the city on her own. How stupid could they have been? No one was safe in Tartarus. No one. Mouse could sense the change in my emotions and touched my hand, her eyebrows rising in question.

I took a deep breath to calm myself before answering her. My heavy exhale ruffled her hair. "It still makes me so angry to know that they sent you into Tartarus and thought you would be safe. It only proves my point that these people know nothing of what's out there—"

Mouse interrupted me by holding up her hand. She signed quickly, looking at Triven impatiently for a translation.

He smiled gently at her, only a slight trace of sadness in his eyes.

"But I was safe. I found you." Triven nodded to me as he finished her words. A hundred emotions flashed in his eyes. Pride. Fear. Longing. Frustration. Anger.

I saw and understood every one of them.

Mouse had become the child, the sister I had

never wanted and now so desperately needed. I hated the rebels for sending her out into the city, but that also brought her to me. My whole life had changed for her. And despite the torture, despite the pain and anguish, the change had been for the better. I stared in turn at both of them. My people. The Sanctuary had taken one family away from me. But they had also given me another.

I huffed out an aggravated breath.

"Try not to be so hard on these people, Prea. It's me you should be mad at, not them. I should have told you sooner. But the timing was never right." Triven made a sound halfway between a sigh and a laugh. "Is there *ever* a right time to tell someone to go on a suicide mission?"

Mouse patted his arm in comfort, shaking her head.

He touched her cheek and then looked up at me. "You don't remember what it was like here before, but I do. And I fear it's only gotten worse."

"And how much have you seen outside of what they have shown you? Outside of these walls?" I wasn't accusing him, I was asking.

Mouse's brown head twisted as she followed our conversation. Her dark eyes intent.

"Admittedly, not much. But you know as well as I do, as well as Mouse does, what's happening out there is wrong. My father—your parents—didn't die for nothing. The Minister is a terrible man, leading equally terrible people, and he has to be stopped. Mouse already said it, he *can't* win."

Mouse nodded gravely, touching her neck again.

"I know! Don't you think I know that? I know that better than anyone else!" Rubbing my temples for a moment, I then lowered my voice. "All I wanted was to exterminate that evil old man and suddenly we are being enlisted into the rebel army. This is different that it was with the Subversive. I don't feel like we have a say here. And what they are asking of us is insane."

"Completely," Triven agreed.

The room was silent as we pondered our own thoughts. The three of us were standing at a precipice. If only I knew the right choice. Jump? Or turn and run. Either way could cost us our lives.

Triven seemed to be thinking along the same lines. "It seems to me, we have two choices. Hang on and try not to get killed while waiting for the outcome. Or, we can get on board and control what *is* within our power. This war is going to happen whether we help them or not." He paused, scratching the back of his head before continuing. "I know what my heart wants and what my head is saying, but it doesn't matter. Not this time. I have already made some rash decisions here. Besides, this is not my choice to make, Prea. You are the only one the Tribes might listen to. So this choice is yours. And whatever your decision, I will support it. I know you, Prea and if anyone has a chance in hell at uniting the Tribes it's you. You are the most resilient person I know and you understand their world better than any of us. The girl I saw in the library, the girl who took on a Ravager hunting party and saved Mouse. The girl who saved my life in the alley... You are already a hero. The only one who doesn't see it is you."

Mouse's head bobbed in agreement. Her expression was stern.

His words stung, their confidence in me only amplified my self-doubt.

"I'm afraid I'm not that girl anymore—that I left her back in the cell with Fandrin. I get glimpses of her but she's changed." I met both of their eyes, pleading with them to understand.

"I know." He touched my cheek and I let him. "No one expects you to be unchanged by what happened. I take the blame for that. You're human. As much as you hate to admit it, you are not indestructible. Physically or emotionally. None of us are."

I lowered my eyes. I hated being weak. I hated admitting that I hadn't been strong enough to come out unscathed.

Grabbing my hand, Mouse then reached out taking Triven's other free hand in hers, joining us into a tiny circle.

Triven stroked my jaw with his thumb. "I have an idea… but you're going to have to trust me."

18. INSTINCTS

I LET MOUSE stay in our room that night, but not without precautions. I made sure she slept securely beneath us—away from my reach. And while Triven was confident my violent outbursts could be controlled, I still took one of the sleeping pills Ryker had given me. Despite my better judgment.

When I finally awoke, I was groggy and slightly unnerved. It felt as though I had just closed my eyes. I couldn't remember dreaming or moving. The pills had done their job. They had let me sleep. But they had also buried me under a thick veil. The world could have exploded around me and I would have never known. With great effort, I forced my leaden eyes open. Triven was already awake, watching me carefully.

My lips stuck together as I opened my mouth to speak, but he hushed me. Pressing a finger to his lips, he then pointed to the cot below us. Mouse's soft breathing could just barely be heard. It was steady. She was still asleep.

"Will you do me a favor?" He whispered.

"What?" I whispered back, still not fully awake.

Triven unfurled his palm revealing one of the white pills Ryker had given me. "Next time you take a sleeping pill, let me know. That way when I wake up and you're not thrashing about, I won't think you've died in your sleep."

I gave him a wistful smile. "I'd have thought you would have appreciated a peaceful night's sleep."

"What I like is knowing you are safe by my side. It doesn't matter to me if it's a restful night or an exciting one." He stretched, placing the pill on our little side table.

"You have a sick sense of what's an exciting night." I rolled my eyes in irritation considering the last time we had an "exciting night" I nearly killed him. He chuckled, trying to make light of the situation. I fixed him in a fierce gaze to emphasize my point. "I took it in hopes of keeping you both safe while I slept."

"I think you are the least of our safety concerns right now." He rolled quietly out of bed and started pulling on a long-sleeved shirt. "Besides, I think we can resolve some of those issues today."

I eyed him suspiciously. His returning lopsided grin did little to sway me.

"Meet me in the training bunker after you eat breakfast."

My eyebrow rose.

"Mouse knows where it is." And with that he was out the door.

BREAKFAST WAS AN uneventful meal. Inessa was the only one in the kitchen when we arrived and while her smile was warm, her eyes were slightly guarded. We didn't speak. I couldn't blame her after the things I said last night. You can't really tell a room full of people to go to hell and expect a warm reception in the morning. When I yawned for the fourth time, however, she placed a steaming cup of something bitter smelling in front of me. The taste made my tongue pucker but amazingly the last of sleep's clingy fingers fell away from my mind. Mouse finished her food while I struggled to stomach mine.

Once we finished, I followed Mouse to what Triven had referred to as the training bunker. We left the familiar safety of Ryker's underground blockhouse and moved carefully through two white power supply tunnels to find it. I felt overly exposed, but Mouse seemed confident in our safety.

Apparently the use of the word "bunker" was a

loose representation. This was more of a dead-end tunnel with training equipment in it. The room was big compared to most I had seen since my escape. Aside from it being a little narrower, it reminded me of the laundry room I had worked in with Triven back in the Subversive. The walls curved into the ceiling making the room feel like a tipped "C". Small pipes ran across the ceiling, disappearing abruptly into the wall at the end of the corridor. The only exit was the twelve-inch-thick door we now stood outside of. Everything was white. Even with only a few sterile lights, the room seemed blinding. I recoiled a little, flashing back to the room with the bright lights and the swallowing darkness. I froze in the steel-girded doorway, unable to enter.

Mouse bound ahead of me to the waiting Triven. She faked a few punches into his side. He bear-hugged her in response, tickling her until her mouth opened in silent laughter. I felt a small pang of jealousy at how close they had become in my absence. Mouse was like my little sister, but still I could not see myself playing with her like that. I wasn't exactly the fun-loving big sister type. I was more of the kind that would kill you if you hurt her. Literally.

I was watching them so intently that I jumped when a shadow stepped out from behind the door. Instinctively, I snarled as my fists curled into weapons.

"If I didn't know you so well, I might be

offended." Ryker's deep voice crooned sarcastically. He eyed my stance with a critical look then turned casually away. He moved fluidly across the room to the training mat. My body relaxed a little as he moved away, but I still didn't enter the room.

"So do you want to tell her or should I?" Ryker asked over his shoulder. He was indifferently stretching his neck and arms.

Triven cleared his throat awkwardly, and my attention shifted to his direction.

"Tell me what?" My gaze shifted between the two men.

"I asked you to trust me." Triven said walking closer to where I stood.

"And I do." My words came out slow, suspicious. *I think...*

Ryker picked up a training baton. I tried to ignore him, but while my eyes were on Triven, my mind was watching the weapon in Ryker's hand. Mouse had picked up a baton as well and was now playfully sparring with Ryker.

Triven spoke, and I made an effort to focus. "When I first saw you, there was this light inside of you. A fire. When we got you back, it was like it had gone out. As if The Minister had snuffed the life out of you."

I looked away from him as his words slapped my heart. *I was dead inside, everyone knew it...*

Triven gently touched my chin pulling my eyes back up to his. "But The Minister is an imbecile if he thinks he beat you. You *are* the Phoenix. You rise from your ashes and become reborn—stronger and fiercer than ever before. I've seen it. There is a spark in your eyes. You just need a little push. You need to fight... as if your life depended on it."

His hazel eyes were steeled with determination.

I glanced around the room. The Minister had used fighting to break me. He forced me to hate myself for what I had trained to be and now Triven wanted to give me that power back. Ryker had stopped moving. His back was still turned to us but he was listening now. It clicked.

"You want me to fight... *him*." I stared at the back of Ryker's dark head. I could feel the stir of revenge in the pit of my stomach. He might be on our side, but I still held some residual hate for him.

"Your instinct to survive is stronger than any other natural feeling you have. Love and passion come second to it," Triven said. If this fact hurt him, he showed no sign of it. The only emotion gracing his expression was confidence. "I have seen the blaze that burns in your eyes during combat. The power and sense of life that emanates from you when your life is in danger is intoxicating to you. You thrive on it. You come alive."

My eyes shifted to Ryker. "Why *him*?"

Triven's eyes flinched slightly. "Because I have seen that spark when you look at him. Your anger flares and I see glimpses of the girl I first met. The girl quick to a fight, not because she was out of control but because she could master every situation." He hesitated. "You also need someone who won't hold back when it comes to a fight and I can't do that. I can't hurt you, even if it means helping you. I'm... I'm *not* my mother."

I reached for him, my fingertips brushing the back of his hand. I spoke quietly, "I couldn't do that to you either. There is enough blood on my hands, I couldn't live with myself if yours was there too."

We stared at our barely touching hands.

I voiced the question we were both thinking. "What if this doesn't work?"

"It *will* work." He grabbed my hand, squeezing it. "Trust me."

He released me suddenly and turned toward the other two. "Come on Mouse. How about we give these two some room?"

He reached out for her. Mouse promptly dropped her training baton and ran past Triven's outstretched hand to me. She collided with my waist and smiled up at me. She nodded at me with knowing eyes. I knew what she was trying to say without any signs. *You can do this.* I hugged her back and kissed the top of her head.

"Maybe you two should stay. It might be a good idea for Mouse to see what we are really capable of." Ryker was now watching us, his head tilted to the side thoughtfully as he spoke.

Triven rounded on him with a paternal wrath that impressed even me. But I couldn't muster that same resentment. A part of me hated Ryker for wanting to expose her to the kind of violence we were both capable of. And yet another part of me felt he might be right. Mouse had never *truly* seen me fight. Would she feel the same way about me, if she knew that I had been raised—that I had trained—to be a weapon? As much as I never wanted her to see that part of me, chances were it was going to happen. Sooner than later. And she had the right to know what her so-called hero was made of. But I wasn't ready, not now.

"I agree," I said evenly. Triven let out a huff of frustrated air next to me. "*But* today is not that day. Maybe we can educate her next time, that is *if* I don't kill you today."

Mouse swatted my hand reproachfully, her tiny brow furrowed. *Play nice. Trust him.* She signed. I tried to smile reassuringly, but it was a little too stiff to be convincing.

Triven squeezed the top of my shoulder before taking Mouse's hand. Letting him touch me was becoming so easy. He winked at me and whispered in my ear. "Kick his ass."

I grinned in earnest this time as they left. Ryker strode past me, his posture stiff from years of ingrained military training. He shut the door with a heavy thud and spun the wheel, locking us in.

"I never thought I'd see the day when Prea Mason went soft for a guy." He leaned against the door tossing the baton idly in his hand.

I bared my teeth at him. He smiled in return—his face was actually handsome when he did so. Looking less military and more human. I hardened my already icy glare. He was pushing buttons and enjoying it.

"You know Triven is a good man—kind, caring. He's a good fighter too. Actually bettered me in our first match together. But he's weak." He pushed off from the door and walked toward me. My heart began to pound as he dropped the baton and grabbed a real knife from the wall. "He may not be willing to hurt you, but I am."

Ryker's expression barely changed in the next instant, but it was enough to give him away.

I twisted and dropped to the ground as the knife sailed past my neck. Warmth spread down my collar, seeping into my clothes. I was rusty. He had missed a direct hit on his target, but still, it wasn't simply a glancing blow. If I hadn't moved, there would have been a knife embedded in my throat. Ryker was already positioned, prepared for my counterattack. He smiled—

not in the warm way he had moments ago—but in the same cruel way I had seen so many times in my prison cell.

Adrenaline pulsed through my veins like venom. I could feel my muscles tensing, my senses heightening. Ryker reached for the wall behind him and produced another glinting knife. My eyes took in the room around us. I was cornered. Behind me was the dead-end wall with nothing but foam covered batons on it and to my sides were only empty curved walls. All of the weapons of real use were now carefully stowed on the opposite end of the room. Behind Ryker. Before I could form a plan, he charged me. The hair on the back of my neck rose as years of experience whispered in my ear. *Kill or be killed.*

Something inside of me cracked wide open and the world changed. Images of injured children fell away. All I could see was the man coming at me. Everything shifted from grey to black and white. Live or die. Fight or run...

Fight.

Just as Ryker bore down on me, my body came to life. I launched sideways with a burst of speed. Ryker's knife slashed past my shoulder, missing me by inches. I forced the muscles in my legs to push forward as I ran headlong at the curved chamber wall. I could hear Ryker adjusting his aim, coming toward me again. My footing came naturally as I leapt onto the rounded surface. One. Two steps. Then on the third I twisted my body in the air, projecting myself back and upward. My arms shot out seeking the pipes suspended from the ceiling. Shock registered in Ryker's eyes a moment too late. He skittered, trying to stop his forward velocity, but I was too fast. I swung headlong at Ryker, using both of our momentums against him. My feet landed squarely in the middle of his chest with a heavy thud. Air whooshed from his lungs as he hurled backward. My blood raced as he slammed into the wall of weapons behind him. The shelves exploded in a clattering rain of deathly artillery. The knife he was clutching clattered to the floor joining its brothers and sisters in an array of silver and white.

I dropped from the pipes, a grin passing my lips. My fingers were tingling. As I gasped for air, my lungs seemed to fill for the first time in nearly a month. My temporary euphoria was short-lived however.

Ryker was moving again. He rolled onto his side. I barely saw the crisp white of a gun's muzzle before he fired. The sound was oddly muted in the convex room, but the searing bite in my arm was plenty real. I dove to the right, throwing myself at the nearest pile of weapons. Careful of where my body landed, I rolled twice, my fingers closing over two knife hilts as I moved. I could hear Ryker's bullets spinning past me. The smell of singed hair burned my nostrils as one skimmed too close to my head. Ryker was getting to his feet as he continued to fire. I flung one knife as I flipped upright. He deflected it with the gun. Metal clanging against metal. But it was enough of a distraction to let me get to my feet. I hurled the second knife as I dodged sideways behind another rack of weapons and counted. One shot. Two more shots and…

Click.

He was out. I flung myself on top of the rack tipping it toward him. I clung to the falling partition until the trajectory was right and threw myself at Ryker with all of my force. We fell in a heap of punching fists and kicking legs. Something inside of me snapped and I let it go.

Everything I had suppressed when fighting those kids, all of the hate I felt for The Minister, all of the rage and distrust I was harboring for Ryker came flying loose. Suddenly he was everyone and no one. A blur of faces flashed in place of Ryker's as we fought—The Minister, Gage, Maddox, Arstid, Ravagers, every soldier I had seen, even my own hollowed face… I wanted to kill them all. To stop the pain they had caused.

I fought blindly, striking to kill every one of them before they killed me. Our bodies collided over and over again. I could hear small bones cracking, see blood pooling but it couldn't be stopped. My body was alive again. It was on fire and I relished in the power of it.

Slowly the world seemed to be clearing and I could think again. I countered every move Ryker threw at me. Taking his blows in stride until I saw my opening.

Ryker lunged, bringing up his knee for a final blow and I parried. Using his own knee as a launching point, I vaulted myself into the air. I grabbed a fist full of his raven hair and slammed my knee into his face. His body quaked with the force and he plummeted to the floor.

I went in for the kill.

With acrobatic grace, I flipped myself behind him and pulled his arm back at an impossible angle, stopping just before the bones reached their breaking point. Anger was coursing in my veins. I pressed my lips to his ear and whispered. "I take back what I said earlier," I pulled, feeling the bones in his arm snap. "*Now* we're even."

Impressively, Ryker didn't scream but only slumped forward with a groan. I slipped my arm around his neck like an anaconda and squeezed as we slid to the floor. I could feel the racing pulse of his heart beneath my fingers and I pulled harder. His good hand clawed at my arm, but I held tight. Slowly his struggling eased. Finally, his bloody bruised hand stopped clawing and began to tap my arm.

He was conceding. *Tap, tap. I give up. Tap, tap.*

A wicked grin spread across my lips and I squeezed harder until his body went limp in my arms. My mind was alive again and my instincts were flaring, whispering to me.

Kill or be killed...

19. CHOICES

I **WAS STILL** feeling smug when Ryker finally began to stir. Triven was right. Fighting, surviving, feeling in control was like a drug for me. My mind was racing again. My body was tingling with excitement. For nearly a month my physical skills and my brain were withering away day by day. But in this instant, I felt like myself again. It was as if my toxic blood had been purified by the adrenaline.

Ryker coughed, rolling onto his side as he clutched his arm in pain. He glared at me. "Did you conveniently forget what conceding in a fight means?"

I tossed an ice pack and a green syringe I found in a first aid kit to him and slid down the opposite wall, careful to keep a safe ten feet between us. "No. I just wanted to prove a point."

He sat up. With one hand, he strategically pressed the needle into his arm near the break, wincing.

He closed his eyes and gritted his teeth as the serum worked its magic. His foot twitched with pain for a moment before calming. Once his breathing regulated he spoke. "And your point would be…?"

"That I'm still better than you." I dabbed my knuckles, blowing on the raw flesh when it stung. "I could feel the pulse on your neck the entire time. You were fine. But it was nice to see that smug smile wiped off your face for a change."

He gave a low chuckle before succumbing to a coughing fit. Tossing the needle aside, he flexed his fingers gingerly, testing his newly healed arm. Once satisfied, he picked up the compress and pressed it to his bruised neck. I watched him with a cautious eye. Ryker had so many faces, so many sides that I had already witnessed. The loyal soldier. The rebel. The lost best friend. The passionate leader. The ruthless fighter. As he looked at me now, I could see every one of those personalities and yet, none of them. I couldn't read him and it bothered me.

His piercing eyes were watching me carefully as I contemplated him. "You feel better, don't you?"

I swallowed before answering him. "Triven was right. He understands me."

Ryker's face hardened infinitesimally, but I noticed.

"You know I should have killed you for the way

234

you came after me." Even though I felt alive again thanks to Ryker's advances, being attacked repeatedly hadn't endeared him to me in any way. If anything, it made me warier. For the first time since we met, neither of us had held anything back. We were well matched and equally lethal. I may have won this round, but not by much.

Ryker rolled his eyes. "Please… It's a few bumps and bruises."

I bristled, speaking through my teeth. "You shot at me."

Ryker tipped sideways, scraping the nearest gun off the floor. He ignored me as I slipped a handgun from my own belt and poised to shoot him. I stayed tense as his hands quickly slid over his gun, pulling it apart. It wasn't until the weapon was completely dismantled that I reholstered my own. He tossed something to me and I caught it. The small cylinder was cool in my skin. Uncurling my fingers, I inspected the object in my palm.

The shape was that of a bullet, but the resemblance stopped there. The casing was clear like glass, but felt like cool metal to the touch. A translucent liquid swirled in place of an ignition powder while the bullet itself was a vibrant red that shimmered slightly. I rolled it in my palm to feel the weight. It was lighter that a regular bullet too.

Ryker spoke as I inspected it. "Training

ammunition. They burn like real bullets but the pain is only temporary, creating the illusion of being shot. They'll leave a welt and singe the skin a little, but never actually break the surface. They simply incinerate on contact."

"It wouldn't have hurt to tell me that sooner." I threw the bullet back to him with a little more force than necessary. He easily caught it and set it aside.

"You wouldn't have fought as hard if you didn't think your life was in danger." He went back to icing his neck.

"Oh, what? Let me guess, now you're going to tell me the knives you threw at me were merely fluffy bunnies." I pressed my ice pack to my swelling lower lip.

"Oh no, those are real. I figured if you couldn't dodge a few knives, then you weren't very useful to me."

"Ever the gentleman." I muttered.

"Please, I didn't try *that* hard to kill you. Or this conversation wouldn't be happening right now." He pulled himself up a little higher.

"What's the matter Ryker? Upset that you still can't beat me?" I crooned in a mocking tone. He shook his head, but I could see a smile pulling at the corners of his mouth. I watched him as he inventoried his own wounds. Maybe he hadn't fought as hard as he could have—though I doubted it—but I had. Before I regained full control of myself, I *was* aiming to kill. It was in my nature.

I glanced at the room around us. It looked like a bomb had gone off. Nearly all of the weapon stands had been knocked over, splaying artillery all over the floor. Singe marks scarred the floor and walls where Ryker had missed. My hair had come loose in a crazed array of gold and we were both nursing some rather serious wounds. I had already pulled two of my fingers back into their sockets and I was pretty sure we both had bruised, if not broken, ribs. This had not simply been a sparring match.

"How did you know that I wouldn't kill you?"

"I didn't." He shrugged. "I guess I just figured you didn't when we were kids so you wouldn't this time either."

"I'm not *that girl* anymore, Ryker. It would do you well to remember that."

He merely shrugged in response, but I didn't push it.

I glanced around the room again, as it filled with our awkward silence. Ryker got up, wincing and began to rummage in the first aid box before returning to his seat. I poked a discarded knife with the toe of my shoe. "What the hell is this place any way?"

"It was one of the city's many safe bunkers. They were built when The Wall was still under construction. A safe place for the citizens to hide if the city was breached. Most people don't even know they exist anymore." Ryker leaned back against the curved wall, dabbing a towel at a deep cut on his forearm.

"I somehow doubt these have escaped The Minister's attention." I pressed my shirtsleeve to my lip. Still bleeding. "And I can't really see him volunteering the space for the rebels to better hone their skills."

He chuckled darkly, then—satisfyingly—had to clutch his ribs. "Far from it. There are fifteen of the bunkers in total. Each one is usually stocked with food and nonperishable supplies. If the city was ever breached and our blockhouses are compromised they are meant to house the most genetically prosperous people to help with re-population. Each of these people has been tagged by our system and preservation soldiers are trained to escort those chosen civilians to safety before defending the rest of our populous. Funny though… in the past ten years all of our most genetically prosperous people happen to be in The Minister's pocket."

"So how does he not know about this bunker?" I glanced at the door, waiting for a soldier to come crashing through.

"The Minister is overconfident about his control over the city. His doesn't think anyone could ever breach The Wall. There are codes—like the ones on our blockhouse—that if breeched send out an alarm. Zeek has hacked this one too. The man is so good it's a little scary. The only other security measure The Minister takes is to assign two preservation soldiers to perform basic rounds of duty. They walk the bunkers, take inventory and report back to him every other week." He raised his eyes to meet mine. They glittered with pleasurable malice. "What he doesn't know is that those two soldiers turned rebel over five years ago."

"And you trust them?" I glared at him. I still didn't trust most of the people from the Subversive, much less Ryker—who was still just a stranger from my past.

"With my life." Ryker's voice cooled. "We are stronger together. If we start turning on one another, he wins. I won't let that happen. I won't live the rest of my life under the rule of a delusional masochist."

"Why not leave? Why don't you just cut your losses and leave the city?" I asked.

"Why did you come back here?" He countered, his left eyebrow raised as he tilted his head. "Leaving won't solve any problems. You can't trade one hell for another and expect not to still burn in its fires."

I bit the inside of my cheek. Despite my desire to contradict him, I couldn't.

"You came here to change things. To save your people, to find answers—"

I cut him off. "I don't have people."

Ryker appraised me. "*Everyone* has people."

I thought of Mouse and Triven. They were my

only people. But even as I thought that, the faces of Arden, Doc Porters, Maribel and Archer flashed in my mind. I shook my head, not wanting to think about the people we had left behind.

"Why do you want to save *your* people so badly?" I dropped my cold pack to better look at him. "They have sent their kids to become soldiers. They do nothing to defend themselves. It's almost as if they don't care. The Tribes are not the most honorable groups, but at least they are willing to fight for something."

Ryker shook his head, as if something I had said disappointed him. "You never were much of a team player."

He stared at me, making me squirm under his sharp gaze. A look of sincere regret touched his usually cold eyes. "I am sorry about the children recruits... It was not my idea to use them to break you. Gage compulsively watched what little video they had of the five of you when you breached The Wall. Your affection for Mouse was visible in them. It was his idea to use the children recruits to get to you."

I pressed the icepack to my knuckles, unable to look at him. There had been something nagging at the back of mind. Something I had intuitively known but was afraid to say out loud. "He's her brother, isn't he?"

Ryker's heavy sigh answered my question before his words did. "Yes. Gage is Mouse's brother."

I closed my eyes wishing I had never asked. But the lid was already off Pandora's box. So I pressed further. "Their parents?"

"We don't know," Ryker said quietly. "Mouse and Gage were brought in from your world. They didn't even have names. We just called them Boy and Girl. Fandrin thought if he could save and rehabilitate some abandoned children from the outside—show some compassion—it might make his people love him more. Really it was his way of hand-selecting and molding an heir from an impressionable, parentless child. Eleven other Tartarus orphans died from his so-called rehabilitation trials before he found Gage and Mouse."

My breath felt short. My soul ached. Mouse was more of a kindred spirit than I could have ever imagined.

"Mouse never took to Fandrin. She refused to train and fought against him in every way possible. Her brother, on the other hand, did. They were both incredibly intelligent for their ages, but that's where their similarities stopped. Gage desired only to please The Minister. He was violent, smart, and had a lust for power that rivals even Fandrin's." Ryker paused. "He chose his name after he passed his test of loyalty. Gage–it means pledge. Every time his name is said, it is a reminder to Fandrin that he is his loyal progeny."

"Loyalty test?" A cold darkness crept into the back of my skull.

"I was your test. Mouse was his." Ryker hesitated. "Unlike you, he didn't hesitate."

My vision went red. I had thought my hatred for that repulsive boy could not deepen, but I was wrong.

"How did she survive?" I thought of Mouse's deep scar on her throat, her lack of voice.

"It was another rebel who checked her pulse. He lied, under my instruction. Proclaimed her dead when there was still a faint heartbeat. I had watched so many other Tartarus orphans die at The Minister's hand and I never raised a hand to stop him. What he did was terrible, but it did distract him, and allowed the rebels more freedom. Fandrin was so busy with his progenies he failed to see the second mutiny developing under his nose. Most of the children were feral and malnourished, one foot already across death's threshold. It was easy to tell myself death was a kinder end than sending them back to Tartarus. It was a lie though. I hated myself everyday for believing it. But with Mouse... She was so different. She..."

"She gets inside your heart." I muttered, understanding. I loved her too.

"She does." Ryker agreed. "I couldn't lie to myself anymore, not with her. But I wasn't fast enough. Our serums are not as advanced as yours. When Doc Porters left us, he took his research with him and, from what Triven tells me, he has been improving on it. Ours work in a generalized fashion, they can heal but only to a limited extent. I managed to save Mouse's life, but Gage silenced her permanently."

"And you expected her to survive outside? Alone?!" My temper flared again.

Ryker interjected, and he sounded equally infuriated about my accusation. "Of course we didn't send her out there alone! What do you think we are!?"

"Monsters." My reply didn't miss a beat.

He snorted arrogantly.

"I sent Mouse out with two of our best soldiers. They were to protect her and search for possible reinforcements on the other side." Ryker's eyes darkened. "But Fandrin discovered The Wall breach. He sent the Ravagers after them. Boxer and Gains didn't even last two days after that. If it weren't for you, Mouse wouldn't have lived either. Once Fandrin knew the girl was still alive he obsessed over getting her back so Gage could finish what he started. Plus, it didn't help that the girl is extremely intelligent and knew how to get in and out of a city that was supposed to be impenetrable. That and I suppose it reminded him of losing you. Needless to say, my soldiers' mission was a complete failure."

I laughed ironically. "And now you're sending us out on the very same death mission."

"You're different."

I glared at him.

The conversation lapsed into silence as we both became lost in our own thoughts. Now, more than ever, I wanted to leave this place, let these people suffer for their sins. I wanted to get Mouse as far from here as possible and keep her safe. But a large part of me also wanted to see Fandrin and Gage punished for what they had done. And I wanted to be the one to dole out that retribution.

Ryker's bright eyes shifted around the room as if they were looking for something they couldn't find. After a moment they settled on me.

"I will make you an offer." His tone was measured, careful. "There is something I want you to see. Something I think you *should* see. If you agree to come with me and still feel no desire to join our cause, I will see that you are escorted safely from The Sanctuary with all the supplies you will ever need. No one will judge you for your choice. And—if we prevail—at the end of this war you will be free to live as you choose. No one will stand in your way—not from our side at least."

"*But...?*" I waited for the catch.

"No but." Ryker shook his head slowly. "If you choose to leave there will be no retaliation. If you choose to help us, we will be forever indebted to you. Regardless, you have a choice. This war *is* going to happen, but I will not recruit those who are unwilling to fight."

I didn't need to think about it. "When do we go?"

Ryker smiled dryly. Dragging himself off the floor, he limped his first few steps toward the door. "Be ready an hour before dinner. *Just* you. There are some civilian uniforms in your room, make sure to wear one. I will meet you in the living room."

Ryker glanced around the bunker once more. "You and your *boyfriend* had better get this cleaned up. There is training in here tonight and I cannot have my recruits' only practice space destroyed." And with that he left.

IT TOOK TRIVEN, Mouse and I nearly an hour to clean up the training room. Mouse's eyes had grown wider as they came into the bunker, her mouth popping open in a small "O". It took all of my restraint not to gather her in my arms and never let go. While she carefully waded through the debris of weapons and broken stands, Triven took in my disheveled appearance. A small smile played on his lips.

"What?" I asked.

"You look better than he did and judging by Ryker's curtness, I don't need to ask who won." Triven's eyes burned with pride. Ever so carefully he pushed the hair back from my face and ran his thumb along my bruised jaw. I didn't pull away.

"We can take care of that." He offered.

I shook my head and bent to pick up a handful of knives. "I'd rather let them heal naturally. It's a good reminder of who I am and what I have always fought for."

I snuck a glance at Mouse.

Triven nodded. His understanding never ceased to amaze me. I knew he hated seeing the bruises on my face, that he hated leaving me to fend for myself against Ryker. But he understood it was something I needed. I wasn't the kind of girl you rescued. I preferred to rescue myself.

When I told them about Ryker's offer, only Mouse's face fell at the mention of leaving. And even though her disappointment was apparent, she took my hand in hers and squeezed to say that she trusted me. At least whatever we faced it would be together this time. I wouldn't have to leave them again.

As we cleaned, Triven's eyes were ever watchful of me and mine of him. We could both feel the shift, the change happening inside of me. I wasn't the same girl Triven's people had taken in from the streets, but I was no longer dead inside either. As our eyes met again, my chest swelled with pride. Something akin to the old Phoenix was rising again. Now, I just needed to figure out what version of her I wanted to be this time.

I STOOD RIGIDLY in the living room sixty-two minutes before dinner was customarily served. The white linen uniform felt starchy. It chafed the scrapes on my arms, making me shift awkwardly to keep the fabric off my skin. Triven glanced up at me periodically from the book he was reading to Mouse. While his posture seemed casual, there was a slight tension in his jaw. Even though he didn't say it, I knew Triven wasn't totally comfortable with me leaving the house with Ryker. Asking him to fight me in a controlled environment was one thing. But based on Ryker's choice of attire for me, we were leaving the safety of the house. I would be alone with him—in public.

I focused on keeping my breathing even and not nervously fidgeting. Even though I now understood that both Mouse and I owed our lives to Ryker, I still couldn't shake the feeling of distrust. My once perfected mask of emotionless bravado was sliding back into place. To Triven and Mouse I looked calm and confident, but inside my mind raced with all of the ways Ryker could betray me. The thought of how he expected to make the face of the Ministry's most wanted fugitive go unseen was making my stomach flip. What could he want me to see so badly that risked exposing us all?

At one minute to the hour Ryker appeared not from his room as I expected but from the stairs to our hidden quarters. Unlike me, he had used some of the healing serum. His face was once again flawless. I stuck my chin out further, as if to show I was still stronger than him. Ryker was dressed to match me, all hints of a soldier hidden beneath his white linen shroud. He looked me over and nodded slightly to himself as if I passed inspection.

"Well, are we going to do this or not?" My tone was a little more terse than necessary. Mouse raised her head. I tried to ignore the pressure of her eyes on me.

Ryker stepped aside and motioned toward the opening through which he had just come. "Ready when you are, *Princess.*"

His eyes were sparkling with mirth. I bit back the retort bubbling its way out of my throat. Just when I thought I might be able to tolerate him, he acted like a total ass. I was, however, beginning to read him better. He wanted a reaction from me and I wasn't going to give him the satisfaction. I took a steady step forward, but a warm hand caught me.

Triven's hand slid around my waist in what seemed like an uncharacteristically affectionate manner. I stiffened for a moment beneath his touch, but thawed as his intentions became clear. His hands lingered on my hips as he pulled me closer to him. He let his lips brush my ear, tracing my bruised jaw as he pulled away. His words were barely a breath, but I heard them. "Just in case."

As his hands left my hips there was a significantly heavy mass pulling down my left pocket. I shifted my weight discreetly and felt the familiar, cool metal against my leg. I knew the bullets in this gun would not be for training. No, they were live ammo.

As Triven stepped back, I lowered myself just as Mouse threw her arms around my neck. She kissed my cheek and signed. *Be careful.*

With a determined look she then hugged Ryker before signing to him too. She ended by pointing at me. Triven's voice carried an additional warning as he translated Mouse's words. "Bring her back, *safely.*"

Ryker bent and kissed Mouse on the head. "I will keep a close eye on her."

Neither Triven nor myself missed that there were no promises made of a return. Triven's hand fluttered at his side, indicating his pocket. With one brief glance, I understood his message.

Shoot first.

20. CONSEQUENCES

I **WASN'T SURE** what I had expected, but it certainly wasn't going back down into the tunnels. Still, I followed Ryker through the maze of hidden panels and narrow passageways. Our soft-soled shoes made no sound on the poured floors. My eyes flickered to every tiny camera we passed, the glowing red lights made my nerves tingle even though I knew their eyes were blind. The lights meant the guards' system would still show the cameras as functioning, despite the fact they saw a false image. Where we stood now they would only see an empty tunnel-way. We had passed a multitude of doors that looked just the same as the one we had exited from Ryker's home. I had counted twenty-nine.

The farther we traveled away from Ryker's home, the more anxious I began to feel. A hushed thought whispered in my ear. Taking me out alone was never about secluding me from the others. It was about controlling me. About making me listen. With Mouse and Triven locked away in Ryker's home, I couldn't run. Not without them. I couldn't forsake my promise to hear Ryker out, now I had to listen. I mentally kicked myself for not seeing it before. It was too easy to forget that this stranger knew me so well.

"If you decide to use that on me, you better make sure you don't miss." He tilted his head in the direction of my left pocket. Triven had been beyond discrete, but apparently like mine, Ryker's watchful eyes missed nothing.

"Give me a reason to use it and I won't miss." I said. Why deny it.

Ryker glanced at his watch. "Hurry, we only have three more minutes before the cameras go live for rounds."

"Where exactly are we going?" I questioned, hastening my steps to match his long strides.

"We are going into the city, but we have to make a stop first." Ryker took a sharp turn and halted before a door just like any other we had passed. Ryker glanced at the door before us with an air of impatience. He was rolling two small black devices in his palm, pausing to check the watch adorning his wrist. I opened my mouth to speak, but quickly shut it. As if he had deemed it so, the door swung inward, revealing the raven-haired man who resembled Doc Porters.

"You're cutting it a little close," the man said, stepping aside to let us in. He quickly closed the door behind us.

"We had one minute, thirty-five seconds to spare." Ryker shrugged, obviously not sharing in his friend's concern. "Phoenix, this is Thaddeus."

I nodded curtly at the man standing before me. We had met before, but were never formally introduced. He was at the meeting I had attended, and I vaguely remembered seeing his face through a haze at dinner the first night I arrived. It was hard to take my eyes from him. His similarities to my acquaintance—friend, I guess was an equally true term—were uncanny. His brow crinkled the same way Porters' had when pondering something. He had the same thin jaw line and angular nose. Even his voice sounded similar. He was taller though, about even with Ryker's stature.

As if reading my mind he spoke. "It's a pleasure to formally meet you. I believe you know my brother from outside of The Wall. You cannot know how overjoyed I was to hear of his survival."

Thaddeus's smile was warm and genuine.

"Doc Porters is a *good* man." I said, watching him carefully for a response. He seemed to understand my meaning.

"I am not a healer like my brother, but I too seek to help others in the best way I can." Thaddeus stood a little taller as if trying to emphasize his point.

I nodded at him. While I felt no true connection with this man, there was something comforting about his presence. Another rare trait he shared with his brother.

"Petra is upstairs waiting for us, it will take about a minute to calibrate the shields." Thaddeus held out his hand and Ryker placed the small black devices into his open palm. He immediately began tinkering with the devices as he led the way upstairs.

"Thad here is The Sanctuary's leading expert in holographic projections." Ryker said as we followed Thaddeus up a narrow staircase.

"Like your rooftop." I noted, thinking about the barrier that had kept me well hidden frequently over the last week.

"Yes, that is one of my earlier works. Not half bad." Thaddeus muttered over his shoulder. His focus was still on the devices in his hand. We emerged into a house that looked identical to Ryker's. It was eerie how much they were alike. Thaddeus paused to gesture at the world around him in general. "Too bad I'm not as good with force fields."

Ryker clapped him on the shoulder. "You can't be the best at everything, Thad."

Thaddeus grumbled something unintelligible that made Ryker smile. It sounded like "especially not combat."

"Don't mind my husband, Ryker. He is still a little sore that I bested him in training the other night." A woman I had not seen before walked in from the kitchen. It was hard to notice anything else at first other than her radiant smile. Her entire face seemed to glow with it. Even in her plain clothing she seemed to emit exquisiteness. I felt stunned by her beauty and sincerity. Her skin was a warm, rich sienna tone that made her green eyes pop with intensity. Her nose was delicately defined, matching her heart-shaped face and full lips. Like most of the women here, her long black hair was pulled up into a neat plaited bun at the crown of her head. She was nearly my height.

Thaddeus lit up at her appearance. Promptly, he wrapped his free arm around her waist to pull her in for a kiss. She giggled in response.

"A love marriage, I assume." I said rather boldly.

The woman pulled away from Thaddeus, but her smile remained. "On the contrary, we were married out of genetic prosperity." She turned back to her husband. "Maybe I only love you for your brain."

He grinned back at her, "And my good hair line."

"That too." She laughed as she disengaged herself from his arms and strode up to me. "You must be the girl I am lending my face to. I'm Petra. It is nice to finally meet the young lady everyone is talking about."

She extended her hand.

I soured a little at the mention of everyone talking about me, but took her hand. Startling me, she yanked me into a hug. I froze as her arms wrapped around me in an embrace. She only laughed in my ear and patted my shoulder as she let go.

"What exactly do you mean 'lending my face to'?" I stepped back from Petra, giving myself a little more space. I turned to Ryker, as Thaddeus motioned for Petra to take something from him. They placed the black devices over their left ears and suddenly it was as if their heads had disappeared. A finely translucent shield had appeared over their faces, blurring them from view. The screen was pulsing with a rhythmic energy.

I watched in fascination as Ryker spoke. "The Minister has increased security tenfold since your escape. More cameras have been installed and patrols have been expanded. Before, we might have been able to conceal you with just a uniform, but that's not a possibility any longer. Faces are being watched—scanned—so to ensure your absolute concealment, it is better that we use faces that are already on record."

The screen concealing Thaddeus and Petra's faces had receded back into the earpiece. Thad handed his to Ryker and Petra stepped forward, offering hers to me. I took it, careful not to touch her skin. I looked at the small plastic clip with suspicion.

"These devices can scan and replicate a person's

face. Once activated, no one will see anything other than Petra's face." Thaddeus pulled his wife close to him, kissing the top of her neck. "As long as no one touches your head, the second you walk out that door, you will be assuming my wife's identity."

There was a slight edge to his tone, a tiny impulse of fear.

I glanced between the two of them, understanding. If I messed up, if I behaved strangely in any way, or shot someone, it would be *their* lives The Minister came for. Not mine. Even if we were discovered as our true selves, *they* would have questions to answer too. One misstep on our part and these two people would pay the consequences.

As if to emphasize this, Ryker placed his device over his left ear and activated it. His face wavered for a moment like a flickering light, then vanished. I blinked. Two identical Thaddeuses stared back at me. Every detail, every line of his face was perfection. As Ryker's head twisted and tilted so did the holographic version of Thaddeus's. If his mouth opened, so did the hologram's. With the matching uniforms and similar statures, the only difference between the two men was maybe an inch in height. They were twins.

"Why would you volunteer for this?" I asked, questioning their sanity.

Petra placed her hand over mine, enclosing the

device between our palms.

"Because there are things you need to see. To *understand* here. And we trust you to keep our lives safe while they are in your hands." Her bright eyes bore into mine.

Triven's gun felt heavier in my pocket. Pulling my hand away, I clipped the earpiece over my ear and pressed the small button at the back. My vision blinked out for a moment. When it came back it was like looking through a slightly shaded window. But other than that, everything looked as it had moments ago. I had been expecting to feel like I was looking out through a mask, but this was nothing like that. If I hadn't caught the reflection of myself in the small mirror by the door, I would have thought nothing changed. But there were now two perfect sets of the pair whose house we had just entered.

Despite his new face, Ryker's voice was still his when he spoke. "How long do we have?"

The real Thaddeus responded. "The devices can hold a charge for only an hour and a half. You will need to be back here before then. After that your faces may get patchy. I am still working on their longevity. Petra and I will be in the training room to keep out of sight. You can find us when you're back."

Ryker set his watch. I stared at Petra and Thaddeus again. How strange it must be for them to watch us leave with their faces.

Petra tossed me a set of white gloves. I pulled them on to cover my skin. Mutely I nodded to them both, unable to find words, and followed Ryker out the door. I could not decide if they were kind people or if they just had a death wish.

Ryker pulled up his hood. I followed suit, careful not to bump my head and interrupt the hologram. We were barely down the steps when he spoke.

"You know the culture. Nod. Smile when smiled at and keep your head up. No one is going to recognize you." Ryker said out of the corner of his mouth.

I glowered at him from behind my animated mask. That was easier said than done. When someone stared at me for just a little too long, I was quick to forget that they saw Petra's face and not my own.

Ryker kept our pace steady, but managed to keep it casual. Once we were on the street with other civilians, he refrained from checking his watch but I could see his wrist twitch with the desire to do so. Wherever we were headed, it was obvious we were on a schedule. It was strange walking down the sidewalk next to Ryker now. While his voice was the same, it felt like walking next to a stranger. Every time I glimpsed him, it was shocking to see Thaddeus's face.

The streets were busy tonight. One mother in particular caught my eye. She was about a block ahead of us. She had two sons with her, one fifteen, and the other maybe five. They were carrying bundles of clothing and food rations. When the little one struggled under the weight of his load, the elder brother relieved his sibling of the burden, smiling fondly at the boy. The mother touched her sons' cheeks in affection before continuing on their way. I stared at the strange family moment. My eyes lingered as they disappeared around the corner in front of us.

Many others were still out as well, arriving home from work or out enjoying the last few hours before curfew. There was also a significant amount of silver scattered among the sea of white and primary jumpsuits. Their uniforms seemed to gleam like beacons in the dimming daylight. I could feel my panic intensifying. There were fifteen silver uniforms on the streets around us. They were in small casual groupings of two to three, but it made my instincts prickle. It still felt wrong to be out in the open, in the daylight. I slipped my hand into my pocket, letting it rest on the gun. A blonde man in a blue jumpsuit turned the corner ahead of us. A memory flashed in my mind—Brant being shot dead in the street. Giving us away.

I quickly pulled my hand from my pocket and balled it in into a fist.

"How much further do we have to go?" I asked through my teeth.

Ryker steered me around the bend where the family had disappeared. He turned his head as if to speak, but I never got to hear his answer. We took three steps down the street and all of my hair stood on end.

We had walked into a sea of silver.

21. REVELATIONS

EVERYTHING INSIDE OF me screamed to leave, to be anywhere but here. I wasn't the only one either. Several citizens on the street had become rigid with apprehension. Ryker's hand caught my elbow as if sensing my thoughts. He pushed me forward slowly, careful not to draw attention to us. My heart was pounding in my ears, but as I watched the growing number of soldiers I knew they weren't here for us.

To most it would appear that the soldiers were merely milling among the crowd. But I knew better. They were moving in a well-calculated formation. Slowly closing in on their target. Trapped at the center of the swarm was the little family I had been watching. They were blissfully unaware. Then in perfect unison every soldier's gun rose. The inner squadron aimed at the family, while those on the outer edges turned toward the surrounding crowd. The reaction was instantaneous.

I didn't miss it this time. Citizens began dropping to their knees, falling into a unified forced submission. I was barely a beat behind Ryker, but his hands were faster than mine. As he moved to put his hands behind his head, he pulled my hood back. His was already down.

"Up. Don't touch." I heard him mutter in the commotion.

Carefully, I pulled my hands up behind my head. I understood his warning. *Do not disrupt the hologram.* My fingers lingered an inch off my skull. One wrong movement and we would be completely exposed. The tiny device clipped on my ear felt suddenly like an obtrusive lead weight.

The soldiers descended on the family, who were shrinking with fear. All of their belongings had been dropped in haste. The food packages had broken open spilling out a sludgy green paste into the street. It slowly crept across the spotless pavement, staining the freshly laundered white linen uniforms that had come loose from their discarded bundle. Both mother and sons trembled with fear.

The soldier closest tapped his earpiece. After a slight delay he began to recite the words being fed to him. "Chase Randal Corvin you are hereby placed under arrest in accordance with law Ten C-53—you have been found guilty of conspiring to commit crimes against the city."

The mother fell back onto her heels, but kept her arms securely behind her head. Tears sprung to her eyes. The teen boy's face drained white. His mouth dropped open in horror. The soldier nearest him lowered his gun and procured restraints. As he leaned over to grab the boy's hands, life returned to the teen.

The young man turned, latching onto the soldier, his eyes crazed with fear. "I haven't done anything! I swear! I am a loyal citizen! I'M LOYAL!"

The soldier recoiled, trying to restrain the boy, but his antics were escalating. A nauseating crunch could be heard throughout the street as another soldier slammed the butt of his gun into the boy's face, rendering him unconscious.

My hand twitched. Ryker shifted next to me.

The small child who had remained frozen in terror until now, exploded into hysterical sobs. He threw himself over his brother's body, pleading with the soldiers not to take him.

"You're wrong! You're wrong!" The boy screamed in a falsetto. "My brother didn't do ANYTHING! Chase is good! This is wrong! *The Minister is wrong!*"

More guns aimed at the child and his brother. Without moving my head, I looked around. To my disgust, no one moved to help them. In fact, most of the civilians had their eyes turned away. As if what was happening right in front of from them wasn't real.

The mother leapt forward, grabbing her youngest child. She clutched the screaming boy to her chest while slapping a hand over his mouth to silence him. But it was too late. His words were already out and everyone had heard them. Nervous eyes now flickered from the soldiers to the little boy. The child continued to fight his mother, thrashing in her arms as he screeched behind her hand. Terror spasmed across the woman's colorless face as the soldiers advanced on her.

A female solider descended on them barking at the mother. "If you cannot control yourself *and* your son, I will see that you are exiled under accordance with law Ten F-34—suspicion of aiding and abetting a known hostile. As for punishment concerning that little outburst, Soldiers will be waiting at your residence to administer ten lashes to the child for his insolent words."

The boy's eyes widened with fear and despite the mother's straining arms, his frantic flailing grew more violent.

In one swift movement the female solider unholstered her gun and pressed the tip of the barrel to the struggling boy's forehead. Her finger poised on the trigger.

The boy froze.

Every single muscle in my body tensed for attack. If she shot, so would I.

The soldier lowered her voice dangerously. "A simple *lashing* is a kindness… your son could be executed for speaking such blasphemy against our Minister." She then turned her gaze on the quaking boy. "Minister Fandrin is showing you compassion, child. Do you understand?!"

The boy's head jiggled in what looked more like a tremor of fear than a nod, but the soldier seemed placated. Glaring at the mother she lowered the gun, though she did not re-holster it.

The mother nodded too, cradling the now still boy. Tears were streaming down her face as the soldiers hauled her older semiconscious son to his feet and began to drag him away. She did nothing to stop them. The young man's once immaculate uniform was now splattered with blood, his dark head lolling to the side. My blood boiled as the mother merely turned away, clasping a hand over her mouth to staunch her own cries.

There was no mention of a trial or hearing—that boy would never see justice. The soldiers were dragging him away to his death. And nobody was stopping them.

My chest felt like it was going to explode. Rage and revulsion ballooned inside of me, growing with each passing second. How could Ryker ask me to help these people who wouldn't even help their own? I was thinking about getting up, walking away and telling all of these cowardice people to screw off, but a voice called out through the crowd, causing my brain to go silent.

"Anyone found consorting with the rebels *will be* brought to justice. We are here to protect you, the people. To keep life within The Wall safe. To keep The Sanctuary pure." Gage's voice rang out, echoing back off the surrounding buildings. He was dressed in his military best, white uniform adorned with silver metals and the emblem of The Sanctuary. "For The Minister! For equality! For The Sanctuary!"

The crowd echoed back his cry with less enthusiasm.

"Take him to be sentenced!" Gage pointed at the young teen barely older than himself. The older soldiers obeyed, dragging the still bleeding, still unconscious youth toward a vehicle waiting in an alley. I bit down on my tongue to keep from screaming.

Gage's cold, dead eyes swept the street as if hoping someone would challenge him. A chill swept up my spine as his eyes passed over the area where we knelt. A manic smile grew on his lips as he took in the crowd. A sadist ruling over a city of submissives. Without another word he turned and marched to the vehicle. The moment Gage's back was turned, my hand quivered, longing for the gun in my pocket.

Ryker hissed out of the side of his mouth.

An older soldier, maybe Mae's age, stepped toward us, his barrel pointed right at my nose. "Do you have something to say?"

I looked up at him, my mouth opening with a smart retort ready to spill free. My hands were equally eager to disarm him and retaliate. But just before the words slipped out, I caught sight of myself in the reflection of the man's visor. It wasn't my face staring back, but Petra's. Thaddeus's warning came back to me. It would be *his* family punished not mine. I could escape with no repercussions, but he and his wife would die for my rash actions. Ryker's breath was steady next to mine, but I could feel the tension rolling off of him.

Closing my mouth I shook my head and stared submissively at the soldier's shoes.

"Thought not." He grumbled and stepped away, but he was keeping a closer watch on us than before. It felt like an eternity until another citizen drew the soldier's attention away from us, an older man who had simply shifted his weight to relieve the pain in his knees.

When the transport vehicle pulled away, the soldiers began to lower their weapons. A sharp whistle sounded, making me jump. On cue, the people began to gather their things and resume their evening. Now the only difference was that no one smiled or nodded at the mother still cradling her distraught child. On the contrary, they gave them a wide berth.

Only the soldiers and I could not seem to look away.

My entire body cringed when Ryker's arm wrapped around my waist. Pulling me close in the pretense of helping me to my feet, he whispered in my ear. "Get up. Walk at a casual pace and put your hood back up as soon as we clear the corner."

THE SECOND THE front door to Thaddeus' house clicked shut behind us I exploded.

"What the hell was THAT!?"

"*That* was a false arrest." Ryker pushed back his hood. Thaddeus's face winked in and out as Ryker's fingers fumbled to remove the clip from his ear.

"A *false* arrest? *That's* what you wanted me to see? The big life-altering moment that would make me want to save *those* people?" I ripped the device from my own ear. It gave a mechanical screech as I yanked it away and flung it into Ryker's emotionless face. "I just watched a teenage boy get sent to his death, and the only one who said anything was his kid brother! Nobody else did a damn thing about it!"

"*Those* people couldn't have done—"

"Couldn't or *wouldn't?* Because there is a *huge* difference." I shoved past Ryker into the passageway door he had just opened in the wall.

"Those other people in the streets are innocents

trapped here, just like—"

"Innocents?!" I rounded on Ryker. "That young man, *he* was innocent. And the people you want me to so righteously save let him be dragged away to his death today. It seems to me that the adults here have forgotten what morals are. The only ones who seem brave enough to stand up to The Minister are children! *They* are the innocent ones. Not the other cowards huddling in the street. *I* have heard people scream for help in Tartarus and done nothing to save them. I now realize that by ignoring their cries, I am partly responsible for their deaths. *I* was not innocent. And *those* people are *not* innocent either." I gesticulated with my finger, pointing back at the streets we had just left.

Ryker paused at the door to the tunnels, carefully checking his watch before turning the handle. His face was growing red with frustration. This obviously wasn't going as he had planned. The color deepened when he opened his mouth to speak and I cut him off again.

"Initially, I only chose to help the Subversive because it helped me, but the truth is, it was the first place where anyone ever looked out for me. They looked after each other. They risked their lives *for each other.* Hell, even the Tribes defend their own! Your people, *your people* do nothing but watch each other suffer and act like it's not happening. Do they really not know that their beloved leader is just a monster in a skin suit?"

"These people have been spoon-fed lies since the day they were born. They know almost nothing about the man they think is their savior. And those who know, believe it's better to sit beside the throne than be crushed beneath it." Ryker's voice rose. When I refused to stop and listen his hands clamped over my shoulders and with sheer force he slammed me up against the wall. My body recoiled as he pressed his against mine, pinning me in place. My chin hit the middle of his heaving chest. Sparks flew between our eyes as we glared at each other.

His mouth twisted as he spoke. "Those people have been mistreated and abused for so long they're not sure what is right or wrong anymore. Our population is over twenty-five thousand. Nearly *forty-five* percent are military. Sure, there are some who agree with The Ministry's brutality and supremacy. But most of our people spend *every day* in fear."

I pushed my chin out digging it into his chest plate.

"I was a child, and even then I had the courage to stand up to that monster and tell him he was wrong. *I* knew and *I* acted on it. My parents fought back too. Those people out there are ignorant about what is happening around them. And ignorance gets people killed. And *those* soldiers are misguided *idiots*. Stupidly thinking they are serving their city when really they are repressing it. Why should I risk my life to help them when they won't even help themselves?" I shoved as hard as I could. Ryker released me after a moment. When his hands let go, I lashed out causing him to stagger backward a few paces. I glared at him. Without another word I continued down the tunnel, with him hot on my heels.

Ryker stepped in front of me, blocking my path, but he did not touch me this time.

"You're right, they are ignorant. They have no idea there are better ways, but they are not blissful in their ignorance. This city is drowning in *fear*. These people are blind—lost in the darkness and they are scared. They need someone to show them the way. To show them there are choices. To *guide* them."

I rolled my eyes and tried to step around him, but he parried my advance again.

"They don't deserve to be punished for their lack of knowledge. It is only those who see the truth and still turn a blind eye that should be punished." His eyes burned with passion. "Most of those people have not chosen a side because they didn't know there was a side to choose. But they will. The day will come when they have to choose. And that day is almost here."

"Yeah, good luck with that." I rammed my shoulder into his sternum, shoving him aside. I glanced at a flashing camera on the wall and hastened my steps. I could hear Ryker moving up behind me.

"It's fear!" Ryker bellowed. "They are *scared*, Prea!"

I didn't stop walking, carefully retracing the path we had taken earlier.

"Only weak people let their fears stop them from doing what's right." I snarled.

"Oh and *you* have always done the *right* thing?" His tone soured.

"HA!" I barked out a false laugh. "That's so righteous coming from *you*."

We had reached the door that lead to his house. I stopped in front of it, staring at the electronic keypad. I didn't know the code to enter. Folding my arms across my chest, I glared up at him.

"You are so dense!" He punched the keypad with unnecessary force. "You don't understand. It's not the same here. They have *no* choice."

I shoved him aside and wrenched the door open as the locks released. We stepped inside the small room off of the corridor.

I shoved my finger in his face. "Everyone has a choice!"

Ryker was already shaking his dark head, leaning over me with his towering height. "You're not listening! That choice has been *taken* from them!"

I turned on him. Pulling myself up to full height I held my ground. We were both screaming now. "That mother did nothing! She cried and did *nothing* to save her child! How could she have let them take her son? I would have fought! I would have *died first!*"

"I am sure she would have too, but it's not just *her* life in the balance! It's not always as simple as sacrificing yourself!" Ryker's eyes were ablaze as he stepped closer. "The soldiers would have killed her, then her other child, then her husband and then her friends. That's what you don't understand, *Phoenix!* You have only had to care about yourself for years. You don't know what it is to have those you love die because of your actions. Would you be willing to sacrifice Mouse just to stand up for what you believe in?"

My face went slack. I faltered. "N…No…"

"*See,* it's not that simple. Not when love is involved."

I glared at Ryker, hating him for demonstrating that I might be just as weak as those people. A few months ago, I thought love was merely a frivolous emotion shared between sexually charged lovers, but it was so much more. Love was more powerful than hate or fear, it was all-consuming and worth dying for. I had proven that when I sacrificed my life to save Mouse and Triven. But Ryker was right. It was easy to sacrifice yourself, but could you sacrifice the ones you loved too?

As my anger ebbed, I became acutely aware of how uncomfortably close our bodies were now that the screaming had stopped. Both of our chests were heaving with anger and exertion. Ryker's breath was hot on my skin. Before I could move, his hands were gathering my face. His lips swooped down, claiming mine. Shock froze me in place. My eyes popped wide as he kissed me with an unexpected fierceness. His vibrant eyes were open, watching me as his lips moved hungrily against mine. I didn't move.

Suddenly my mind clicked back to life and regained control of my body. My knee wrenched upward catching him in the gut. His lips released mine as he heaved out air and staggered backward. Reflexively Ryker's hands flew up to protect his face but he didn't fight back.

I advanced on him like a predator, only stopping once his back hit the wall.

I stared at him incredulously. My fist froze in the air ready to strike. He just raised his chin prepared to receive my retribution. Ryker's eyes were filled with defiance and arrogance, but also fear. Not of physical pain, but rejection. Maddox's face flickered across my vision, merging with Ryker's. I shook my head. A strange feeling tugged at my heart, making my chest ache. I hated that feeling.

"Screw you." I growled and turned to walk away. Even though Ryker's advances were a far cry from Maddox's, they were still unwarranted and unwanted.

"Prea…" He said it so quietly I wasn't sure at first if he spoke at all. I stopped by the doorframe. My whole body shook with anger.

"*Your* Prea is dead!" I rounded on him. Then letting the rage boiling within me surface, I punched the wall next to his head. He flinched. White-hot fire shot up my arm as I screamed with rage more than pain. The plaster cracked under my blow, splintering as the knuckles in my hand broke. Keeping my fist balled up, I strode from the room refusing to look back.

22. PROMISES

WHEN I ENTERED our room, Triven was pacing the floor. A book lay facedown open on our bed, forgotten. His back was turned to me. One hand was tapping nervously at his side, while the other ran idly through his hair. My stomach clenched. Triven had always kept this worried, nervous side of himself well hidden from me. I knew that he never wanted to appear weak. The same as I did. Pride was a dangerous thing. A fault we both shared.

Then, a dawning realization crept over me as I watched him. My chest began to ache as he anxiously paced. His pain was my pain. His fear was my fear. And for the first time I understood it wasn't always about pride. Sometimes we hid parts of ourselves to *protect* those we cared for. I took an unsteady breath.

"Triven." I said his name with reverence.

He spun on his heels. The entirety of his body

relaxed at the sound of my voice. A warm smile lit his face as his eyes met mine, but quickly faded when they fell upon my hand. I clutched it closer to my chest, as if to conceal it from him. He closed the gap between us in five strides and pulled me gently into his arms. After a few heartbeats he let go and gently slid his fingers down my arm to my injured hand. I had spilt two of the knuckles and the inflamed skin was already yellowing.

"It's broken," he sighed. "Do I want to know what happened?"

"Probably not." I said honestly.

"That bad?" Triven smiled, trying to ease the tension.

"*Ryker* kissed me." I said his name with residual malice. A flash of pain shot up my arm as Triven's hands reflexively squeezed a little too tightly. As I sucked in air, he instantly adjusted his grip. His smile wavered.

"Please tell me you broke your hand punching him in the face." Triven said, carefully examining my hand again. His tone was a little too tight.

"The wall actually."

"Too bad, the pompous ass could use a little humility," he said.

"Triven…" I sighed, then laughed darkly.

"Well, it's true." He muttered.

He was right. Ryker was an ass, but there was something about hearing Triven say it that made it seem harsher. Triven got along with almost everyone. I, on the other hand, hated pretty much everybody. But the truth was, as much as I wanted to hate Ryker, I didn't. Not really. After hearing Triven's tone, however, I wasn't sure the same could be said for him.

I looked at my hand, unable to meet Triven's eyes as I spoke. "I should have broken his nose, but... As much as it irritates me to say it, I couldn't. For a split second, it made me think of Maddox and I just couldn't hit him. I don't know why. It's not the same with Ryker as it was with Maddox. I don't like him but maybe it's that I owe him too. No matter how hard I deny it, there is some... connection between us. We have a history. Even though my mind can't remember it... it's like a part of me does. It's hard to explain. I hate him and I don't. He understands me. He can get under my skin. I *hate* that he kissed me, that he even *touched* me. Ryker is a manipulative ass, but he's not the enemy. He risked his life to save me. I despise owing him my life. But I still do."

Triven pulled away, dropping my hand. When I reached for him, he turned away from me. I caught the pain that flashed across his handsome features before he could hide his face. He took a few determined steps away from me.

"I'll go get the medical kit." His voice was flat, trying to hide any pain he felt.

I reached out again and grabbed his arm with both hands, squeezing so hard my eyes watered from the pain in my injured knuckles. But I held fast as he tried to pull away.

"Triven, he and I have a history, but that's the *only* thing between us. And it definitely doesn't change how I feel about you. I may owe him my life, but you *are* my life. You're the one I *chose* to let in. You and Mouse. You're the only reasons I survived. I *love you*."

He turned so fast I was nearly knocked over. Triven's lips were loving, hungry and desperate all at once. They pushed against mine with a need so strong that it was almost frightening. Then just like that it was over. He pulled me to his chest, pressing his cheek to the top of my head as he held me. I could hear his heartbeat racing.

"You have no idea how long I have waited for you to say that." There was sadness in his voice when he spoke. "I just wish... it hadn't been in reaction to someone else kissing you."

I pressed my face to his chest as my eyes began to burn. I had no words. I had selfishly kept those three words from Triven. But it *wasn't* Ryker kissing me that had enabled me to say them aloud, it was what he said— that I loved Triven and Mouse. I did love them. In different ways of course, but they were mine. The only things I had ever cherished more than myself.

"You could have said it first." I muttered into his linen shirt.

His responding laugh rumbled in his chest. "No, I couldn't."

As always, he was giving me the choice. Letting me take control. Triven pulled away, lowering his gaze to meet mine. "I'm not blind. I see how he looks at you. There is a connection he shares with you that I will never have. I know you love me, but there is chemistry between you two. Even you admitted it. And as much as I love you, as much as I am willing to sacrifice my life for yours, as much as I *trust* you—I don't trust him. Not anymore. I put your life in his hands when I could not save you. Granted he brought you back to us, but not in the way I would have hoped. Not without hurting you first. You and I once agreed that a person's choices define them and I don't trust Ryker's."

I thought of the horrific things Ryker had done for the right reasons. Things *I* had done. Triven was right though. Terrible things done for the right reasons were still terrible. I understood that now. The difference was, Ryker rarely showed the same regret I felt. A quiet pain blossomed in Triven's warm eyes. I tried to look away but he pulled my face back to his.

"I may distrust that man, but there are still decisions that must be made and they *will* involve him. Despite how I feel about him, Ryker is a good leader and this war is being started for the *right* reasons. I know you have already made your choice about what we are going to do. I could see it in your eyes the moment you walked in here." His tone was even. "And I have made promises on behalf of the Subversive, that they would be allies in this budding war. But those promises do not include you. Eventually we will have to leave here to warn and prepare our people. They deserve that much. But after that, you're free to act of your own will, as you always have been. I said I would follow your lead and I still hold firm to that promise. I may not trust him, but I trust *you*, Prea. Nothing will change that."

I nodded mutely, unable to find the right words. Triven kissed the top of my head just as the tears began to fall in earnest down my cheeks. I hated emotions. Life was easier when I felt nothing at all. I blinked furiously.

"When this war is over I'm going to beat the crap out him." He muttered. Taking a deep breath, Triven cleared his throat thickly and motioned to our bed. "How about I work on mending that hand while you tell me where the *ass* took you. I highly doubt this entire evening was merely about him trying to make a move on you."

We both laughed a little too stiffly as I took a seat and Triven retrieved a healing kit. I regaled him with the details of the events I had witnessed tonight, recalling the family's terror and pain vividly. Triven was equally appalled when I finished, his face pale and brow furrowed. He was shaking his head as I gingerly flexed my newly mended hand.

"Arstid told me stories about how controlled the people were here, but I never wanted to believe it was this bad, that a mother would be forced to sacrifice one child just to save another. A small naive part of me had hoped I would be wrong, that it wasn't as bad as I had been told. That maybe my mother had exaggerated." He opened his mouth to speak but closed it, thinking. When he opened it again, someone else spoke.

"She didn't."

Triven stiffened as Ryker entered the room. He surveyed the two of us. My cheeks burned in anger. Tension flexed in the air around us.

"I came to apologize for my actions earlier." While Ryker's voice sounded remorseful, the sincerity never reached his eyes.

Triven rose, turning to face me. "I think maybe I should go find Mouse. She'll want to know you're home safely."

He was gripping the healing kit so tightly his long fingers were turning white as the tendons strained against his skin. I placed my hands gently over his. "We will find her together in a moment."

Ryker's keen eyes stared at my hand on Triven's—a rare sign of affection. His jaw clenched when he looked up at me. I stepped around Triven, addressing Ryker with all of the authority I could muster.

"Triven, Mouse and I will be leaving the city in three days."

Triven showed no reaction to my words but Ryker's face fell as he lost his usual military stoicism. This was not the response he had been expecting. I relished in his discomfort for a moment.

"You will supply us with ample amounts of food, weaponry and any other supplies we deem necessary to survive." I took a deep breath and closed my eyes for a moment before continuing. "I will need everything you can spare if I am to unite the Tribes."

Ryker's face twitched with confusion. "You're going to help us? I thought… After everything… You're going to gather the Tribes to fight for us?"

I shook my head. "I'm going to try. That's all I'm promising. Surviving is what I do best and I am banking on the fact the Tribes will understand that basic need more than any other desires they may have." I took an unsteady breath. Triven's hand squeezed my shoulder, letting me know I had his support. "But let's get one thing straight. I'm no one's hero. I will fight for what *I* believe in. And if you ever find yourself on the other side of that line, I won't simply punch a wall next time. So, I will do what I can to see The Minister fall, but find yourself another savior. It sure as hell isn't me."

For the first time, Ryker looked genuinely stunned. He quickly recovered, his mask slipping back into place. He blinked at the floor and I could see the plans forming in his mind.

"Arrangements will need to be made. I will see to it." Ryker said.

He moved to go, but Triven spoke out, stopping him. "Touch her again without her permission and I will remove your arms."

It was the first time I had heard him speak protectively out of anger. While Triven's tone was carefully controlled, the threat was palpable. It felt strange hearing such aggressive words spill from his usually gentle lips.

Without a response, Ryker nodded to both of us and turned to leave. Only I caught the flicker of his eyes before he disappeared down the hall. As he left, the tension tapered. I could feel rather than see Triven relax.

"Are you sure?" Triven asked. He was not questioning my decision, merely ensuring my choice was purely what *I* wanted.

"No," I breathed. "But what we want and what is right don't always coincide."

"They rarely do." Triven squeezed my shoulder again, smiling sadly. "For what it's worth, I would have made the same choice."

As I trailed behind Triven to find Mouse and tell

her of our news, I couldn't shake the hollow feeling in the pit of my stomach.

If I was making the right decision, then why did it feel as if I had just condemned us all?

THE PROBLEM WITH making promises in advance is that you have time to second-guess and regret those decisions. Which I did.

We had found Mouse under Inessa's motherly care reading a contraband book by some long dead author. Unlike Triven, Mouse did not seem as concerned about my return. Her faith in Ryker was obviously greater than mine or Triven's.

It was Mouse's reaction when we told her of our decision that was now making me regret my promise to help the rebels. Instead of being hesitant about joining the rebels and returning to Tartarus, she seemed elated. She had bound to me wrapping her thin arms around me in a tight hug. She pulled away from me with a more serious expression on her young face. The danger of what we were being asked to do resonated with her. She signed the word I had begun to both cherish and dread.

Together.

I hugged her close to my chest. She was so small. Triven and I shared a weighted look over her shoulder and I knew his conscience was aching with regret just as much as mine. We could not condemn her to our fate, but we couldn't leave her here either. Neither path was what we would have chosen for her.

For nearly an hour, the three of us sat holed up in our barren room talking strategies. Surprisingly, I missed the council at the Subversive. Making decisions that only affected yourself were easy, but making decisions that could affect an entire city—our entire world—felt like smashing my head against a brick wall. No option was without risk. No option was the perfect choice. People were going to die. We were just trying to minimize the casualties. The cost, however, could be our own lives.

Mouse tapped my shoulder, signing to me again. I had let my mind wander and missed her last words. She stuck out her index fingers and thumbs, like guns. Pointing her fingertips at each other, she swept her hands up her torso to her chest.

Survive.

I shook my head, grabbing her hands to keep them from continuing. "Yes, self-preservation is the core objective of the Tribes. But they have never played nice together before. I don't see how we can change that now."

Triven spoke from his seat leaning against the closed door. "You're right, they haven't. But their survival depends on it this time. No matter what the Tribes choose to do, The Wall is coming down. And if they don't pick a side, the only thing guaranteed at the end of this war will be their eradication. If the Ministry and the Ravagers take control, they don't stand a chance against their weapons, not alone."

Exasperated, I threw my hands in the air then folded my head in my arms. "I agreed to a fool's errand, Triven. We *can't* unite them. They will never listen to reason."

"If they would possibly listen to anyone, you are our best bet. You're a product of both worlds, but their world raised you. You understand the Tribes better than anyone. You watched them when they thought no one was looking. If anyone can make them listen, it's you. You are not a Tribe deserter or a Sanctuary citizen or a Subversive member or a rebel—you are every one of these things and yet none of them. You have been reborn time and again into each of those roles and you survived. You have done what the rest of us struggle with. You adapt. You change. That's how you endure. You are unlike anything they have seen before."

"Your flattering words still don't change the fact that I was not meant to lead, Triven. There is a reason lone wolves don't join the pack. I am good with my fists, not words."

He chortled, "True, making friends was never

really your strong suit."

I twisted and threw a pillow at his face. He caught it, looking more serious as he pulled it into his lap. "I will be your voice, if you want me to be."

"And if words don't work?" I asked.

"And if words don't work, then we may have to kill anyone who stands against us." His eyes hardened as he spoke. Triven was never one for killing. He injured but rarely killed his assailants. The severity of his words made everything too real.

I gathered Mouse's small hands in mine and held her gaze. "This is insane isn't it?"

She nodded slowly, pursing her lips.

"We *have* to do this don't we?"

Mouse nodded again, sadly signing. *Yes. Help them. Help us. Survive.*

I bowed my head, resting it against my knee. I had wanted her to say no, to tell me it was okay to turn my back on everyone, but I knew she wouldn't. Mouse was like the moral compass I had ignored for so many years. But I couldn't ignore her now. Still, I also didn't think I could do this. Fight—yes. Hide—yes. Survive— yes. But lead? It brought on a new emotion for me—I doubted myself and for the first time feared what the future might hold.

Two tiny hands wound around my cheeks, pulling my face back up to hers.

You promised.

"I said I would *try*." I corrected her.

Try harder.

I pulled Mouse into my lap, cradling her small frame in my arms. Taking a weighted breath, I turned to Triven. "I never thought I would say this, but we need to speak to your mother."

23. ATONEMENT

DEATH...
      Equals freedom...
      Equals sweet reprieve...
      I had contemplated this equation so many times in my life. Despite my persistent will to survive, it seemed my mind could never escape those thoughts. It had been nearly twenty-four hours since I told Ryker we were leaving. Twenty-four hours of restless, anxious planning. Still we heard nothing from our rebel counterparts. The waiting was eating at me from the inside out—crawling under my skin and boring into my brain. Triven understood my need to escape—to think— when I left in the middle of the night seeking reprieve from our four smothering walls.
      My bare toes hung over the edge of the rooftop's ledge, toying with the open air, careful not to reach past the holographic field. I took a deep steadying breath as

the simulated wind swept across my skin. If I closed my eyes, if I shut out the serene sounds from below, it almost felt like I was back at home on the rooftops of Tartarus. My eyes popped open.

Home?

When had that hellhole become home?

My head twitched as the hatch door opened, but I didn't take my eyes off the empty streets below.

Ryker's baritone broke the night air. "You know there are better ways to kill yourself. The least you could do is make it seem like a sacrifice for liberty." He paused next to me leaning over the edge to appraise the height. "You'd have to find a higher building though."

He was in his soldier's uniform tonight. The white suit, adorned with the silver bars appeared to glow with an eerie aura in the still darkening night air.

"I thought my job was to die uniting the Tribes for you, not jumping off a building." I turned and hopped soundlessly down from the ledge. Folding my arms across my chest, I gave him a bitter smile.

His gaze turned hard. "Your *job* is to do what the rest of us cannot. To tip the scales in our favor... and to come back to us." He thawed, pinching his forehead. "We all have to make sacrifices. We can't selfishly protect the ones we love at the risk of losing hundreds of others."

"You have a funny way of showing people you

care for them." I said coldly.

"And you have a bad habit of pretending like you don't need people." There was a bite in his tone. "I'm *not* sorry I kissed you."

"I get the feeling you're *not* sorry for a lot of things you do." I bit back.

He leaned back against the ledge and swept his fingers through his hair, a habit I now recognized as a sign of his exasperation.

"There never was any winning with you." Ryker took a deep breath. Folding his arms, he slumped, curving his shoulders around himself. "We have moved up our timeline to accommodate your escape. As you saw, the streets are teeming with soldiers and security measures have increased. It will be nearly impossible to move the three of you without a distraction."

"What about the devices you and I wore the other day?" I asked.

"No." Ryker was already shaking his head. "We can't have three citizens disappear from one place just to pop up a mile away. There are too many cameras now for someone not to notice. Besides, The Minister is watching for a male and female traveling with a child. Families are being stopped regularly for questioning. It's too high of a risk."

I toed the rooftop. "So what *are* our options?"

"You will be moved throughout the day to

several rebel safe houses. Each location will move you closer to the drop point. We have strategically planned each stopping point to align with that rebel's schedule. That way, no red flags will go up if one of us is missing for too long. Each rebel will make themselves publicly seen throughout the day to ensure they are not under suspicion when the feed goes live."

"Feed?" I looked up, questioning him. It clicked before he could answer. "The video of me."

Ryker confirmed, "Yes. Well, one of them at least. We are hacking the system through an untraceable remote. Thaddeus and Zeek have been working for the last three months securing it. Our hope is that it will cause enough of a distraction to allow your escape. This video will be the first public appearance the rebels have made. Ever. There won't be any going back after that."

I stared at his feet. The leather boots were shined to perfection. Our reflections mirrored us, two ghostly pale faces distorted in the dark.

"And where will *you* be when the feed airs?" I inclined my head, waiting for his answer.

"By The Minister's side of course." His voice was controlled, but something was off in his tone.

"Better to sit beside the throne than be crushed beneath it." I repeated Ryker's own words back to him.

"As it is better to deceive from within, than to attack with a blind eye." He chortled humorlessly, then sobered up as the silence dragged on between us. "In less than forty-eight hours, we will have done what no one else has. We will have made an official proclamation of war against The Sanctuary."

He shifted and I could sense his tension.

Planning a war was one thing, but actually starting one meant putting gears into motion that could not be stopped. Selfishly, I was glad that task had not fallen on me. I did not envy Ryker for the choices he had to make. While we were still at the Subversive theorizing strategies, Ryker and the rebels were preparing to take action. They had always been leaps and bounds ahead of us. Our well thought-out plans now looked liked child's play compared to their strategies of warfare.

I understood now, more then ever, that we needed allies to survive this looming war. The time for being a loner was over. The Subversive would gladly fall in line to ensure their survival, but could I really expect the Tribes to see it the same way? Could I make them understand that when The Wall fell, they would have to sacrifice a few to save the many? The real question was how do you unite people who have spent the last decade killing each other? The answer—give them a common enemy. I knew that, but getting others to fear or hate something they had never even heard of would be nearly impossible.

I had never actually chosen to start a war. Sought

change, destruction, vengeance? Yes. But as with most shortsighted people demanding change, I did not realize what must be sacrificed in order to gain it. Dictators did not just roll over and give up. Freedom only comes at a high cost. The truth—wars were not started by the masses. Wars were started by a few men—men who could rarely foresee *all* of the consequences of their actions. They saw a means to an end. Everything else in between was merely collateral damage. And the rest of us—the ones caught in the middle—we are left to choose sides or bury our heads in the sand. Either way, we would be swallowed by a war we did not start, but were required to finish.

Ryker cleared his throat, recalling my attention. "Inessa is downstairs. She was looking for you. I suppose she wanted a word before you left."

"Mmmm," I nodded, not bothering to correct him that I was actually the one who had asked for her.

"I have another favor to ask of you," he asked with a careful tenor.

"What, possibly sacrificing my life isn't enough? Let me guess, you want my soul now too?" I leveled him with a well-practiced glare.

The corner of his thin lips pulled up. "Not quite. It's more about your expertise…"

My eyes narrowed.

"The largest group of rebels we have ever risked

having together at one time, will be in the training room tomorrow night." He shifted, turning his insightful stare on me. "I cannot be there because I will be preparing for your escape. I was hoping you could train them in my absence. Teach them some things I have overlooked."

My eyebrows rose. "You actually think I can teach them something you haven't?"

"I would love nothing more than to say when you beat me the other day, it was because I let you. But that would be a lie." He bowed his head looking uncharacteristically humble, before returning to face me. "You are still the only person I cannot best. If anyone can teach them something I have not, it would be you."

The look of admiration in his eyes made me uncomfortable. I turned away, staring at the street below. It confused me that while I certainly had no romantic feelings for Ryker, I didn't exactly hate him either. Was this what it was like to have a friend... or maybe even a brother? Five soldiers were patrolling the neighborhood. Their guns glinted in the darkness, reflecting back the houses' porch lights.

"What time?" I asked staring at the soldiers.

"Mae will bring you there after dinner." Ryker turned following my gaze. We watched the silver uniformed team in the forced stillness of the night air.

"I should find Inessa." I said pushing away from the roof's edge. Ryker nodded but did not move, still watching the guards. I turned, beginning to walk away, but Ryker's voice stopped me just as I reached the roof's hatch.

"I will see you the morning of your transport. I will see to it that everything is prepared and you are returned to Tartarus safely. After that, you are on your own." He still had his back turned to me.

"Got it." I replied. As I slipped my foot onto the first step, he spoke again. When I glanced up his head was twisted back, his strong jaw brushing his shoulder as he spoke.

"There isn't room for failure."

I turned away and continued down the steps. "I know."

INESSA WAS WAITING for me in the main room of the house with two cups of steaming liquid already perched on the table in front of her. Her prematurely weathered faced glowed as I approached. A glimmer of a younger woman showed beneath her wrinkled eyes when she smiled. It was lovely.

It dawned on me how beautiful and unmarred the people of The Sanctuary appeared. No scars or limbs lost telling of battles survived or years won. But I also knew some scars could not be seen. Despite her exquisitely aged beauty, I could see still the deep sadness that lingered in Inessa's eyes. It faded at times, but never truly went away. Some scars are too deep for flesh to heal.

I picked up the steaming mug and took a sip, letting it warm my body as I thought over my words. Inessa waited patiently, sipping at her own cup. Her smile was serene.

"I realize that I have not always been the most... *receptive* person to your kindness." I paused. Being nice took so much thought and energy. "You must understand that kindness is not something that I am accustomed to... but I'm trying."

Inessa nodded, encouraging me to continue. The house felt heavy with an abundance of silence. I took another sip of the sweet water.

"We are leaving in less than two days and there are still some things I need to understand before we go. Things I have a right to know. I have made commitments I can no longer rescind. And after we talk tonight, I must only focus on the future. While we can learn from the past, dwelling in it will not save us. There are so many people here eager to give me their renditions of the past, but I don't want interpretations. I want the truth. I want to know beyond a doubt why I'm choosing to fight with you."

Inessa spoke for the first time. I had nearly

forgotten how soft her voice was. "The ghosts from our past will haunt us everyday if we let them. Even drive us insane if not dealt with—if they go on misunderstood. One thing your mother taught me was that *true* knowledge is power, but *assumed* knowledge can be fatal. Unfortunately my child, most truths are nothing but interpretations. However, ask me anything you like and I will do my best to provide you with an honest, unbiased answer."

I smiled at Inessa for the first time, letting down my walls just a little, allowing her to see the person I kept so tightly bound inside. It was the only gift of thanks I had to offer her. I also hoped taking down that wall would allow me to hear her words without bias. Keeping people out was so much easier than letting them in.

The smile fell away as I asked my first question. It was the one I had to get out of the way, the one that could hurt the most. The one that had plagued me since my arrival here. "If my parents loved me, why did they give me to that monster for so many years?"

Inessa's eyes closed for a moment. Her soft face pinched with pain. There was regret in her voice as she spoke, but only truth spilled from her tongue. "They led The Minister to believe that you were a peace offering— an olive branch to soothe the years of a bad relationship. Jutta claimed she wanted to keep the power in the family. And at the time your grandfather was so desperate for a blood heir, he never considered that you were offered to him as a distraction. And so while his focus became tigerishly focused on you, the rebels were watched less closely."

"I was bait." My tone was flat, but pain stabbed at my chest with acute precision. *I wanted the truth*. I reminded myself. *Truth hurts.*

Inessa's eyes brimmed with tears, but she held them back. "In a way, yes... but it was more than that." She hastily added. "It killed your parents every day to send you to The Minister, but you—of all people—should have been the safest under his watch. You were his heir, his progeny, his only hope of lineage survival. Fandrin cherished you. Jutta and Coen would have never sent you to him if they thought he would hurt you."

"But he did." My nostrils flared. "And he taught *me* how to hurt others."

"Despite what we are led to believe, parents are not always right in the decisions they make. They are human too. And they screw up sometimes." Inessa grimaced. "In an effort to do right by you, they inadvertently put you in harm's way. Your parents didn't want you to hurt others, Phoenix. They wanted you to be able to defend yourself. No one knew better than them that a war was coming. They wanted you to be prepared."

I thought of Mouse and the books I insisted she

read. Yet if it came down to a fight, she wouldn't be able to defend herself. *What help was schooling if you didn't learn anything practical?* Words from the past slammed into the forefront of my mind. Something my father had written in his journal. My fingers tingled as if retracing the familiar words.

"*Non scholae sed vitae discimus.*" I said out loud.

Inessa surprised me by translating. "We do not learn for school, but for life. Seneca the Younger."

"They were using The Minister—to train me against him."

"Yes. Who better to teach you, than the man who trained the army you would one day fight against."

It took me a minute to swallow Inessa's words. It was strange. Despite the fact I could remember nothing of the past, it still held power over me. It still caused inexplicable anger to boil in my veins. But it was pointless. The past had happened. It couldn't be changed. Hell, I couldn't even remember it. One thing was true, though. As much as I was hurt by my parents' choices, those choices were the only reason I was still alive today. If they hadn't sent me to Fandrin as a child, I would have never survived in Tartarus. Even The Master was impressed by my skills when I found him. It wasn't that I was a natural, it was because my body already knew what my mind had forgotten.

In truth, I wasn't even sure if I could still be mad

at them for dying to save me. My mother and father may have abandoned me in that alley, but they did so to give me a future. Life in Tartarus was hell, but I shuddered to think what it would have been if we stayed. I could have been dead at my own grandfather's hand or worse yet, grown to stand beside him like the cold and merciless Gage.

I shook away those thoughts, returning to matters at hand. *Learn from the past, don't dwell in it.* "At this time, Ryker and I seek the same outcome. Fandrin's death. Our paths toward that goal may be different and our reasons are our own, but for now we are united in that same objective. Ryker and the other rebels are... *confident* in their cause. But others have failed where they seek to succeed. I wasn't here when these plans were put in motion. It is not in my nature to trust. Nor is it to act the fool. So, why did the rebels—my parents—fail the first time?"

I had heard Arstid's side—her tales of betrayal and blame. What I needed now were facts, not emotions. I watched Inessa with rapt attention as she pondered my question. Her delicate thumb idly traced the rim of her glass as she began to speak.

"Things were not as... *organized* then as they are now. We didn't have safe houses where we could talk without being seen, or bunkers where we could hide our secrets from the Ministry. All of our decisions—our rebellious inclinations—were whispered in passing on the streets or murmured about in dark alleys. We knew very little about one another. Most of us were only on first name basis for fear of being turned on, for our own protection. We figured the less a person knew, the less they could divulge if captured. Trust was an issue back then." She puckered her lips.

It still is, I thought.

Inessa continued. "Back then we knew so little about what lay outside of the Wall. We were told of the terrible Tribes that hunted outside of our walls, but no one had ever been outside and returned to tell us first hand. Some thought we were being trapped in here—held captive when a better life was outside. Others thought only barren land awaited us, that maybe the Tribes had died off. But many feared the nightmare stories of the Tribes were true. Not even your mother really knew."

"But The Minister was working with the Ravagers, how could that have gone unnoticed?" I asked.

"Their alliance was very secretive. Only the highest council members knew of it," she replied. "We couldn't even confirm those rumors until Ryker became a higher ranking official. And even still, his knowledge has its limits. Honestly, it was Triven who verified those rumors for us."

"Then why did The Minister associate with them

at all? What could the Ravagers possibly offer that he didn't already have?" It was the piece of the puzzle we were missing. Why integrate the two worlds you worked so hard to keep separate?

Inessa's face tightened, her graying eyebrows knitting together in thought. "Power would be my best guess. Maybe our worlds are not as divided as we once thought. To be honest, I'm not sure. I really don't think anyone but Fandrin himself could answer that question. The man is a sociopath."

My gaze fell to the floor as I wondered if that mental affliction was genetic. Too many of my family members had made decisions that had cost the lives of so many others. My parents included. I shied away from the next thought creeping into my consciousness.

Was I following in their footsteps?

"We have a long day ahead of us tomorrow. I should try and get some rest." I rose. Inessa mirrored me, extending her hand to take my cup. Respectfully, she was careful not to touch me as she took it.

"May I impart a few final words from a silly old woman?" She waited for me to nod. "War is never a good thing. A necessity… maybe. But it is ugly and in a way both sides always lose. Fighting for others—for a cause—can liberate you. But when fighting for vengeance, one must be careful. It's a slippery slope. And once it's over, you may not find the peace you sought."

Startling both of us, I leaned in and kissed her cheek. "Thank you for your honesty tonight, Inessa. I hope to find you again when this is all over."

She patted my hand with tears in her eyes. "You came home once, I am sure you will do so again."

I nodded politely and turned away. As I walked the dim halls to find Triven and Mouse, I could only think of one thing.

Was this my home too?

If I was being honest, we were leaving in barely twenty-four hours and despite what horrors awaited us outside that wall, it still felt like I was going home. Even if Death was waiting for us on the other side, his arms would be open in welcome to his lost children of Tartarus.

24. EDUCATION

AS RYKER HAD promised, Mae led us to the bunker after dinner. Mouse had eaten hungrily as Triven and I struggled to swallow our meals. I knew we should eat as much as we could, since after tonight meals would undoubtedly become harder to come by for a while. But my stomach didn't seem to care.

While there was still a frostiness between us, Mae's demeanor had been more benevolent in the past few nights. She wasn't the only person either. Between my time spent in the underground of the Subversive and within the walls of The Sanctuary, there were a few things I had gleaned from being around other people. One was that people were usually kinder when you had something they wanted. Another was that a strange mix of kindness and pity seemed to emerge when they thought you were going to die. Since our proclamation to help them, the rebels' attitudes had changed on both accounts. For the most part anyway.

Fiona, the stern-faced soldier with the hawk nose I had noticed from the meeting was one of the few whose attitude continued to be sour. It was her haughty face that caught my eye as we entered the training room. It pinched with displeasure as I held her glare. Breaking away from her fixated stare, I scanned the room full of murmuring rebels. Ryker had not been exaggerating about the number of people here tonight. There were at least thirty-two people in the room. My earlier fears were confirmed, however. I recognized about half of the faces and even with the new additions I still only counted nine soldiers. Their stances always gave them away. Everyone else was civilian. It did not go unnoticed that the only two familiar faces I did not see were Inessa's and Ryker's. Those waiting were gathered in little groups huddled along the curved walls and hidden behind weaponry racks. As we made our way through the door, the murmurs lowered but did not cease. More than their voices, it was their looks that rattled me. My skin began to crawl with all of their eyes watching me. As if their gazes carried actual weight. It was like standing trial before the Subversive again. Reflexively I took a step back, bumping into Triven's chest. His hand discreetly soothed my lower back.

This was not a trial.

Nor was I expected to fight anyone.

I was not alone. He and Mouse were with me. I reminded myself.

I stepped to the center of the throng, pulling myself up to full height. And still feeling short. People here were not malnourished, they all seemed suddenly tall in the crowded room.

We were the last to arrive.

Thaddeus closed and latched the door behind us, locking us in and keeping others out. As the latch fell, the room grew silent. Mouse stepped to my side, taking my hand. I smiled down at her before addressing the room.

"As I am sure you already know, we are leaving soon. I have made no promises to Ryker and I will make none to you tonight." My voice was louder than I had expected, bouncing off the curved walls. I lowered it slightly. "When The Wall comes down in two week's time, I hope that we will be waiting on the other side with reinforcements. That said, only an idiot would wager a bet in our favor."

Several people averted their eyes. Idiots.

I continued, "*AND* would think that we could save them." A few more eyes fell away, others hardened.

"But you saved Mouse." A smaller black-haired woman in the back corner spoke. Her almond shaped eyes flittered between me and the girl holding my hand.

I stared down at the little girl I had been willing

to give my life for. She squeezed my hand. I squeezed back before returning my attention to the woman who spoke. "I did, but I understood the gravity of my actions. I went into that alley with the intention to die. I don't regret my choice—it was the best I ever made—but it was a reckless one. Don't mistake my choices as heroism. *Never* expect someone to save you. Learn to save yourself." My voice had risen in frustration.

The woman recoiled as if I had slapped her. She was not a rebel I had seen before and like most of my rebel admirers, I obviously was not what she had been expecting. My mother may have had a way with people, but tact was forever lost on me. It showed.

"Not that your motivational speeches aren't moving and all, but aren't you supposed to be training these people?" Fiona's cool eyes shimmered with spite. "Unless words are all you have to offer us."

I opened my mouth with a string of venomous words ready to spill out, but a minute squeeze from Mouse made me shut it again. *We needed allies, not more enemies.*

"You're right. Let's not waste time." I said with an even tone. "But when you say 'these people' I am sure you are not forgetting to include yourself, Fiona. Even soldiers need a little refreshing now and again." She glowered at me, but said nothing in return. I turned to address the rest of the room. "I need to see where your skills are. Break into three groups—mechanical weaponry, hand-to hand combat, and manual weapons. We will rotate."

I leaned down to Mouse as the groups began to form themselves. "I want you to watch and learn everything you can tonight, but I don't want you sparring. Okay?"

Mouse bobbed her dark head. Her deep eyes widened, a trickle of fear mingled with excitement. Despite my desire to keep her innocence, I knew I couldn't send her into the future ahead of us without some training.

Triven oversaw the mechanical weaponry group while I split my time between the manual weapons and hand-to-hand combat teams. We focused on basics at first. Holding weapons, disarming and arming them, basic attack moves and self-defense, then we moved to more technical tactics like sparring and target practice. We corrected them where we saw fit and most were receptive to our advice. It was oddly satisfying to teach them skills that came so second nature to me. Very few rebels could wield a knife to my standards, but they were better than I expected. Even Triven seemed pleased by their knowledge and skills with the guns, stunners and bombs. I was even more shocked to see many of them could fight. Once I began selecting the pairs to spar, their real skills came out. When sparring, a person never fought their hardest when paired with someone they loved. But if I pit them against someone with better skills, then the lesser fighter always fought harder. We were careful to keep most of the blows to parts of the body that were easily hidden by clothing. While there was healing serum at the ready, it would be unwise to waste it on training. They were going to need as much as they could get in the upcoming weeks.

Satisfyingly, there were even a few people who surprised me. Mae was one of those. Despite her thicker stature and age, she was surprisingly quick on her feet and packed a lot of power behind her punches. More than twice she earned a pleased smile from me. The less I saw of her chilly disposition, the more I could understand why Inessa loved her. I had learned we alpha-females rarely played well together, but we could certainly admire one another's strengths. Thaddeus was another surprise. His skill with a gun outrivaled most of the snipers we had in the Subversive's numbers. His calm demeanor and calculated shots made him a lethal ally. But he was lacking in hand-to-hand combat. While I was impressed with their overall skills, they were still far from ready for a war. Especially not where the Tribes were concerned.

Time in the training room was moving like a blur, feeling much too short. We had been through three full rotations and three and a half hours when there was a collective groan of sympathetic pain from the room. Fiona had just laid out her third opponent. She looked at me, grinning like a shark through her ragged breaths. It was difficult for me to admit she was good, but she was. Fiona's skills were honed to military precision. Against most opponents she would be deadly. She was confident too. If The Master had taught me one thing, however, it was that over-confidence was a fast way to get yourself killed. Only an idiot thought there was nothing left to learn. Still smiling, Fiona walked closer to the gathered crowd. Almost everyone had abandoned their posts and were now watching the hand-to-hand combat, drawn by Fiona's unrivaled successes.

As she drew nearer I tilted my head toward Mae, who was standing next to me. Making sure to speak loud enough for the entire room to hear me, I posed her a question. "You have plenty of the healing serum in supply, right?"

Her brow furrowed as she answered. "Of course, but we—"

"Good," I spoke over her response.

At that moment, Fiona drew level with us. Twisting to the side, my fist flashed out like a snake, smashing into Fiona's unexpecting face. She staggered backward as the room fell into utter silence. Blood began to pour from Fiona's nose, staining her face and marring her white shirt. She doubled over in pain, grabbing at her gushing nose with both hands in an attempt to staunch the bleeding.

"YOU BITC—," she began to scream behind her hands but I cut her off, stepping out of the crowd.

"Have you ever fought for your life with a broken nose? Have you had to fire a gun or throw a knife while your tear ducts were opening like flood gates? How about when your airways are blocked off and you are choking on your own blood?"

She stayed crouched, glaring at me over the top of her blood-soaked hands. The crimson tide was seeping between her fingers now. Unwanted tears were blurring her eyes. I leaned in as I lowered my face to her level.

"Well, have you, *sweetheart?*" I smiled sweetly, baiting her. As predicted, she took the bait.

Releasing her face, Fiona shot upright, bringing her fist up with the force of her movement. I twisted with her. The air flexed next to my temple as she missed her target. In the same movement, my left elbow collided with the side of Fiona's head, sending her tumbling head over heels. Her long limbs curled and tumbled with trained precision. When she emerged from her calculated roll, a knife was now clutched in her right hand. The smug smile that had lit her face mere minutes ago had been replaced with a feral snarl. From my peripheral vision, I could see several people move to step in. Both

Mouse and Triven were in the forefront, but I held up my fingers telling them to stop. Triven's hands clasped over Mouse's shoulders and they stayed put, as did the other concerned rebels. No one intervened, but each of the anxious onlookers had slipped to the front of the watching group.

While these marginal movements happened, my eyes never left Fiona. Lunging like a cat, she closed the gap between us in two strides. Her hand flashed with quick short strikes, keeping the weapon close to her body and well under control, the blade of the knife whistling as it cut through the air. Though her attacks were well marked, I was faster. I easily danced away from the singing blade. It never even grazed the fabric of my shirt. The tighter she gripped the blade the more it began to slip in her bloodied grasp. Fiona's face blazed red with fury. The more I eluded her, the wilder her advances became. With an erratic, powerful thrust she drove the knife toward my stomach.

Pivoting outward, I twisted around her extended arm until I could feel her shoulder in the square of my back. Utilizing the impact of my movement, I brought my right elbow down into the back of her skull. The hollow sound echoed in the still room as Fiona went sprawling face first onto the ground. The knife slid from her bloody hand, clattering loudly across the floor.

With intentional nonchalance, I turned away

from her. Addressing those who watched us, I pointed blindly to the knife fallen from Fiona's hand. "Rule one, never try to staunch your bleeding during a fight with your hands. Blood only makes your hands useless and slick."

Even without the collective intake of breaths from the watching rebels, I knew Fiona was on her feet again. She had the knife and was charging once more. I turned to face her just as she bore down on me, her arm thrusting to kill.

Using her own momentum against her, I grabbed her wrist pulling her toward me. Twisting myself into her arm, I curled my back into her chest like a deadly lover's embrace. I dropped my body and yanked her arm downward, flipping the woman who was nearly a foot taller than myself over my back. As Fiona's body flew air bound, I clung tighter to her wrist, twisting the knife with ease from her still bloody hand.

Air coughed from Fiona's lungs as her body slammed into the floor. Her back arched in pain as she rolled to the side gasping for air. She wouldn't be getting up anytime soon.

I flipped the knife twice in my hand, feeling the weight. The only sound in the room was Fiona's gasping breaths.

"Rule two, fight with your head, not your heart or you'll make stupid decisions that will get you killed." I glanced at Triven and Mouse, both of whom I was willing to make stupid decisions for. Triven's hands were still firmly clasped on Mouse's shoulders, his own broad shoulders showing subtle signs of stress. Mouse was gripping Triven's hands with equal intensity. While her knuckles were nearly white with anxiety, her eyes were alert as she took in my lessons. Fiona was stirring again. Unable to look into Mouse's perceptive eyes any longer, I turned away. Several other rebels were now offering her assistance up, but she batted them away, wiping at her nose, obviously humiliated.

"Get off of me!" She yelled. I raised the knife in my hand and the others quickly backed away, leaving her to fend for herself. Fiona glowered at me. With a flip of my wrist, the knife soared across the room. It imbedded into the mat with a dull thud, the hilt quivering between her legs. An inch higher and I would have hit her pelvis.

I looked directly at Fiona when I spoke this time. "Rule three, The Minister taught you how to fight for loyalty. Now you need to learn how to fight for your survival."

Leaving Fiona on the floor, I walked toward the outskirts of the circle. Several cries broke loose as a knife imbedded itself into the weapons stand less than a foot from my head. I traced its trajectory and found Fiona was no longer clutching her nose like a scorned child. She was standing proud, chest heaving with the effort to maintain her stance.

I nodded curtly at her in approval. "Better. But next time, don't miss."

A flicker of a smile graced Fiona's face as she nodded back.

"Who has next match?" I called.

To my surprise, over half of the room eagerly raised their hands.

People slowly trickled out of the room as another hour passed. It was late and those of us left were growing weary. Despite her best efforts, Mouse had fallen asleep in the corner. Her tiny hands were clinging to a training baton as her head lolled against the bowed wall. Her lips murmured something unintelligible, her hands tightening on the baton. The sight tore at me.

While nearly every rebel did their best to catch my eye as they left, I resolutely avoided them. I had already stupidly let too many people into my heart—my parents, Mouse, Triven, Archer, Arden, Inessa, Ryker... even Maddox. So many were dead and many more would follow. I didn't want to feel the loss anymore. I was already too full of it.

No. *These* people—these rebels—were allies, not friends and it needed to stay that way. The Minister didn't need any more ammunition against me. And I certainly didn't need the responsibility of their lives. I could help them learn to fight, but I was not the one asking them to fight. We were all safer if I kept them at arm's length. It didn't register until we were walking back to our room, with Mouse cradled safely in Triven's arms, that even he was keeping these people at a distance. The charismatic boy I had fallen in love with was quieter here. More reserved. This place had changed both of us.

"A lot of them are going to die, aren't they?" I asked, secretly pleading with him to disagree.

His honesty, however, was staunch as ever. "Yes. They are."

His arms tightened around Mouse as we unconsciously hurried our steps, furthering ourselves from those we knew were damned.

25. PROCEDURE

THIS GOODBYE WAS different.

There were no heartfelt farewells. No wishes of good fortune.

When we left Tartarus to come here, it was supposed to be a reconnaissance mission. Now, however, the time for recon had passed. We were going home not to start a war but to be pawns in one that had already begun, making these goodbyes feel much more final. It was harder to feign optimism when both sides were aware of what lay ahead. Our mission was probably a death sentence and if we failed, theirs would mostly likely follow suit. If by some miracle we did succeed, half of these people could already be dead by the time we were reunited. Merely saying goodbye seemed inadequate when it could mean forever.

While sleep was imperative, none of us slept very much. I could hear Mouse tossing restlessly in her bed, which we had moved back in. And while Triven never moved, his breathing never grew deep enough for sleep. I had clung to my father's journal all night, my thumb sliding rhythmically over the worn surface as my mind raced. By the time a soft rapping came at our door, the three of us had already been up for the better part of an hour. Triven strode across the room and opened the door. Mae was standing in the hallway with a pile of clothing draped over her arms. She too looked like she had barely slept. Her round face was wan, the purple marks under her eyes deepening her already depthless eyes. Even her curly hair seemed extra unruly this morning.

Triven stepped aside so she could enter. Mouse instantly moved to the woman, throwing her arms around Mae's substantial hips. She smiled down at the child while speaking. "These are for you to wear. They are lightweight, but bullet-resistant at long distance. You three should eat before you leave. There is a very long day ahead of you…" She faltered. "Um… Ryker also informed me that he was not sure how easy it would be to procure food on your side of The Wall, so I added some extra nonperishables to your packs. Ryker will bring them in a bit."

Triven relieved her of the clothing. Mae blushed when he bent to kiss her cheek tenderly. "Thank you, Mae. You are too kind."

She pressed her palm to his cheek patting it sadly, as her other arm hugged Mouse.

It was the least I could do since you're probably going to die out there.

She didn't say those words, but she didn't have to. We could all see it on her face. Despite Ryker's bravado and many of the rebels' confidence, Mae proved not everyone was so optimistic about the impending war. Like us, she could admit that people were going to die. Blinking away the tears in her eyes, she turned her attention back to the uniforms in Triven's hands.

"Get dressed. Then come upstairs for a bite to eat. Ryker should be meeting us soon and we will leave." Her curly head bobbed once at the three of us and she swept from the room. An escaped tear had slid down her cheek as she left and her thick hands had fiercely wiped it away. Realization struck me, I actually liked the tough old broad.

Ever the gentleman, Triven left to change in the bathroom, giving Mouse and I some privacy. I neglected my own suit to help Mouse with hers, carefully tucking my father's pocket watch back around her neck. Unlike the flowy civilian uniforms we had become strangely accustomed to, these were practically skintight, fitting similarly to the soldiers' uniforms. A long zipper sealed the back, stopping at the nape of the neck. The silvery-black fabric reminded me of the bulletproof undershirts we had worn when first coming here. This time at least, all three of us would be wearing one.

Once Mouse was fitted in hers, I began to pull on my suit. I paused with the zipper halfway up. Mouse was sitting on her cot frowning at her new boots, her skinny legs swinging, knocking the soft rubber soles together.

She noticed my staring. *Too big. Ugly.* She signed sticking out her tongue in distaste. I smiled at her and knelt to examine her boots. Her toes fell just a tad shy of fitting perfectly, but not much.

"They're fine. You will be too big for them before you know it." My heart skipped as I said the words. I would do everything in my power to see that happen. "I like to wear mine a little big, anyway. More comfortable."

Mouse now beamed at her boots, proud to be like me. As always, it disconcerted me that she looked up to me so much. As if reflecting my thoughts, her hand shot out palm up asking for something. When I did not respond fast enough, she retracted her hand. Sliding her pointed index finger across the other, she then pointed at her boot. I understood.

"You want a knife for your boot," I said.

She nodded, very serious now. I reached behind my cot and grabbed two small, white handled knives. "Then I guess it is a good thing I stole these from the training room last night."

I watched as she took the weapons and carefully placed them in her own boots. She seemed so much older than just a few months ago. I took her hands once she was done. "You are to stay by my side, unless I say otherwise. If I tell you to run, you run this time. Got it?"

We both knew I was speaking of her defiance the night we first came to The Sanctuary. Shame swam in Mouse's eyes as she nodded. Her fingers moved shyly. *I promise.*

At that moment, a small rumbling sound emitted from Mouse's mid-section. She flushed red and pressed her hands to her stomach in an attempt to staunch the sound. It merely grumbled again, causing us both to laugh.

I kissed her swiftly on the forehead. "Go on up and get some food. I will be there in a minute."

Mouse threw her arms around my neck in a swift hug, and then ran out of the room. Her long brown hair whipped around the corner after her. Once she was out of sight, I pressed my face into her cot. I wasn't sure what to feel. Joy? Panic? Fear? All of those things and more? I was almost certain I had a better chance at protecting Mouse out there. Here we were like trapped rats, but out there… that was my territory. In less than twenty-four hours we could be back in Tartarus. Or if things went not according to plan, I could be back in The Minister's clutches. Either way, I would put a bullet in anyone's head before I let them lay a finger on Mouse—friend or foe. I had made promises to the people here, but as my parents had proven, people break promises all the time. I knew Triven wanted to help the cause, but when it came down to it, I would choose him and Mouse over all of these people. I could only hope it wouldn't come to that. Pushing away from the cot, I pulled on my own boots.

There was a soft brushing noise of skin on metal as Triven's hand grazed against the doorframe when he entered. My back was still turned as I gathered the last of our few belongings—my father's things, pictures Mouse had drawn, a book Triven had become attached to. Chills ran up my spine as his fingers grazed the exposed skin on my back.

"May I?" He asked.

I drew my hair to the side, allowing him to zip up my suit the rest of the way. I leaned back against his chest listening to his heartbeat. It was steady as ever. His arms wound around my waist pulling me closer. Feather light, his lips pressed to my ear. Spinning in his arms, my lips sought his. For this one moment, I allowed myself to forget about everything else.

Our mouths moved in feverish unison, never feeling satisfied. In that moment I knew no amount of time with Triven would ever be enough. Even if we had an entire lifetime to grow old together, I would still want more. And the sad truth was, we were not likely to get that time.

Once we were both gasping for breath, I pulled away letting my head fall forward onto his chest as I clung to him. Triven pulled me tighter, feeling the same sense of impending loss. For now, this one moment was about us and nothing else. Because the second we left this room, everything in our lives would be overshadowed by war.

THE MANUFACTURED SUN was barely up when we arrived in the kitchen. Mae was busying herself with food while Mouse pushed around her breakfast. It looked like she was painting with grey mush more than she was eating it. In an attempt to set a good example, I took my bowl from Mae and shoveled in a bite. I had to choke down the chalky flavor.

"High in protein today?" I asked Mae.

She gave me one of her finest reproachful looks. "You'll need it."

"Mmm, thanks." I muttered around another mouthful. I tried not to snicker as Triven's mouth puckered with his first bite. We were still grimacing our way through the remainder of breakfast when there was the sound of footsteps coming up the stairs. Ryker emerged from the blockhouse carrying three small black bags. He looked exhausted, but that didn't stop me from being critical.

"Those don't look like they are exactly filled with weapons." I suspiciously eyed the three small packs dangling in his hand. My father's journal would barely fit inside one, much less the food and weapons we had agreed upon.

Ryker dropped the bags by the doorway. "These are just your day packs. There is some food and a few devices that may prove useful. The packs I have arranged for your escape are waiting for you at the final drop location." He yawned, reaching for the cup Mae was offering him. "It didn't make sense to have you drag them all over the city. They would only slow you down."

Triven and I exchanged glances.

He had better not be lying.

Ryker didn't miss the silent exchange.

"Please, haven't we gotten past our trust issues yet?" He rolled his eyes, leaning against the counter across from me.

Triven muttered something I couldn't quite make out. Gathering my empty bowl, he moved to the sink to assist Mae with the dishes. Ryker watched him with appraising eyes. I tapped the rim of Mouse's bowl, reminding her to eat more.

"When do we leave?" I asked.

Ryker refocused on me. "Your next host is expecting you in less than an hour. We are—"

The dim lights in the house suddenly went red. Ryker shot bolt upright and Mae dropped a dish into the sink. Instinctively, I grabbed for Mouse who was already reaching for my arms.

"What the hell—" I shouted but Ryker waved me off. He was darting across the kitchen. His fingers flew over a keypad making a screen on the wall glow to life. The entire room froze. Three military vehicles were parked outside of a house and soldiers were spilling out like silver ants into the street. From the center car stepped a young man with rich brown hair and white suit embellished with silver emblems. I hissed through my teeth as a string of profanities flew from Ryker's mouth.

Gage.

It took less than a heartbeat to know they were not outside some random home, but the one we now took refuge in. Ryker's fingers grazed the keys once more. The screen vanished and the lights turned back to a yellow-white hue.

"Move!" Ryker barked in a hushed tone. He was already running to the hidden doorway. I bolted after him, Mouse's head bobbing on my shoulder as I ran. Her fingers were painful as she clung to me. Triven and Mae were on our heels. Ryker unceremoniously threw the bags down the stairs and ushered us inside. Triven pushed Mae in first, then began to pull Mouse and I in with him. As my foot hit the first step, the doorbell rang. For one second we froze. Everyone's eyes were on the front door. Triven put out his hand to me, but I didn't go further down. Instead I turned to Ryker.

He stood with his hand hovering above the panel, ready to shut us in. I took in his resolve.

"You're not coming."

"No," he said. "I have to answer the door. I have to keep up appearances. This could just be a routine visit."

We both knew he was lying.

Mouse was beginning to shake in my arms. I clutched her tighter as Triven and Mae came up closer behind me. Mae's hand reached past us as the doorbell rang again. Ryker grabbed his aunt's hand, kissing her knuckles. They nodded at each other, the simple inclination of their heads carrying a multitude of emotions.

Ryker then grabbed my shoulders, giving me a firm shake. "When The Wall comes down I *will* see you standing on the other side."

"You had better pray you're right, because if you're wrong Tartarus is going to swallow you whole." I said in a rush of words.

He ignored me, turning his attention on Triven. "Keep them both alive."

"Try to keep *yourself* alive." Triven retorted.

Ryker reached out, stroking Mouse's terrified face with his hand. "The cameras will go live in seven seconds. Don't do anything stupid! Whatever happens, *stay hidden.*"

With one last glance at me, he pressed the wall panel and the heavy door slid shut, locking us in.

I began counting down.

Six…

Mae touched a panel on the wall and a screen came to life.

Five…

Our necks simultaneously craned to watch the image flickering to life.

Four…

Ryker stood at the front door, his hand on the doorknob. He was poised perfectly, undoubtedly ticking the seconds in his own mind.

Three…

Through the screen, we could hear Gage banging impatiently with his fist this time.

Two…

One.

There was an infinitesimal pulse visible on the feed. One would barely notice the change if not looking for it. The video was live. It was one time the unchanging uniforms came in handy, no one would notice the blip in the feed. Ryker pulled the door open, his face feigning surprise at finding The Minister's protégé on his doorstep.

"Gage, what a pleasant surprise." Ryker bowed his head slightly to his juvenile superior, slipping again into the role of the devoted soldier I had hated so much.

Gage shoved his way past Ryker, inviting himself in. Mouse's trembling amplified as he crossed the threshold. I clutched her tighter.

"This is no time for pleasantries, Major." He rebuffed. "Get inside and shut the damn door!"

The flanking soldiers rushed to follow his orders. Two remained on the porch while the other four soldiers entered Ryker's house. They lined the wall in a stripe of silver, their weapons held to their chests at a casual alert.

Gage, however, was restless. He paced the hall, stopping with his back directly in front of the hidden doorway. He was so close and yet no sound traveled through the secreted entrance.

I shifted my gaze away from the screen, my eyes boring into the metal door. Less than six inches separated us. An impulse slammed to the forefront of my thoughts. I wanted so badly to tear through the door and break his neck. Mouse's breaths were coming in tiny convulsions now. Her fear only fueled my rage.

Mae's eyes flickered to the door as well, her weight anxiously shifting. It was apparent she wanted to back away down the steps. I turned back to the screen.

Ryker kept an aloof air, his well-trained reactions under control. Somehow he managed to look like an entirely different person.

Loyal soldier.

Vengeful rebel.

He played both parts so well.

"We have received intel that the rebels may be making a move today." Gage's eyes glittered as they bore into Ryker's.

Mae and Triven both swore under their breaths behind me.

"The Minister has called you in *immediately*," Gage continued.

A low growling noise was growing in the back of my throat.

Ryker saluted, "I will put on my fatigues and meet you at the Tower straightaway."

We watched on the screen as Ryker moved to open the front door for them to exit. But they would not be so easily dismissed. Gage signaled and two of the soldiers stepped into Ryker's path, blocking the door. Ryker stopped mid-stride. It looked like he was debating taking out the soldiers obstructing his way.

"The Minister wants to see you *now*." Gage's voice was nearly shrill in his command. He shook his head, adjusting his tone to a more confident purr.

"Unless you have something more pertinent to tend to, Major."

Something was wrong. We could see it even through the screen. Ryker's face was too calm, his body overly rigid. This was not how The Minister usually called on his soldiers.

This was not protocol.

I shoved Mouse into Triven's arms and whipped back to the door with the rash intention of exploding from our hiding place. This wasn't a friendly house call or a leader requesting his best soldier's service, they were taking him in.

There were only four soldiers and Gage… I could easily incapacitate—Triven's fingers wrapped around my elbow, causing me to pause mid-thought. My hand was already on the door. When I glanced back, he shook his head. Mae touched my arm gently, nodding in agreement with Triven. Ryker's words hung over us like a net.

Stay hidden.

He knew this might happen. I pulled my hand away from the cool metal of the door and turned rigidly back to the screen.

"No, of course we will go now." Ryker's voice boomed as he bowed his head again. Even though his head sank in Gage's direction, his eyes were on the door hiding us. He knew we were watching. "My life is dedicated to The Minister and the betterment of The

Sanctuary. One life for the many. My plans can *always* be changed to ensure the safety of our people."

His final glance to the hidden door was nearly imperceptible, but we got the message. We were to continue without him. Ryker did not want to be saved and no one should pursue him. He was going and we should be too.

The soldiers once blocking his way now opened the door, letting him out. Ryker strode from the house like a dedicated soldier and a parade of silver fell in step behind him. Only Gage lingered. His soulless eyes swept thoroughly over the rooms, lingering on the few dishes abandoned in the sink. With an animalistic sniff of the air, he swept from the house, slamming the door behind him.

None of us moved for what felt like an eternity. Mae's trembling hand was covering her mouth in horror. Slowly gathering herself, she swallowed a few times. Her tones were still hushed when she spoke, but her voice did not waver. "Plans have changed. We should go. Right now if you want to make it out of here."

26. SACRIFICES

HORROR SPREAD TO each home we visited like the plague, each host going pale at the news of Ryker's apprehension. We assured each person that he left under his own will and there were no formal allegations brought against him. But it comforted no one, not even us. Mouse had been crying slow heavy tears since we left Ryker's kitchen and I couldn't stop looking over our shoulders.

It had been twelve hours and seven safe houses since Ryker was taken. There still wasn't news. While no one knew his fate, none of the others had been seized... yet. As the hours passed, more soldiers were teeming in the streets. Even a few unexpected patrols were trolling the underground system we were using for travel. There had already been two close calls, leaving everyone shaken. Reason should have warned me to wait until the waters had calmed, but my need to distance ourselves from this place was even stronger. Besides, there was no guarantee things would calm down. The waters were just starting to simmer and if we waited, we might be boiled alive.

The thought of ending up back in Fandrin's grip kept chasing me from safe house to safe house like a dark phantom. I would seriously consider death before I would allow him to take me again. The only thing that would be worse than death was if he got Mouse and Triven too.

Not a single rebel had let us out of their basement blockhouses for fear of a random inspection. Several homes had been raided already, but to our advantage none were actually rebels' houses. Zeek had done a good job overriding the systems. The Minister's soldiers were always off by a few residences, rifling through neighbors' homes and arresting citizens at random. Three homes were raided near ones we had hidden in.

"If someone had turned on them, surely we would have been found already. Right?" I asked Thaddeus. He and Petra were our second to last stop. I again flipped the knife I had been toying with, unable to be still.

We were gathered in their safe room, watching on a screen as their neighbors were dragged from their house under suspicion. Petra had left the room to fetch us water, unable to watch anymore. Triven and Mouse were reading a book without focus. They hadn't turned a page in over ten minutes.

"I wish that were true, Phoenix." Thaddeus chewed his thumbnail, his eyes glued to the screen. A hushed cry broke from his lips. His neighbor had just been tasered for not moving fast enough. Thaddeus turned away from the screen. He shook his head and ran his hands through his hair before addressing Triven and me. "Ryker was very careful about moving you three. There were twenty-five houses you could have gone to today. We didn't even know for sure you were coming to ours until you appeared at our door."

Triven handed the book to Mouse, joining our conversation. "How many of you knew we were moving today?"

Defiantly, Mouse dropped the book and came to stand by me.

"About half of us. Ryker gave two other dates to the rest of the rebels. Just in case." Thaddeus replied.

"What about the video feed? Did everyone know it was going live today?" Triven asked.

"Only four of us knew about the video. The other rebels knew that we were making our first move soon, but they only knew to watch for our signal." Thaddeus answered. "That may be why the soldiers aren't looking at specific people. They may know of something happening, but aren't sure what that is."

"For claiming you trust your people, you certainly don't tell them very much." Triven's tone was not as accusing as his words sounded. But I knew what he was thinking of… his mother. When Arstid had acted without confiding in the rest of the Subversive, it had cost people their lives.

"Trusting someone and keeping them safe do not always go hand-in-hand. Sometimes the less people know the better. If they appear as pawns they will be treated like pawns if captured." Thaddeus took a steadying breath. "Sometimes the few must make the decisions for the many. But they must also be willing to take the fall if things go wrong."

He, like Ryker, was one of those few. It was the same strategy I had preached to the Subversive. Cutting off the limbs of a beast did little. It was the head you wanted.

We fell quiet.

A devise on Thaddeus's wrist dinged. He glanced down, his forehead pinched.

"I have to go." He said with a tight jaw. "I am expected at work and must keep up appearances."

The hair on the back of my neck rose as he used the same words Ryker had. Keeping up appearances was going to get them all killed. Routines and habits made you an easy target to find.

"Petra will see you safely to the next house. Send my brother my love." Thaddeus raised his hand as if to shake mine, but thought better of it. He shook Triven's, patted Mouse on the shoulder, then tipped his head to me and left.

An hour later, we were once again skirting through the white tunnels lined with doors. The shoes Mae had provided us were nearly silent on the hard floors. Only Petra's made a soft noise as she led us. The cameras were off as planned, but we moved with haste nonetheless. Mouse ran beside me like a soundless ghost, her tiny hand clasped securely in mine. Triven's hand hovered over the small of my back as we moved. There was an unspoken pact in our physical contact. We would not be separated. Not here. Not again.

"Less than two minutes out." Petra whispered back to us.

The seemingly infinite tunnels reminded me of a book I had once stolen from the library. It was about a labyrinth constructed to hold a beast called a Minotaur. Many lost their lives in the endless maze.

I suppressed the thoughts of our fates being the same.

Up ahead I could see a six-way split in the tunnels. The junction looked like a hexagon with a path leading off each side. Petra decelerated her pace as she came to the opening, her hand extending behind her to slow us down too. Chest heaving, she leaned into the room checking that the surrounding tunnels were empty. Her head snapped back as she swore under her breath.

They weren't.

She pointed at her eyes, then to mine and down the tunnel to our left. Passing Mouse to Triven I crouched to the ground and leaned out around the corner. Slowly I pulled back. Still crouching, I nodded at Petra confirming what she'd seen.

Two armed soldiers were standing at the end of the tunnel next to ours. It would be impossible for us to pass through without being seen. I glanced at the camera pointed at us.

It was still off. Otherwise they would know we were here.

At least we were invisible for the moment. I looked up at Mouse and Triven with a sense of dread. My sacrifice had worked once before, it could work again. Death before their capture. Unsheathing the knives from my boots, I rose. Triven reached for me as Mouse's mouth stretched in a muted scream of protest, but it was other hands that reached me first.

Petra grabbed my arms pulling me toward her. Her lips brushed my cheek as she pulled me in. At first it seemed like a loving embrace, but as her lips met my ear, words spilled out. "Second tunnel on the right. First two lefts then a third right. Be safe."

Before I could react, she yanked one of the knives from my hand, threw me into the wall and bolted into the hexagonal room.

I staggered in shock. Jaw open.

Petra paused for two seconds in the hexagonal junction, ensuring the guards saw her.

They did.

"Halt!" A female guard screamed from the end of the tunnel. Feet could be heard pounding down the pathway toward us. Without a second glance Petra took off down the hallway across from us. I just saw her dark head disappear around the first bend when arms wrapped around me pulling me to the side. Triven's arm pressed me against the wall as the two guards in pursuit bound into the crossroads.

"We have an unwarranted civilian in the tunnels. Sector Fifteen-A. Requesting backup. Suspect is female, dark hair, approximately five-four. Not able to get a facial recognition on her. Be advised she is armed. Cameras are still down! Again, all available units respond. Light it up!" The male counterpart barked into his earpiece. "Repeat, LIGHT IT UP!"

Both guards touched their temples and an iridescent visor appeared, shielding their eyes. Without a glance in our direction, the two soldiers plummeted after Petra.

They were leaving. But more were coming.

As soon as they rounded the corner we were in motion. We took fewer than three steps before we realized what "light it up" meant.

They weren't talking about the cameras.

The once pleasantly warm lights began to grow in luminosity. I squinted my eyes against their blinding aura. Triven yanked Mouse into his arms, trying to shield her eyes as we bolted through the room. I took lead, running through Petra's directions with each stride. My eyes were on fire, tears streaming down my face. I tried to keep count of the passageways and turns, but it was getting harder to see. On our second left, voices could be heard echoing down the tunnels toward us.

Backup was coming.

My eyes seared as they flicked up to a camera when we passed the second right. I prayed they were still blind.

I flicked out my hand, signaling the next right. But Triven was not slowing. We were both nearly blind. I could barely make out the opening though my lashes.

"Right!" I barked out.

He was so close on my heels we would crash if either took a misstep. My heart sank as we rounded the corner. Even through my burning retinas, I could just make out the surrounding walls. No less than ten doors flanked the walls and we were headed to a dead end. Petra never told me which door.

My stride was just starting to slow when the door to my right sprung open. A silver clad arm shot out, grabbing me as Triven cried out a warning.

27. CATALYST

I WAS BRIEFLY airborne before I heard the shuffling feet and a slamming door. The room felt pitch black after the brightened hallways. I wheeled with my knife ready for attack, only to find a familiar hawk-nosed face in mine. My eyes searched wildly in the dark room.

"Easy... we're here." Triven said, winded. His voice sent a tidal wave of relief over my body.

Twisting the blade back toward myself I shoved the woman standing in front of me. She shoved back glowering down at me.

"What the *HELL*?! Fiona bellowed.

"There were soldiers—" I yelled back, but she cut me off.

"I KNOW!" She snapped. Pointing to her earpiece. "It was a rhetorical question. We had this damn thing planned flawlessly and practically everything has gone to shit!"

"Is Ryker being charged?" Triven asked as he slid Mouse down to the floor. It surprised me that he was the one to ask that question.

"I don't know yet." Fiona answered with a much more subdued tone. She seemed to shrink a little. "He was taken into The Minister's office this morning, but no further information has been released as of yet. I have no idea if he is in the clear or if he is being held for questioning."

I slumped back against the wall. Mouse took my hand giving it a reassuring squeeze. I brushed her tear-stained cheek with my thumb.

"Don't get comfortable." Fiona snarled. "We are leaving in twenty minutes and you have to get your packs fitted."

Ryker had been right in leaving the packs to the very end. They were made from the same material as our suits. The frames were low profile, but heavy. Mine stretched from the nape of my neck to below my tailbone and weighed nearly thirty pounds. An additional thirty pounds may not sound like a lot, but it was enough to slow a person down or blow a knee if taking an unexpected impact. Upon inspection, however, the weight would be worth it. Both Triven's and mine were filled to the brim with Sanctuary goodies. A few months' supply of nonperishable food, a plethora of weapons that would make even The Master drool, military grade clothing, and maps. *Real*, photographic maps with notes and marked locations. The packs were a sick irony—they held everything we had once come here seeking.

Mouse had a small pack with mostly food in it. Triven was helping her put some of it into his pack to lighten her load. I was sure when he was done, she would mostly be carrying air. I watched them as I tightened my own straps.

Fiona stepped between us, blocking my view. Something was clutched in her hands.

"I'm supposed to give you this." She kept her voice low. I examined the thing in her hands. It was a gadget like the one Ryker showed me on the rooftop. It could play videos on its tiny screen, and do many other things I was sure.

I stared at the flat device, unmoving. "Why would I want that?"

Fiona thrust it at me, jabbing me in the stomach with it. "I don't really care if you want it or not. Ryker instructed me to give it to you. So I am following my orders."

I stiffly wrapped my fingers around the screen, maintaining a fierce glare at Fiona. Feeling malicious, I grinned wickedly at her.

"How's the nose, Fiona?"

Her lips twisted up. "Fine. It seems there were

still some things for me to learn about combat. *Thank you*. I look forward to the day when I can repay the favor."

I leaned in closer, returning her smile. "I would be happy to see you try."

The watch on Fiona's wrist beeped four times, but neither of us broke eye contact. It wasn't until Triven cleared his throat loudly that both of us thawed to life again.

"I am assuming your alarm wasn't just a friendly wake-up call." Triven pulled his pack over his shoulders.

Fiona's expression was kinder as she addressed him. "We will be leaving in six minutes. But we are not going out the same way," she added seeing us move toward the sealed door. "Follow me."

I let Triven follow directly behind her, not fully trusting that I wouldn't punch her in the back of the head. Just for good measure. Mouse and I held hands as we moved past concrete rooms like the ones in Ryker's home. In everyone's home. When we came to the room that was ours, however, it was different. A small cot was crammed in the corner as a large cylindrical pipe took up much of the room. There was a makeshift man-sized hatch cut into it. Fiona checked her watch briefly and then began fumbling in her pocket.

I turned to Mouse, kneeling to her height awkwardly with the pack. "You okay?"

She bravely nodded her head, but I could see the fear in her eyes.

"Are you sure you want to come back with us?" I hadn't had the guts to ask her that question earlier, for fear she would say no. But I needed this to be her choice. My parents didn't give me a choice before dragging me into Tartarus. I didn't want to do the same to Mouse.

Her hands brushed my cheeks, then pulled my face closer to hers. Mouse's eyes had the depth of a much older person. As so many times before, she was scared but still sure of herself. Looking up at Triven then back to me she signed. *Family. Stay together.*

"Together." I nodded at her, repeating her favorite word.

"It's time," Fiona said.

Instead of opening the hatch as I expected, she pointed to the device in her hands. It was like the one she had given me. Then she pointed at the wall. As she slid her finger over the screen, a projection appeared on the concrete before us. It was the evening announcement. A well-manicured female soldier appeared. She opened her mouth to speak but before a single word came out, she was gone. The screen went black.

The photo of The Minister that hung in every home appeared on the screen. His bright eyes looked powerful and falsely charismatic. Ominous red words appeared at the bottom. *"Do you know who The Minister is?"* They faded out to be replaced by more. *"We do."* His picture inverted suddenly, turning his healthy skin a violent shade of green and his eyes devilishly white.

My breath caught as I appeared on the screen. Not the me now, but the me then. There were other children this time too. Repeated footage of The Minister and his militia beating kids into soldiers, over and over again. Then the video I had seen appeared, not all of it, just the part where Fandrin beat his own granddaughter unconscious. It repeated twice, zooming in each time. You could see the flecks of spittle flying from his mouth as he screamed.

The image went blank for a moment, then the female soldier was back. Her slack face was white. Shock emitted from her every fiber. Helplessly she looked off screen for direction before the feed cut to a generic photo of The Sanctuary's emblem. Fiona turned off the screen and placed the device back in her pocket. Her face was stern as ever, but there was an unmistakable glint of pride. Grabbing three handguns from behind the cot, she tossed two of them to Triven and me. After checking her own, she twisted her wrist to examine her watch, eagerly counting the seconds.

"The fake location signal will be detected in ten seconds. Every military guard will be routed in that direction. We have two minutes to get you to the last drop off, then I must join the rest of the soldiers. We will have to run the entire way and even then it will be cutting it close." She glanced at Mouse.

Mouse rose up on her toes looking offended. I squeezed her hand. "It won't be a problem."

Fiona grabbed the latch while still keeping an eye on her watch. "Once we're through, the hatch will reseal itself. Just focus on keeping up. We shouldn't have any interference but have your weapons ready."

I checked my gun, taking off the safety and counting the bullets. Once satisfied, I grabbed Mouse's hand. My eyes met Triven's. His hazel eyes were so intense that it made my chest tighten.

"Five seconds." Fiona counted.

We tensed for movement. My heart rate spiked as I glared at the back of Fiona's head. *Thanks for the gun.* I thought. I still didn't trust her, not really. As we had been passed on and led blindly by different rebels today, I knew for certain I didn't trust them. But I also knew we didn't have a choice.

Fiona braced herself to pull back the door.

"Now!"

She yanked open the door and was gone. I shot out into the hallway after her, clinging to Mouse's hand. I was prepared to drag her, but her tiny legs pumped harder than I would have thought possible. She was proving herself. We were in the maintenance ducts again

They looked the same as the ones we had hidden in when I was shot.

Fiona's long legs were gaining ground and I pushed harder to keep pace. I could have easily outrun her on a rooftop, but the pack was slowing me down. My legs were screaming under the extra weight but we kept moving. Fiona rounded the corner ten feet in front of us and a single shot rang out.

Before I could halt, her gravelly voice cried out, "Keep moving! One minute ten seconds."

I rounded the corner, nearly tripping over the dead body of a young soldier. His weapon was barely out of his holster. Fiona's bullet was perfectly placed, right between the eyes. I could not spare him much of a glance and pulled Mouse harder as we passed the dead boy. While the thought of making Mouse see more dead bodies churned my stomach, it was the same thing I would have done.

Leave no witnesses.

Fiona halted under a ladder with a black rectangle painted next to it. She bound up three rungs and knocked a rehearsed pattern. As she jumped back down the rungs, the door swung open. Pointing my gun into the blackness above us, I circled the ladder.

Fiona scowled. "GO!"

I still didn't move.

Triven slid off his pack and climbed up, his gun

at the ready. I pointed the barrel of my gun at Fiona. If Triven didn't return, I would shoot her. She glared at me but said nothing.

I held my breath as his feet disappeared. My lungs refused to work again until his face reappeared in the opening, his soft voice calling out to us, "It's okay."

I lowered my gun. Reaching his hand down he waved to Mouse. She scrambled up to him as I grabbed his pack. Once he took it, I peeled off my own and handed it up too. The opening was too small to fit through with it on my back. Quickly, I shoved my gun into my boot. Since I had no intention of thanking Fiona, I began to climb.

My hand was barely on the first rung when Fiona grabbed my shoulder. Her dark eyes were nearly black. "Tell them whatever it takes to grow our army."

I stared her pointedly in the face climbing up one more rung to make us the same height. "I won't glorify your war just to gain you soldiers."

"When are you going to realize this isn't just *our* war, *your highness*?" Releasing me, Fiona gave a mock bow and took off down the tunnel. I spit in her direction.

Fiona's voice could be heard booming down the tunnel as I climbed the ladder. "Requesting coverage! Be advised, I have a soldier down in tunnel thirty-seven. DOA. Shooter is MIA underground! Repeat, shooter is *MIA*! I am en route to compromised location and need coverage in tunnel thirty-seven NOW!'"

Once I was at the top, Triven's hands helped pull me to my feet when I emerged from the tunnel. My fingers carefully retrieved my weapon as I stood.

I visually swept the room.

It was astoundingly bright despite its lack of windows. A chemical tang salted the air, clinging to my nostrils. It made my throat tighten. The entire ceiling glowed a sterile white, illuminating the bland grey floors and walls. The walls were completely barren except for one door and a large silver panel with a glass front on the wall opposite of us, brilliant flames lapping at the glass like they wanted to be set free. Three silver tables stood on wheels in the middle of the room.

Goosebumps rose over my flesh.

Two carts were empty but it was the third that caught my attention. A black sheet was draped over the third, covering something.

It wasn't the sheet that bothered me.

It was the shape.

I had seen enough dead bodies in my time. I knew what lay beneath the black fabric. I lingered for only a moment on the unmoving cloth before turning my attention to the silent stranger in the room.

For a man of his great stature, he nearly blended into the walls. It looked as if all of the color had been drained not just from his face, but from his entire essence. He was dressed in head-to-toe black. The rich dark color only further washed out his pallid skin. He had a shock of pure white hair on top of his head and his skin took on an oddly translucent hue. It was as if he was withering away. The peculiar man was nearly as wide as a door, but his square shoulders hunched in on themselves, like he wished to disappear.

He looked like death incarnate.

Mouse was clinging to Triven's backpack, keeping it between her and the tall man. Her neck was bent back at nearly a ninety-degree angle to meet his face. She and I watched in stunned silence as the strange man reached out to Triven, addressing him by name.

"Triven Halverson. It is a pleasure to see you again. It has been many years." He offered a spider-like hand to Triven.

I choked back the urge to tell him not to take it.

Triven reached out to take the man's hand, but he kept a good distance between them, staying barely within arm's length. Triven's hand looked small in his grasp. The man's willowy white fingers folded over his. I cringed at the sight of his touch.

"So it has." Triven agreed. "My mother will be happy to know you are still alive, Nathanial."

The man named Nathanial sighed, releasing Triven's hand. "My sister takes little joy in things. Anger was always easier for her. But perhaps knowing a part o her family still lives would thaw her a little."

I gaped at the man before us. He was not just some creepy old man.

He was Triven's creepy *uncle*.

While it was a fact that they shared family, the bond between the two men seemed nearly nonexistent. Even Mouse's mouth had popped open in surprise. Triven looked at the man as if he was a stranger and there was something dark in Nathanial's eyes as he looked at his nephew. It made my intuition flare.

"This is Phoenix and Mouse." Triven introduced us. "This is Nathanial Waters. He is The Sanctuary's *undertaker*."

Triven's slight emphasis on the last word did not go unmissed. Nathanial's eyes swept over us and I stepped closer to Mouse. However, I noticed something else in those opaque grey eyes as they fell on me. Sorrow and pain swam intermingled with the bitterness I had seen moments ago.

"Why exactly are we *here*, Nathanial?" It took all of my restraint not to glance at the dead body behind him. One hand tightened on my gun as the other grabbed Mouse. Ready to move her.

"I see Ryker has not confided his entire plan to you." His grey eyes glittered strangely under the opalescent-lit ceiling. "All tunnels are being watched. There is only one way out of The Sanctuary now. With the dead."

His black-clad arm rose and a bony finger swept over the dead body before landing on the hatch filled with fire.

28. FIRE

MY LIPS TWISTED into a snarl. The gun twitched in my hand.

He was crazy if he thought we were climbing in there. I moved to pull Mouse behind me, but she placed her hand over mine. She squeezed until I looked down at her. Her brown eyes bore into mine as she nodded encouragingly. *Trust,* she was telling me. I took a deep breath but didn't let go of my weapon.

"And why exactly are *you* helping us, Nathaniel? I don't recall ever seeing you at any of the meetings." I scrutinized him. "I don't even remember hearing your name."

"I am the rebel's best kept secret." Nathanial's faded eyes studied me. "My reasons are my own, but seeing as I am in the presence of *family,* perhaps I should share."

He slowly pulled himself up to full height, his

eyes becoming hard like steel.

"After the first wave of rebels was disposed of nearly seven years ago, those of us left behind were interrogated. *Especially* the family members." Nathaniel said. Triven stiffened next to him, his face going slack.

Nathaniel continued, never looking away from me. "I call Arstid my sister, but I am Triven's uncle by marriage, not by blood. His aunt, Belle, was my perfect mate. While she and I never found love, we did live in perfect unison. Our contract was a sound one and we produced two *perfect* children. Belle and Arstid had been estranged for many years. I barely knew Arstid or her new family." He shifted his gaze to Triven. "But after you disappeared, my wife was taken in. She was tortured for days before her body gave out. In the end, she confessed to make the pain stop. They obliged. When I received her body, she was utterly unrecognizable.

"Shortly after, my children were taken into the military as recruits, The Minister proclaiming there had been an error on their placement tests. They were both dead before the year was out. Training accidents, the soldiers claimed. But I saw their bodies. I knew the truth." Nathanial took a steadying breath. He stared at the hatch door in the wall. "I have put my entire family in there. Watched them burn... I *will* see everyone guilty of their deaths blaze for their sins."

"And are we listed among those guilty?" I asked

blatantly. "You would not be the first person in this family to blame children for their parents' sins."

There was a minor twitch in the corner of Nathanial's mouth. "Even though your parents did not directly cause my family's deaths… I would be lying if I said I did not find them guilty on some level. But I do not relish the idea of killing others' children. It will not bring back my own." Nathanial took a deep breath, his hooked nose flaring. "Even if I did seek to harm you, the revenge I truly desire is against The Minister. And from what I understand, *you* are my best chance at getting it."

"*We* are your *only* chance." I heavily exaggerated my words, implicating Triven as well.

"How much has Ryker told you about the way out?" Nathaniel questioned. His head tilted to the side. A strange smile played at the corners of his mouth.

"He has informed us about most of the plan." Triven lied. He watched his uncle with an appraising eye. "But he was taken in for questioning before he could elaborate every detail."

Nathanial did not look surprised. "Very well. Then I will fill you in."

Ryker's plan for evacuating us was well thought out. Down to the most minute details. A voice in the back of my head wondered how much of this he would have told us himself if he had not been taken. I had a feeling there still would have been gaps just in case w were captured. What did Thaddeus say... something about pawns not knowing all of the answers for a reason?

That seemed the case. So few rebels seemed to know all of the details. Even Nathanial only seemed to know his part. The only unwatched tunnel—if you could call it that—out of the city was where the dead bodies were released. The undertaker's job was to destroy the bodies by placing them in the incinerator. Once the bodies were reduced to ash, they were released through a tunnel outside of The Wall. For years, Tartarus' air had been unknowingly polluted with the ashes of Sanctuary bodies. As if our own body count wasn't high enough, we had been stockpiling the Sanctuary's too.

The only activity monitored by the Ministry's guard was how many times a day the tunnel was released. One release for each recorded death. One unwanted body dumped at a time. There were seven bodies to be released today so Nathanial had already burned three sets of bodies together, which meant we would be sent through without raising suspicion. Our passing through The Wall would simply look like three more unwanted dead bodies being dumped.

The three of us could not fit all at once. Triven, with his larger frame, would have to go through alone. His broad shoulders were already a concern. The drop chute would be tight for him. Mouse and I, on the other hand, were small enough to fit through together. There were rare times it paid to be small.

The only catch was that the fire must first be activated before the chute could be opened. After I cursed Nathanial, not wanting to die a fiery death, he explained that our suits were not merely bulletproof, but fire-resistant as well. I had stared at the fabric on my arm with heightened curiosity. After providing us with matching gloves and full-face head masks, Nathanial had assured us that all of the weapons would be safe within the packs as well. Since they were the same material as our suits, the majority of the heat would be repelled. There would be no risk of a weapon being ruined or discharging in the flames.

After confirming our boots would perform the same way, I kept my pistol in hand with the intent of stowing it later. Triven had offered to go before Mouse and I, so I thought it important to visually remind Nathanial that I would shoot him if he betrayed us. To prove that the suits would perform as promised, we were to send the packs into the incinerator first.

The fire that had been burning when we arrived was now out. As Nathanial opened the small hatch I partly expected to find a half-burnt body in it. When the door sprang open, however, the small container was immaculate. Scorched, but immaculate. A stench crept out of the rectangular space. It was surprisingly mild, bu

I could still catch a hint of char mixed with a musky sweet perfume. My stomach flipped over. Mouse covered her nose and mouth.

Triven and I placed our packs inside. Once the door was closed, Nathanial's fingers crept over a keypad to the left of the opening. Within seconds the entire port-window was engulfed in fire. The air around us rose in temperature. Hesitantly, the three of us stepped away from the door—waiting for a bullet to discharge in the heat or a bomb to activate.

Nothing happened.

Soon the fire went out and Nathanial turned back to us.

"Our family reunion might not be so warm once this war is over." He warned Triven.

"I would be surprised if it was. Good fortune, Nathanial." Triven shook his hand again.

"And to you," Nathanial replied. He opened the now empty container, stepping aside. There was no smell of burning materials, just the rancid sweet scent of long-term decay.

Triven's lips briefly brushed mine, then Mouse's forehead.

The hair on my arms rose.

It felt like a goodbye kiss.

He took a deep breath and said, "I will see you on the other side."

The confidence in his words didn't reassure me.

I couldn't say anything. My throat was already closing in panic.

Mouse and I watched in unspoken horror as Triven donned the headpiece Nathanial had given him. His face disappeared behind the shimmering material. I couldn't help but wonder if I would see those warm eyes again. I slipped the safety off my gun, ready to fire at the first sign of betrayal. Triven's head turned blindly toward us, then he climbed into the rectangular hole. His broad shoulders grazed the sides of the compartment. I had a pang of claustrophobia watching him. This wasn't a sewer drain… it was so much worse. We were literally jumping out of the frying pan and into the fire. Willingly.

My heart actually skipped a beat when Nathanial closed the door. The pain in my chest was becoming increasingly real. I could barely see Triven through the dark window, his shadowy figure stirring slightly in the confined space. Then with a flick of white skeleton fingers, all I could see were flames. We were closer this time and I could feel the heat on my face. My palms went numb, but I kept my finger firmly on the trigger. I waited to hear Triven scream, to hear banging from inside. But there was nothing. The flames vanished and when the door opened, the chamber was once again empty. That horrible smell lingered once more in the air, and my panic began to rise.

As I knelt, I carefully slipped the gun back into my boot for safekeeping. My fingers worked numbly, helping Mouse with her mask. Kissing her briefly on the forehead, I whispered. "See you on the other side, beautiful."

She gave me a shaky smile before pulling down her mask. I inspected it thoroughly and then taking her hand, lead her to the opening. Nathanial watched us with the expression only a father who had lost his children could. I felt pity for the strange, angry man.

"Thank you." I said. *Don't kill us.*

"Make sure that bastard pays." He responded.

"I will." That was one promise I would happily make.

After yanking my own mask down, I was surprised how well I could see through the dark material. It was like looking through tinted glass, not a tightly woven fabric. Scooping up Mouse, I helped her into the person-sized tunnel and crawled in after her. As my feet slid along the tray, her thin arms wrapped around me. Careful not to scrape her suit against the charred sides, I rolled onto my back holding her to my chest. Her toes rested on my shins.

"Close your eyes," I whispered in her ear. Mouse buried her face in my neck just as the door clicked closed above my head. Shutting my eyes, I clutched her tighter. I couldn't be sure if I was shaking or if she was.

Without warning, there was a deafening roar. Even with my eyes closed, it looked like daylight. The bright light bore into my retinas, making my eyes water beneath the mask. Warmth began to envelope our bodies—the intensity escalating, but not yet painful.

But something was wrong.

Pure fright enveloped me. The heat was swallowing the air around us and my lungs were beginning to ache with lack of oxygen. The panic rose higher, but I couldn't even find enough air to scream. I wanted to reach for my gun, to shoot out the tiny window, but I couldn't risk it discharging in the heat and hitting Mouse.

Oh, god! Is this why Triven made no sound? Had I just watched him suffocate to death and willingly followed?!

The tiny body in my arms began to spasm as she too gasped for air. My lungs felt full of molten lava. New tears of panic and anger fell with the others. Mouse was going to die in my arms and I could do nothing to save her.

29. ASHES

JUST WHEN I thought our lives were over, the floor suddenly fell out from beneath me and the fire vanished. After the searing heat, it was like being dropped into a bucket of cold water. We were blind in the sudden darkness, but I could breathe. Air rushed past my ears in a whir. My back slammed into a metal surface, knocking out what little air was left from my lungs. A hollow thud echoed in the confined space as my head cracked against the hard shell. Mouse's head slammed into my collarbone and I heard a snap that was accompanied by searing pain. My ears rang like a bell as I coughed out a startled breath. Air rushed into my lungs quenching their thirst, but there was no time to feel relief. We were still moving.

My whole body pitched forward feet first. The tunnel was whipping by at an alarming speed. I couldn't see it, but I could feel it. The back of my suit was quickl·

heating with friction. My shoulders shifted back and forth ricocheting off the sides of the cramped tunnel. I didn't dare raise my head. Fearing our inevitable fall, I stuck my boots out trying to find purchase—trying to slow us down. There was nothing. So we did the only thing we could do. Mouse and I clung to each other. It felt like an eternity in the darkness, like the fall would never end. Then the darkness seemed to dissipate, its thick bonds diluting with light. My eyes finally caught sight of the silver tunnel surrounding us, then it was gone. Everything but Mouse's body disappeared. For a brief second I saw a sickly green night sky, then a pillow of dust swallowed us whole.

I couldn't see anything. And I couldn't breathe again. Instinct told me to rip the mask from my face, but another voice in my head told me not to.

Grabbing Mouse around the waist I thrust her in the direction I thought was up. Her arms and legs flailed in the mass surrounding us. The world around us floated and shifted in the air, allowing us to suck in a breath before falling back down to choke us again.

I knew what it was.

"Don't take off your mask!" I screamed to her. "Don't take off your mask!"

A large hand grabbed over the top of mine and Mouse was gone. I pushed my way up and the hands found me again. Yanking me from the sea of grey, Triven hauled me onto the top of the old vehicle we had narrowly missed. He hugged us both to him. He was shaking nearly as bad as I was.

"I thought we were going to suffocate." I pushed away gasping, thinking of the fire.

"I did too... I thought he betrayed us." Triven panted, hugging Mouse closer.

Me too. She signed with shaking hands.

The three of us sat wheezing on the rusted-out old vehicle. None of us had removed our gloves or masks, the silvery black material now coated white with ash.

Despite my nose being covered, it still registered that the air here was rank. I looked up from where we had fallen. The hole looked much too small for a body to pass through, inset in the enormous wall. I had nearly forgotten just how foreboding the metal goliath of a wall was. A small cloud of grey steam billowed from a pipe next to the chute we had just vacated. The stench of burning flesh was carried with it. Ventilation. I repressed a gag.

Desperately needing to look at anything else, I dropped my eyes to the ground to orient myself. A strange gargling sound brewed in the back of my throat. We hadn't just fallen into a *pit* of ash. We were surrounded by an *ocean* of ashes—of *human* ashes. While the wind picked up some of the dust, spiriting it away, so much more was left behind. Ash piled nearly thirty feet up the wall, tapering down into the streets of Tartarus like a morbid beach. Thousands upon thousands of bodies had made this. Centuries of The Sanctuary's dead lay at our feet. I couldn't help but wonder how many of them were at my grandfather's hand.

"It's horrific." Triven said, staring at the ash surrounding us. "They used to tell us the bodies were repurposed back into our environment. That our loved ones were being recycled back into plant life. But this... This is a monument of the dead memorializing Fandrin's control over people's lives."

"*His* body should be down here." My hands shook with anger. Trying desperately to keep my wits, I jumped to my feet. "I know where we are. We need to get moving. Now."

Throwing Mouse onto his back, Triven and I picked our way across the dead to our backpacks.

The instant the stench had hit my nose, I knew where we were. It seemed like a lifetime ago that Triven and I had been here seeking answers. I had once equated the stench to rotting sewage, but now I knew that burning bodies were mixed into that too. This was the old warehouse district. Even though I had never made it this far north, I could still pick out familiar landmarks in the distance. The Ravager meeting place where we had nearly been captured was less than a mile from where we stood.

Finding a sheltered spot to hide, we quickly shed our soiled clothing. I was so eager to get the ash far from my skin that I didn't even bother hiding my body from Triven. It was like having my parents' blood on my hands again.

Ryker must have known what we would land in—or at least he had an idea—because fresh clothing had been packed in the caps of our bags. I was both thankful and angry. We carefully stowed the soiled suits in an empty stuff sack I found in my pack. Despite my revulsion towards what coated them, they were still valuable. As I pulled my boots back on, a lone piece of ash fell onto the back of my hand. Spastically I shook it off, but another fell in its place.

I stared at it.

Was this one of my mind's sick games again? Then there was another piece. Then another. My eyes flashed up and both Triven and Mouse were seeing them now too. Thick ashes filled the air around us, floating lithely to the ground. Snatching one out of the air I smashed it between my fingers. It was thick and chalky. This wasn't the ash from bodies. This was the ash of a burning city. Stuffing two knives in my boots and holstering one on the guns Ryker had given me, I threw the pack on my shoulders.

"We need to get skyward." I began racing

through my brain for the closest way up.

"Lead the way." Triven said. Mouse nodded seriously at his side.

We slithered through the city in the darkness. With the packs, our progress was hindered, as I had feared it might be. Once we were safely on a familiar rooftop, we hid the oversized bags carefully in an air duct. We would come back for them later. While Triven pulled the grate back into place, I stared out at the dreary skyline. Small fires could be seen throughout the city, their billowing plumes feathering the sky. I had forgotten how dark it was here. How the pollution blotted out the sky and a rotten smell lingered in the air. The air was wretched, but somehow my lungs felt full for the first time in months. This place was horrible. But it was more my home than The Sanctuary had ever been. Standing on the rooftop, with the decay below, I felt like myself again. I felt free. I understood the rules of this city. Here I knew how to survive. Here, nothing slipped from my memory.

Triven appeared at my shoulder. "It's strange isn't it?"

"A little," I replied. "Is it even more strange that I feel at home?"

His voice was deep. Gentle. "Not in the least."

I smiled up at him. "Let's go find our people."

Mouse took her place in Triven's arms and we set

off at a run. The rooftops flew beneath our feet. My long hair caught the wind, waving out behind me. I felt free. The wild recluse The Minister had so brutally caged came back to life. Her instincts raged in my mind. She wanted nothing more than to bolt across the tarry skyline and leave everything behind... But I wasn't that girl anymore. I had tethers in life now.

I could hear the sounds of movement below us. The Tribes were restless. I was thankful our new boots barely made a sound. Combined with my stealth, I moved more like a phantom than a human. Even Triven's usually louder feet were nearly silent. At this pace we would be at a Subversive entrance in less than hour. We bound over a small gap between buildings and I caught a flash of moving bodies below us.

Purple and gold.

Adroits.

I cursed internally. It wasn't smart to travel long distances when the Tribes were out. I had a safe house barely a mile from here. If it was uncompromised, it could provide a safe place for the night. I was calculating the other hideouts within reach as we leapt to another rooftop. My thoughts stopped, however. As my feet landed on the other side, invisible fingers tingled up my scalp.

Something was off.

There was a huge, decrepit ventilation system on

the roof ten yards ahead of us. It was the perfect place for an ambush. Flashing my hand behind me, I signaled for Triven to fall back. He obeyed immediately. Just as I unsheathed my knife, a whizzing sound registered in my left ear. Triven shouted a warning but I didn't need it. Diving forward, I rolled head-over-heels. A knife sliced through my hair, tugging at the loose strands as it flew by. I skittered to a halt in front of the vent.

For one second the world stopped.

A shadow broke away from the rest of the darkness. There was a glint of gunmetal in its hand. I lunged and collided with the attacker. Our bodies rolled in a jumble of punching limbs and flashing weapons. The assailant's hand never left the gun, wielding it like a club. It wasn't until we stopped that I saw why.

We rolled out of the shadows and into the eerie light of the hindered moon. There was a mask covering my attacker's face, but it was plain to see she was female and only had one hand. We froze, panting for breath. I sat over her lean body, pinning her to the ground, my knife at her throat, the barrel of her gun pressed to my chest.

Then she spoke. "Phoenix?"

Without removing my knife, I yanked the mask over her head. Curly dark hair spilled out of the mask, surrounding a face I never thought I would see again.

"Archer—" I gaped at her. Our weapons fell

wayward as I helped her to her feet. She beamed at me like a long-lost sister. Before I could react she threw her arm around me in a tight embrace. To my own surprise, I hugged her back.

"We thought you were dead." She said pulling away.

"We thought the same about you." I flashed back to watching her fight Ravagers in a blood-soaked alley as Maddox dragged me away.

"If you two are done trying to kill each other, we have more important matters at hand." Triven said. He strolled casually across the roof holding Mouse's hand.

Archer pushed passed me with a small cry and embraced her friend. Tears welled in her eyes as she hugged Triven. Then quick as a whip, she pulled back and slapped him across the face. Triven looked stunned.

"That is for making me mourn you." She said pointedly. Before he could find words, Archer turned and swung Mouse up onto her back. The little girl clung to her in delight.

A lanky young man with dark hair and chocolate eyes walked up behind Triven. A gun hung loosely across his back. I recognized him at once. He was one of the Subversive's best gunmen.

"Baxter." I nodded to him.

"Damn, if you three aren't a sight for sore eyes." His returning smile was dazzling as he slapped Triven on the back. There was a mischievous glint in his eye. "I would like to point out that Triven and I didn't need to roll around throwing punches like two lunatics in order to recognize our friends."

Archer punched him in the shoulder, hard, but he just laughed. An echoing rumble of laughter rolled through the group. Archer was the first to sober up.

"The others?" She asked without any real hope.

Triven placed a hand on her shoulder as I shook my head. Closing her eyes, she nodded. She had been expecting that answer.

"And you? The Subversive?" Triven asked, his voice tense.

Our friends exchanged glances. With great care, Archer slid Mouse off her back and pushed her toward Triven. In a terrifyingly compassionate gesture, she pressed her hand to his shoulder in comfort. "There were some attacks. Arstid is still alive, but we have suffered many loses since you left. There is something—"

Archer's next words were lost in an explosion of fire and glass.

Triven curled protectively around Mouse, as the rest of us turned, guns ready, toward the blast. The air around us vibrated as the second story windows of a building a block down from us blew out. Loose gravel skittered by our feet as the building we stood on quivered beneath us. Shards of glass twinkled to the streets below like falling constellations as an undulating cloud of flames exploded from the windows before imploding and sucking back inside. Brilliant fire leapt inside the now shattered windows illuminating the surrounding buildings.

"Adroits." I muttered watching the flames consume the building.

Eyes wide, Archer lowered her gun. "We should get moving."

"I think that's a fine idea." Baxter pulled his rifle into his hands and began checking the weapon.

"There is a safe house not far from here if we need to hold up for a while," I said. Triven and I exchanged a glance. "But we must get back to the Subversive—as soon as possible. There is *a lot* you need to know and time is short."

The same lingering unease still hung in the air between Baxter and Archer.

"And apparently you have a lot to tell us as well." Triven's shrewd eyes watched his friends. I could see the leader in him reemerging in the presence of his people. I had not been the only one lost in The Sanctuary.

Baxter inclined his head, encouraging Archer.

"The Subversive has been compromised. We believe there is a traitor in our mix. It's not safe anymore." Archer warned. Her keen eyes swept the

JENNIFER WILSON

rooftops around us. "But this is not the place to speak openly."

"I agree." Triven's voice was flat with strain. This was not the welcome home we had been expecting. Honestly, I'm not sure what we had been expecting.

Archer sidled up to me as we checked our weapons in preparation to move out. "Why do I get the feeling you're going to try and get us all killed again?"

Lying would have been a kindness, but she deserved the truth.

"We're bringing a war to your doorstep."

She looked past me to the burning building. A humorless laugh broke from her lips. "Phoenix, it's already here."

I could see the raging fire reflecting in her dark eyes. A stray piece of ash floated onto my forearm.

"So it is."

ACKNOWLEDGEMENTS:

AS WITH MY first book, I must start with thanks to the people who make bearing my soul worth it. You, my readers. So many wonderful and compelling stories are never heard, but now — in this day and age — Indie Authors are finally getting a voice. And that is because of fan support. Without your overwhelmingly loving posts, blogs and social media support, Phoenix would never have a story to tell. So, I thank you.

Writing is so much more than putting words on a page. It is putting a little bit of yourself into every syllable written, every emotion expressed and every character's innate flaws — I am every bit a part of this story as it is a part of me. So thank you for letting me share a piece of myself with you. As before, I ask one more favor of you. While passion consumes me to write, I am still human and thus make mistakes. If you find errors in my book, please contact me so I can correct them. No one is perfect.

To the book bloggers who support my books, I am eternally indebted to you. Every post you put on your blogs, every video on your YouTube channels and every image on your Instagram accounts were life-altering for me. The web so often jostles and pushes us Indie Authors to the side, and you made my words heard. You inspire people to read, you speak your mind and you bravely put yourself out there for the world to see. You are the trendsetters, the voices of a new generation and soul mates to every author striving to be heard. Thank you for your amazing amount of support, honesty and energy. I am inspired by you.

I cannot express enough gratitude to my Oftomes family. I am overwhelmed with joy to have such a supportive and talented group of authors/people in my life. You are all amazing and inspire me every day. It is an honor to be published along side each of you. Xina, you are a champion with the eyes of an eagle! Thank you for catching everything my tired eyes couldn't see and helping to bring this book one step closer to perfection. And Ben! What can I say? Thank you, not for just taking me under your wing, but for also flying me higher than I could have ever done on my own. Your enthusiasm, support and charisma are unending. Thank you for helping to bring the New World out of the shadows and into the hearts of readers.

To my confidants, editors and beta-readers: Diane Schultz, Auston Wilson, Cameron Walker, Kimberly Karli, Cerri Norris, Amie Bergeson and Annette Meyerkord. What can I say that could truly express my gratitude? You have taken this long road with Phoenix and me, and your support and time is utterly invaluable. You may get to read the books first, but you also have to trudge through the edits and storyline changes that would make most people crazy. Thank you for your time, energy, honesty, opinions and support. Pieces of each of you have been woven into these books as well. You are forever immortalized within the pages and always cherished in my heart.

Nana, thank you for being a strong woman beyond your years and teaching me to speak my mind. I do so frequently. Papa, thank you for your creative genes, I knew it wasn't just your blue eyes I got. Mum and Granddad, thank you for exposing me to the arts and always encouraging me to read. Both helped mold the person I am today.

Mom and Dad, there are so many things to thank you both for. Mom, the endless late-night Face Time sessions editing, talking plot, and rewording sentences were never-ending, but you never complained. I couldn't have done this without you. Really. Dad, thank you for letting me steal your wife for hours on end and then always managing to sweep in at the right moment with the perfect word. For a man who claims not to love syntax so much, you have quite the arsenal of words hidden in that mind of yours. I love you both to no end.

Auston, there are not enough words in the world to express what you mean to me. What your support means to me. I couldn't have done any of this without you. I could tell you that everyday and it still wouldn't be said enough. You believe in me when I have a hard time believing in myself. You have let me be selfish and come to bed late, and you do so without ever complaining. You are an amazing man and I count my blessings for you every day. You're brave, kind, generous, and loving. You amaze me.